PLUTUS

PLUTUS

COLIN WADE

Matador
9 Priory Business Park,
Wistow Road, Kibworth Beauchamp,
Leicestershire, LE8 0RX
Tel: 0116 279 2299
Email: books@troubador.co.uk
Web: www.troubador.co.uk/matador
Twitter: @matadorbooks

Web: www.colinwade.co.uk
Twitter: @CPWADE1
Also by Colin Wade: *The Lost Years*

ISBN 978 1838595 128

British Library Cataloguing in Publication Data.
A catalogue record for this book is available from the British Library.

Printed and bound in Great Britain by 4edge Limited
Typeset in 11pt Sabon MT by Troubador Publishing Ltd, Leicester, UK

Matador is an imprint of Troubador Publishing Ltd

For my family

1

Maryland, USA

Alice Bidebecker sat eating her club sandwich in the park, trying to enjoy the late spring sunshine during the poor excuse for a lunch break. She had been a member of the elite Senior Counter Intelligence Team at the NSA for the past ten months and the constant pressure was beginning to take its toll.

As she got toward the end of her lunch, she was suddenly aware of an old geezer sitting on the other end of her bench, staring at her.

"What are you looking at old man?" she said with just a hint of passive aggression. He just smiled at her.

"If you are trying to pick me up, then don't bother. I don't screw men old enough to be my grandfather."

The man, dressed in an expensive sharp suit, with thinning grey hair and a handsome but well lived-in face, sat there for a moment still smiling. Alice continued to stare at him with contempt. He spoke.

"I can see I have the right person. My briefing told me you were feisty and wouldn't take any crap. Alice, my name is Clay Deepermeyer, and I want you to work for me."

Alice stared at him dumbfounded. "How the hell do you know my name?"

"Alice, my organisation is working on a secret scientific project that will eventually have a global impact."

"Ooh, secret scientific project. Get you."

He ignored her flippancy.

"We only employ the best people who are able to work within an environment where secrets have to be kept. You are the best cyber security person in the US and my organisation needs you to set up security so tight and so secure that no one in the world will ever be able to mine our secrets and destroy the good work we are doing. We believe that the work you are doing at the NSA on US cyber security and particularly your work on new encryption standards is the best in the world, but we think with a free rein, you could make it better. We want your talent to serve us, not the US government."

Alice stood up and started to walk away. She had been warned about approaches like this as part of her top-level security briefing.

She made it ten metres before he spoke again. "We'll pay you ten million dollars to leave your job and be on a plane to Innsbruck within the next few days."

Alice stopped and turned around. She stared at this strange old man, trying to judge what to do next. She returned to the bench.

"OK, I am listening."

"An open-ended flight ticket is booked in your name which can be used any time in the next three days. It will fly you to Innsbruck. When you land, you will be picked up and taken to our secret scientific site. You will not be told any more until you arrive at the destination. You will be given a spectacular apartment within the site where your every need will be catered for. You must break all ties with friends and old colleagues. We know your parents are dead and you have no siblings, so hopefully that is not an issue for you. You must not use your current identity to do anything online from the moment you join us. We have created your new identity and you need to disappear. The NSA will be after you as soon as they realise you have gone. You will be allowed to move freely within the site and can leave to visit local towns and villages, provided you stick to the rigid security protocols we set out. You will be paid into a new Swiss bank account. Your task is to set up the best security the world has ever seen to protect our secrets, including a complete implementation of anti-surveillance measures for our site. We do not want anyone to be able to see us from space, find us online or hack any part of our extensive network. If you do all that, we will give you ten million dollars, with the first two million dollars paid for just getting on the flight."

Alice was stunned. Was this man for real or was she about to be duped and foolishly put the NSA at risk by being kidnapped and tortured for what she knew?

He handed her an envelope with plane tickets and a code to a Swiss bank account. She went back to work and tried to concentrate as millions of thoughts ran through her mind. Was this really going to be her last few days at the NSA? Could she really betray the US for $10 million?

As she walked back into the office, she felt like everyone was watching her. She sat down, her mind scrambled and confused.

"You alright Alice?"

Chad Brown, her co-worker and cubicle buddy was staring at her.

"Umm, yeh fine."

"Did you have a nice lunch break?"

Alice tried not to react. Why was he asking her that? Had he seen her talking to that old guy? Was she being watched? She sometimes wondered how much covert surveillance was on her team; after all they were the elite team in the NSA and had knowledge that few were party to. It would make sense for the NSA to be ultra-cautious about their best human assets. She tried to keep her tone calm and casual.

"Oh, you know. Too short as always but the weather was quite nice."

Chad stood up and walked over to her desk. Alice tensed up.

"Um, Alice, I was wondering…"

Alice looked at him. "What are you wondering?"

"Err, God, I didn't think this was going to be so hard. Err, I wondered if you wanted to come out for a drink with me tonight?"

Alice was taken aback. Since the chat with the old dude she had become completely paranoid in a matter of minutes. Chad's fumbled attempt at asking her out had floored her and she sat there not knowing what to say.

Chad stood next to her desk, the embarrassment consuming him.

"God, I'm sorry Alice. Stupid of me. Sorry. God, forget I asked."

Alice jumped back to the present.

"Chad, no, I'm sorry. Thank you for asking. I would like that but not tonight. I'm really tired. I just need an early night."

Chad felt a huge wave of relief. "Oh, good. Another time then."

The afternoon dragged on, her mind addled with what to do about the unsolicited approach from this Deepermeyer dude. Alice knew the protocol. She was supposed to report such instances to her line manager immediately, but there was something about what he said that was stopping her. She was tempted. Ten million dollars was a lot of money in anyone's book.

Eventually the stress of the situation got to her and she walked in to see Jon Ruganzi, the head of their team.

"Jon, I need to talk to you about something."

"I'm really busy Alice. Can't it wait?"

"Well, I dunno, not really."

"You don't seem sure Alice, which means you are wasting my time. I have a three-hour meeting scheduled any second now to go through the new encryption protocols that Chad has produced."

Alice was stunned. "Encryption protocols that Chad has produced!"

"Yes, now unless someone is about to die, can you leave me to get on with my meeting?"

Alice turned to walk out of his office. What the hell was going on? That was her work. All her work. What was Chad doing taking credit for it and why was Jon so oblivious to her shock and fury at what had just happened? As she walked back to her desk, Chad was coming the other way. She gave him a fierce, pissed-off stare. He seemed confused by the look and walked past her into Jon's office.

As Alice sat back at her desk, she could hardly contain her rage. She had only been in the team for just under a year but it was obvious to everyone that she was 'head and shoulders' above the rest of the team in terms of her cyber skills, and Jon knew it. Which is why she was so stunned that this sexist 'old boys' club' had reared its head again. Every time she made a breakthrough in developing new cyber standards, someone muscled in on her work. If it wasn't Chad it had been Brad or David. She was glad she hadn't accepted Chad's offer of a drink. The way she was feeling at that moment, she might just smash the glass across his stupid smug face.

The rest of the afternoon was a blur and Alice was glad when she could eventually leave and take the short commute back to her apartment.

She threw her bags down and immediately turned her laptop on. She navigated to the bank account that Clay Deepermeyer had given to her. It was in the name of Jasmine Bakerfield, apparently her new identity. The balance was $2 million.

2

Alice woke with a start. She was cold. The apartment was cold. Her bed was cold. She looked over at the large space next to her in the double bed that dominated her small bedroom. No one there to warm her up.

This job was killing her love life. She could never tell prospective partners what she did, always having to spin a web of lies. No way to start any relationship. It meant any relationship was only ever surface level for her and often boiled down to how desperate she was for sex. She understood the carnal needs but wasn't sure she ever understood what love really was. She knew love for her parents, which is why their recent passing still tore at her heart every day, but she wasn't sure she ever knew what romantic love was. She certainly didn't think she had experienced it. As her brain re-orientated to the present, the weight of the previous day's events bore down on her. The melancholy threatened to consume her and she realised that the Deepermeyer dude was right. She had no one now. No parents, no siblings and no real friends. She forced herself to get out of bed and get ready for work, no nearer to making a decision.

*

By lunchtime, Alice felt tired and drained. She had barely slept the night before. Her boss had spent most of the morning asking her if she was feeling well, and she was running out of excuses.

And here he was again. Standing over her. "Alice? I need those reports."

"I'll have them to you this afternoon."

"You said you'd have them late morning. This isn't like you."

Of course it wasn't like her. But she couldn't tell him why. She needed time to think.

"Maybe I just need to stop for a moment, gather myself?"

"If you're ill—?"

"I just need lunch," she said, logging off her workstation. "That's all."

He touched her shoulder, gently, his concern apparently quite genuine.

"I'll be fine," she said.

She went back to the same seat in the park. Clay Deepermeyer was not there but she was fidgety and jumpy, reacting to anyone and everything around her.

The afternoon didn't improve things. Chad's attempts to talk to her had been met with silence but he didn't seem to understand what he had done wrong.

Alice had been more receptive to Mahindra's apparent concern for her welfare.

"Are you OK Alice? You seem a bit wired and off form today."

"Oh, don't worry about me. Just having a bad couple of days. Just make sure those bastards don't walk all over you. Sexist pigs."

Mahindra walked away, staring at the males in the office that Alice had gestured towards. She knew Alice was right but sometimes you just had to put up with it.

By the time Alice got home she was a nervous wreck, mentally exhausted and no nearer a decision. She lay on her sofa and fell asleep within seconds.

Three hours later she came to and took a minute to re-orientate herself. As her fuggy head cleared, the weight of the situation she was in flooded back into her mind.

I can't do this. What am I thinking? Why am I even considering this?

As she looked around her empty apartment, the realisation that she had no one to answer these questions, no one to share these moments with, jolted her into action.

She logged back into the bank account that Clay had given her. The $2 million was still there.

In that moment the loneliness once again consumed her. The money would set her up for life. Her career would be over before it started but did that matter if she had more money than she could ever hope to have?

She turned on the TV, trying to take her mind off the biggest decision of her life. She realised she hadn't eaten, threw a curry in the microwave and forced it down whilst watching some inane reality show.

She cleared away and looked at the view onto the street, desperately searching for some form of inspiration, something that would help her decide.

She didn't know what compelled her to find the special box that she kept in her closet that contained all the mementos; all the memories of her now departed parents. She started to look at the cards and letters. She found one from her mom, written just before she passed.

Alice, be free my precious girl. Don't be tied down. Be free. Always in my heart, Mom.

A tear escaped from the corner of her eye. Was this it? Was this note telling her to go?

3

Faculty of Infectious Diseases, University of Minnesota

Professor Carlton Jenkins sat watching the newscasts. Every one of them seemed to be running the same story. Scientists in another university had made a breakthrough, a step toward curing the very condition that he had being working on for more years than he could remember. What he called the 'Holy Grail' of scientific breakthroughs. The one thing he was sure would get him a Nobel prize – if he could deliver it first. He felt like the game had suddenly moved into a new phase. A race to the finish line.

He was pissed that they were lauding their progress all over the media. He had always done his research in complete isolation, paranoid about his secrets getting out. He never felt the need to shout about his progress to all and sundry.

The only thing that was stopping his anxiety reaching debilitating levels, as he pored over the new stories about these other scientists, was the clinical trial results he was now looking at. Clinical trial results on human subjects, not mice or human tissue like those other scientists. Real-life people delivering real-life results.

My God. Can these results really be true?

He looked at the clinical data across the three control groups. The placebo group was as expected. The normalisation group was as expected. The experimental group was not.

"George! George! Come in here quickly."

George Mankley was the Professor's Senior Research Technician, occasional lover and the only person in the world he truly trusted.

"Yes Professor. What can I help you with?"

"Have you seen the results of the latest trials?"

"Uh, yes, they seemed quite promising."

"Promising! Promising! They are amazing. The virus has practically disappeared from their bodies in less than twenty-four hours."

"It was only six people Professor. You have always said that these trials have to deliver consistent results over several trials and a wide population demographic to be statistically and scientifically viable."

"George! Stop quoting my wisdom back at me. You know it annoys me. I am well aware it is only six people but I have never seen as consistent results as these in one experimental group. What are their origins?"

"Uh, two African Americans, one Chinese, three white."

"Genders?"

"Three of each."

The Professor sat and mused.

"George. This is significant. I know it is only six people but if these results could be replicated across a wide demographic, we could be on our way to..." he could hardly bring himself to say it... "to delivering a cure for the common cold and beating those bastards that are lauding their breakthroughs all over the media."

George was pensive. The Professor seemed obsessed with being the one to deliver the ultimate scientific breakthrough. Sometimes it seemed it was all he cared about. As George sat across from the Professor trying to work out what to say next, more questions were being bombarded at him.

"George. What was the compound we gave them? How was this different from the last trial? Who else have these results been shared with?"

"The compound was dihydroxyacetone mixed with the latest probiotic formula we used in the last trial. This was the first time we have used it. We are the only people that have seen these results."

"Ah, yes of course. Dihydroxyacetone. From Manuka flowers. The antibacterial compound in Manuka honey is methylglyoxal and this comes from the conversion of dihydroxyacetone. We need to know what the UMF rating of our compound is and I need the full scientific breakdown of everything that was in that test batch."

"OK, it will take me several hours but I can do some checks on the samples we administered. I'll get right onto it."

"Do it. Do it now George."

*

The Professor was back in his lab at 8 a.m. the following morning, desperate to find out what information George had sent him about the compound used in the trial. George was already in.

"Morning George, have you got that information for me?"

"On your desk Professor."

The Professor strode into his office, excited to find out the full details of the magical compound, but as he entered his office he stopped in his tracks. Something wasn't right. Stuff had been moved around. The pot plant was in a different place, the visitor's chair had been moved, one of the drawers of his filing cabinet was slightly ajar and the blinds were down. He sat and stared at the room. He was a stickler for order, everything had its place and he always noticed when things were different. The problem was this was the second time this had happened in the last couple of months.

"George. Have you been in my office this morning?"

"No Professor. I left the report on your desk last night and have only been out here this morning."

"Were the blinds down last night?"

"Um, no I don't think so. You never have the blinds down."

"I know."

He stood motionless, trying to work out what had happened. Had someone been in his office? Only George and he had access. This area was sacred. It was where all his scientific work was stored. The secrets; the breakthroughs; the hope.

He turned around and just as he was about to call George in, he caught sight of the gun. George was down on the floor. A figure, all decked out in black, was holding a gun and it was aimed straight at him. Was this it? Was this his appointment with death?

A strange noise came out of the gun. It wasn't a bullet. He looked at the dart now resting in his chest. All he knew next was blackness.

4

Alice sat in the morning team meeting, nursing her third cup of coffee, trying to medicate against the thumping in her head, brought on by too little sleep and the 'little dilemma' that clouded her every waking hour.

Jon Ruganzi started the meeting.

"Right team, the first point on the agenda is the G8. I need a team of three to manage the US cyber security…"

"I'll do it."

Everyone turned to look at Alice.

"You know. Sounds like a blast."

Alice could tell from Jon's face that he was not impressed with being interrupted.

"Err, no Alice. I need you to stay here and work on the new encryption with Chad and Mahindra. Brad, David and Jez will go."

Alice was gobsmacked. Her non-verbal communication was obvious to anyone that was looking at her. She stared at Chad. He just smiled and looked back to Jon. She looked at Mahindra who just shrugged and shook her head. No one was going to speak up. The 'old boys' club' had struck again.

Alice spent the rest of the meeting quietly seething, not taking any notice of what Jon was saying. She was relieved when the meeting finished and she could get back to her cubicle. She opened up the files on the latest encryption work, her work, and the cogs began to whirr. She got out an encrypted memory stick and copied all the work onto it. For the first time in a couple of days, she allowed herself to smile.

At lunchtime, she decided to go back to the park. The nice spring weather was holding and she needed to get away from all the testosterone.

As she made her way to her normal bench, she stopped in her tracks. The Deepermeyer dude was sitting there. Curiosity won the day and she walked nonchalantly over to him, trying to seem cool when every part of her being was telling her to run.

He spoke as soon as she sat down.

"You're not on the plane yet?"

"Well obviously not, otherwise I wouldn't be sitting here, talking to you."

"Can I ask why?"

"Why! Do you really need to ask me that? I have no idea who you are and you expect me to leave my highly sensitive US intelligence job and betray my country on the promise of ten million dollars?"

"Is it not enough?"

"That's not the point. You are not giving me anything I can reconcile as normal. Something that would make such an outrageous offer seem viable."

"Ah, ever the analyst, Alice. OK, I thought I had laid out the offer quite clearly but let me pitch it again to you. I own a pharmaceutical company that is funding vital medical research and we have recently had a significant breakthrough. I am setting up a dedicated state-of-the-art medical facility in Europe that will focus on delivering a cure for one of the most common ailments in the world. I am recruiting the best people to make sure that this new facility is ultra-secure as this has the potential to be a multi-billion-dollar breakthrough."

"Ah, so now we get to the point. You are going to make shitloads of money and don't want anyone else to steal your thunder."

14

"Exactly. I can guarantee that every other pharmaceutical company in the world would like to get hold of what we have, so I make no apologies for doing everything I can to protect this vital work. Is that so bad? Can you analyse that as a good offer now?"

Alice looked directly at Clay Deepermeyer, trying to see if his eyes would bear witness to his true soul. He stared back confidently, unflinching and unwavering. She was none the wiser.

"I just don't know Mr Deepermeyer. This is madness."

"Didn't your mother die of cancer Alice?"

The mention of her mother disarmed her.

"What? How did you know that and what's it got to do with convincing me to work for you?"

"If you could have saved her, been part of a team to deliver a cure, that would make my offer more palatable... wouldn't it?"

"Are you saying you have a cure for cancer?"

"No, I'm not saying that but I consider our work just as important."

Clay got up without saying another word and left Alice to the rest of her lunch, seemingly confident he had done his job. Alice sat there stunned, trying to reconcile just what he had said. Could she believe him? Was he really offering her an opportunity to be part of a team that would deliver a major cure... not cancer... but something similar?

*

As Alice walked back to her desk, Chad stopped her progress.

"Who was that guy you were talking to?"

"What?"

"That guy you were just talking to. In the park. At lunch."

"Jesus Chad. Are you spying on me?"

"No. I was just walking through the park and saw you talking to that guy. You seemed to be in a rather deep conversation with him."

15

"And what difference does that make to you?"

"Just looking out for you Alice."

"I'm fine Chad. You don't need to worry about me or who I talk to."

With that she pushed past him and sat back at her desk. She put her head in her hands. *What was she doing?*

*

The rest of the day dragged on without incident but Alice spent the whole time going over and over what Clay Deepermeyer had said to her. Whilst his style of approach was unconventional, she was finding it hard not to accept his offer as perfectly rational.

As she left the office, Brad, David and Jez were high-fiving each other, seemingly revelling in the party potential they thought they were going to have at the G8.

As she entered her apartment, the first thing she saw was the note from her mom. She sat down and stared at it. She put it up to her nose and smelt it. Was her mind playing tricks on her or could she really smell the faint and unmistakable scent of her mother? She wiped away a tear.

She ate a quick microwaveable meal, washed down with a slightly disgusting glass of white wine. The computer screen glowed back at her the whole time. The balance of $2 million didn't change.

She got the memory stick out of her bag and loaded up the code of the new encryption standards. Her fingers danced over the keyboard at a lightning pace, two hours passing with what seemed like a click of her finger. She ran the updated programme and smiled. It had worked.

In that moment, with her mom's note staring up at her, she made a decision. She was going to accept Clay Deepermeyer's offer.

5

Alice was up bright and early the next day, packing her suitcase with as many clothes as she could fit in and the few personal mementoes that she had. Pictures of her parents in an attractive oak frame, a small jewellery collection that included some nice pieces she had inherited from her grandmother, the rather threadbare teddy bear that she'd had since birth and a pennant of New York, a crappy piece of souvenir shit that an old boyfriend had given her that she had got strangely attached to.

She grabbed her backpack and stuffed all her toiletries and gadgets in it. Laptop, smartphone and numerous flash drives, one of which contained the work she had done the previous evening. She had a feeling her updated encryption work may come in useful for what she was going to be asked to do. She decided to leave the Taser behind. She grabbed her passport, the tickets she had been given and all the US money she had. She packed a bottle of water that was left in the fridge, and threw the rest of the contents away. As she locked up and left, she wondered whether she would ever see this place again.

She grabbed a cab outside her apartment. The traffic to the airport was light at this time of the morning and the flight was running on time. She boarded and found her business class seat. Nice. No one was following her. No one seemed to be bothered about her. At 9 a.m., as the plane had reached its cruising height, she had a text from her boss.

'Alice. Where are you? You are not normally late for work. Are you ill? Please call me.'

She ignored it. Turned the phone off, took out the SIM card and proceeded to smash up all the separate components of the phone, trying not to draw attention to herself. She couldn't be tracked by her phone. Her name was on the flight tickets but she knew once she landed, she had to go dark.

After an eight-and-a-half-hour flight, they landed in Innsbruck. She went through the usual checks and walked into the arrivals lounge. Immediately, she spotted a short, muscular man with dark glasses seemingly staring at her. She walked over to him. He seemed too obvious not to be her lift. As she approached, he spoke.

"Miss Bidebecker, my name is Shaun Griffiths and I will be taking you to your new life. Please come with me." As he walked in front of her, she spotted the conspicuous bulge of a firearm tucked in the back of his trousers.

It was past midnight by the time they set off and she was pleased that the journey was short, as they drew into the parking lot of a small Austrian hotel, fifteen minutes after leaving the airport.

"We have rooms booked here for the night. I will meet you for breakfast at nine a.m. and then I will take you to your final destination."

Alice did as she was told, checked into her room and stared out of the window into the blackness. What the hell was she doing here? She suddenly remembered two million reasons why and another eight million reasons after that. She got in bed and fell into a deep sleep.

6

NSA Offices, Maryland, USA

Jon Ruganzi sat at his desk trying to work out how to balance the excessive workloads that his team were constantly tasked with. They were the best cyber security team in the world but constant threats from the Russians and Chinese kept them on their toes, as well as the growing threat from the lone-wolf hackers. More and more, these lone-wolf hackers were some spotty Herbert from the US or UK who spent all their time in their bedrooms, just trying to embarrass the US government by hacking major government networks. It was a constant wonder to Jon how they learnt the knowledge to get as far as they did. He wondered whether he should change his recruitment processes to employ these uber geeks.

What was bothering Jon most this particular morning was that Alice had not turned up for work. She was usually so reliable, but no one had heard from her. He sent her a text.

Thirty minutes later he had still heard nothing. He texted her again and got a service rejection message. The second text had not been delivered.

He now knew they had to kick in with their missing persons security protocol. The analysts in his team were the only people, except for senior military positions, who had the highest level of security access to US government and military secrets. Any suggestion that these individuals may have been compromised had to be met with immediate action to assess and deal with the potential threats.

He called Dirk Landsley, the Director of Intelligence. He answered straight away.

"Mr Landsley, it is Jon Ruganzi. I need to report a missing person in my team and initiate our immediate security protocols for these circumstances. She has not turned up for work and is not responding to phone contact. As per the protocol, I will despatch one of my team to her home address to do a physical search and another to do a digital search."

"Who is it?"

"Alice Bidebecker."

"OK, I agree to step one. Call me when they have done their initial review. We will need to formalise this if she is not found by the end of the day."

Jon got off the phone and called in Chad and Mahindra.

"We have a problem. Alice is missing."

Mahindra's snort of derision got both their attentions.

"Something to say Mahindra?"

"Well, let's just say I'm not surprised. The way you two have been treating her lately."

Jon reacted first. "What's that supposed to mean?"

"My God, you don't even see it do you? Chad presenting you that latest encryption work as his own, when you know that was all Alice's work. It was her brilliance that took us to the next level of sophistication on those latest standards and you two dismissed her like some office junior."

Jon and Chad looked at each other dumbfounded. Mahindra carried on before they could speak.

"And yesterday Jon, in the team meeting, the way you dismissed her request to go to the G8. She was just looking for some recognition, some reward for all her hard work, but instead you send the three wise monkeys. Have you any idea what it's like being a woman in this team?"

The tension in the room was palpable. Jon eventually broke the uncomfortable silence.

"I'm sorry you feel that way Mahindra but right now our priority is to find out what has happened to her. I have agreed with Mr Landsley that we will initiate the missing persons protocol. Chad, I need you to go to Alice's apartment to do the physical search and Mahindra, I need you to set up the digital search. Please report back your findings to me by the end of the day."

*

Mahindra walked out of Jon's office shaking her head. She couldn't believe the arrogance of the man. A small part of her was envious of whatever it was that Alice had done. Stood up to these bastards. Go girl.

Mahindra started the digital search. She immediately found Alice's name booked on a flight out to Innsbruck at 8.30 a.m. that morning. She accessed the traffic and buildings CCTV from around her apartment. At 5.30 a.m. she picked Alice up on CCTV getting into a cab outside her apartment and sure enough tracked her to the airport. She had a suitcase and hand luggage bag. She seemed to be leaving of her own accord. No one was with her. No one was forcing her to go to the airport.

Mahindra contacted Innsbruck Airport. They eventually provided confirmation that Alice had landed and had passed through passport control. They provided access to their CCTV. She picked up Alice leaving the arrivals lounge and seemingly meeting a short, muscular guy wearing dark glasses. They left the airport together but there was no CCTV picking up where they went. Mahindra checked satellite images for that period. Nothing. The satellite surveillance was not covering that particular part of Austria. Had they been on it earlier they could have redirected satellites to track her in real time. They had lost her. They would have to hope that her digital footprint would soon tell them what she was doing.

*

Chad travelled the short distance to Alice's apartment, his mind spinning with what Jon had told him. What the hell had happened to Alice? Why had she disappeared so suddenly? Was it his fault? Did she react badly to his unwanted attentions? Was Mahindra right about her being pissed off about the encryption work? Surely not.

He entered the apartment using the specialist lock-picking kit they were authorised to use in these circumstances. There was no alarm as he entered the rather small but neat apartment. He walked into an open-plan living, dining and kitchen area, with smart contemporary furniture and a large UHD TV dominating the corner of the room. He checked the fridge. It was turned off and empty. He ran the taps. No water. He realised there was no heating on. He moved into one of the two bedrooms, which seemed to be Alice's as the other was set up as an office. The cupboards and drawers were pretty much empty of clothes. There were no gadgets in the office. Her laptop and phone were not there. The bathroom was sparse with no toiletries. It was clear she had left.

As he left the apartment, he tried to visualise the face of the man she was talking to in the park. Something about that situation was pricking his conspiracy radar. It was too much of a coincidence that she had disappeared the day after that strange meeting.

*

Chad and Mahindra reconvened with Jon at the end of the day and recounted their preliminary findings.

"This is not good," said Jon. "She appears to have left of her own accord and, based on what Chad observed, taken most of her worldly possessions with her. Mahindra, has there been any digital activity since she landed?"

"No, nothing, but I now have a trace set on all her email accounts, bank accounts, credit cards, store cards and anything else she might use that we can trace her by."

"Good. I will need to speak to the Director of Intelligence and update him on your preliminary analysis. This will become a formal operation, which we will need to regularly review. Chad, you will need to set up some form of surveillance in and around her apartment to pick up any unwanted visitors or Alice actually returning. Mahindra, you will need to keep the digital surveillance on constantly and let me know the minute we get any hits. I have a bad feeling about this. Alice did not seem the type to become a traitor but her actions don't seem like someone under duress."

Chad had been agonising over whether to mention it but decided to blurt it out before the meeting ended. "There is one more thing."

Jon looked at Chad with just an ounce of irritation. "What? I thought I had your complete report."

"Well, to be honest I don't know whether it is at all relevant, which is why it wasn't in my report, but it has been playing on my mind."

"What is it?"

"When I was walking through the park at lunch yesterday, Alice was deep in conversation with an older guy. They were sitting on one of the park benches. I asked her about it when she got back but she just told me to stop spying on her and that I didn't need to worry about what she was doing. It seems odd that she has disappeared the day after that happened."

"Jesus Chad, how did you not think that was relevant? Could you describe him to a composite artist? Is there any CCTV in that area?"

"That's the problem, I have been trying to visualise his face but beyond recalling that he looked quite old, grey hair and stuff, I can't really remember. I'm pretty sure there is no CCTV in the park."

"Well sorry Chad but I think this absolutely needs to be part of the intel report. This could be significant. Both of you check whether there are any cameras, CCTV, traffic, store security, that may have picked him up. We need to find her and work out what the hell she is up to. Do not leave any stone unturned."

Chad and Mahindra left the meeting and immediately put in place what Jon had asked for. This was a shitstorm in anyone's book.

*

Jon phoned the Director of Intelligence and appraised him of the situation.

"This seems serious Jon. I don't like what I am hearing. I will need to brief the President. In the meantime, I am happy that you have put the obvious steps in place and please report any progress to me immediately. We need to give this a formal operation codename so it becomes part of the regular intelligence briefing to the President."

"Yes Sir, the protocol allocates this as Operation Hawk."

Dirk Landsley phoned the President. He wasn't impressed. The NSA was now under severe pressure. Their best analyst missing and no let-up on the workload. Dirk and Jon had definitely had better days.

7

Switzerland

The Professor struggled to open his eyes. His head was thumping, his whole body felt heavy. *What the hell did I drink last night?*

As he forced his eyes to take in the day, he double-took as he looked at the snow-covered peaks of mountains outside his window. *Where was he?*

The memories started to click in. His lab. The man in black. The gun. GEORGE!

He bolted out of bed. He was in a massive room with stunning views over a beautiful mountain range. He approached the door to the bedroom and tentatively opened it. It led to an enormous living area with plush sofas, a huge TV, a large kitchen/dining area and more brilliant views. As he tried to orientate himself, a voice came from the kitchen.

"Ah Professor, you are awake. Would you like some coffee?"

He looked at the stranger. Gobsmacked.

"What! Who are you? Where am I?"

"You are in Switzerland Professor. Beautiful, isn't it?"

"Sorry, but are you insane? Why are you chatting to me like it's just a normal day? I have no idea who you are and why I am here. You have kidnapped me."

"OK, Professor. Let me explain. My name is Jacob Deepermeyer. I run a company called Deepermeyer Pharmaceuticals with my brother and we want you to work for us."

"What? You think I am going to work for you when you extract me from my normal life, against my will, bring me to another country and try to sell me your madness on a nice view and some coffee?"

"Look, our methods may be unconventional but what we need you to do requires the utmost secrecy. We have been keeping an eye on you. We know what you think you have stumbled on and we want to make it a reality."

The Professor stared at this man. Now things began to make sense. The disruption to his office. Someone had been in there. They had planted some sort of surveillance device and knew everything that George and he had been speaking about over... how long?... months? weeks?

The thought of George made his stomach churn. Raw emotion sounded in his voice.

"Where is George? Did you kill him, you bastard?"

Jacob picked up his phone and sent a text. A few seconds later George emerged from another bedroom, manhandled by a hard-looking soldier type.

The Professor rushed up and hugged him, like his life depended on it.

"My God George. I thought you were dead. Are you OK?"

"I'm fine Professor. Don't worry about me."

The Professor was now getting some inner fight. His body was almost fully functioning and now he was apoplectic with rage.

"I don't know what you think you know, but there is no damn chance on this planet that I will ever work for you. Let George and I go immediately."

Jacob Deepermeyer sat down and shook his head.

"The thing is Professor, we just can't do that. We know what you discovered on those latest clinical trials and we want you to take the research forward with us, here in this secure, state-of-the-art facility. You will have access to things here that you could only dream of in your dingy university labs and George is here to help you. We want that cure Professor, and you are going to deliver it. We will pay you ten million dollars each when you succeed."

"You really are insane. Do you think I am motivated by money? I am a scientist. My life is dedicated to improving people's lives, not lining people's pockets."

Jacob looked at him with pity.

"Dear, dear Professor, you really are a crashing bore, but oh so predictable."

He picked up the TV remote control and switched it on. A picture emerged of an old lady sitting in a chair, half watching TV and half looking at a magazine. The Professor was stunned.

"What is this? Why have you got a camera watching my mother?"

"We are watching her Professor. If you don't comply, she is dead."

The Professor was racked with terror. He tried a bluff. "You know she is terminally ill?"

Jacob smiled. A smug, arrogant smile. He nodded at the soldier type. The Professor heard the cocking of his gun, which was now aimed at George's head.

8

Austria and Switzerland

Alice got up from a strangely untroubled sleep, considering the drama of the previous days. She met Shaun for a very nice continental breakfast in the dining room of the pretty Austrian hotel.

"Where are we headed?" she asked.

"We are going to Switzerland."

"Can you be more precise?"

"No."

"OK, a man of many words."

They finished breakfast with a slightly uncomfortable vibe hanging over their limited conversation.

They set off a little after 10 a.m. and within an hour were crossing the border into Switzerland. She had been given a new passport with her new identity, Jasmine Bakerfield, which matched her new Swiss bank account. It was clear she had to go dark the minute she got through Innsbruck Airport. The NSA had countless surveillance tools and she knew by now that they would be tracking all her previous digital life. The guys she was working for knew it too. They had wasted no time in helping her go dark. The new passport would not trigger anything at the border.

As they continued their journey, Alice tried to strike up a conversation with Shaun. He was clearly not one for polite chit-chat.

"Look Miss Bidebecker, I understand you are here to protect the secrets that the Deepermeyers need to keep. I, and my team, are the physical security and you are responsible for the technical security. I won't interfere in your work if you don't interfere in mine. My job is to deliver you safely to the site. You will meet the team later today. Your new phone is in the bag on the back seat. Why don't you get that sorted and listen to some music and let me concentrate on driving?"

Alice was impressed that she had managed to get such a long sentence out of him, in that strong British accent which seemed to make him a bit more threatening. She decided to cut her losses, got her new phone out and fiddled about with the apps to get some music she could listen to. She got comfortable and closed her eyes.

After about four hours of driving and a brief stop for lunch, they arrived at a car park high up in the mountains below a cable car station. Shaun helped Alice with her luggage; not that she needed his faux chivalry but, whatever, she just let him get on with it. They were met by two heavily armed guys who both gave Alice a cheeky smile.

Hmm, she thought to herself, *maybe this won't all be work after all.*

They completed the short cable car journey and alighted to another security gate, manned by another couple of ripped US Marine types. Alice smiled to herself and went through the gate.

The site was impressive. Various smart buildings sat around lovely gardens, looking out onto panoramas that took your breath away. She was shown to her amazing apartment with incredible mountain views.

"Well this is a bit better than my pokey apartment in Maryland."

After a very nice meal, Alice was summoned to the conference room which was up a flight of stairs from the comfortable restaurant she had dined in, within what she had worked out was the main leisure and office building.

As she was invited into the impressive room that was laid out in a board-room style, equipped with large TV screens and various bits of communication kit that would allow a range of virtual meetings, she was met by four men.

As she viewed the scene, she had a pang of doubt. *From the frying pan into the fire,* she thought to herself. She had just left a place full of sexism and latent misogyny. She wondered whether she had just stepped into another one; after all, she had not seen a single woman since she arrived. She tried to put the doubts out of her mind as Clay Deepermeyer started the introductions.

"Miss Bidebecker, I'm absolutely delighted that you have taken up our offer. Your talent is unsurpassed and we are all stoked that you have agreed to work with us on this exciting project."

"Thank you, it's nice to be here and such a stunning place." *It's also nice to be appreciated*, she thought to herself.

"So, let me introduce you to the rest of the Plutus Group…"

"Plutus? The Greek god of wealth… that figures."

Clay smiled. "You are clearly well-educated Miss Bidebecker, and yes we think it is very appropriate for our ambitions on this project."

Alice smiled back. She had the size of this bunch of men.

Clay continued.

"This is my brother Jacob. You have met Shaun and this is…"

Alice had clocked the final person as she walked in. Someone she already knew. Or at least knew by his reputation. He had been all over the news for the last eighteen months, implicated in a 'cash for babies' scandal that had got both his sons arrested and put away for some time. It had been headline news for so long due to the small matter that one of his sons was the Prime

Minister of the UK. As scandals went it didn't get any bigger, but somehow this man had survived and was sitting staring at her, or rather staring at her tits.

"… William Hardacre."

"And what is your role in this, Mr Hardacre?" Alice probed.

Clay answered for him.

"Mr Hardacre represents our UK interests. He is a very well connected and influential man."

"No shit," Alice muttered under her breath.

There was a brief uncomfortable pause. Alice was holding her own and the collective audience was clearly unnerved by her strength of character. She was fascinated by this little brood. Three old men and an alpha male with the charisma and sense of humour of an amoeba. She would give herself some time to size them up and make sure she wasn't taken advantage of. She was pretty sure they weren't used to a strong woman telling them what to do.

She decided to get on the front foot. "So, are you now going to tell me what it is that I'm protecting, Mr Deepermeyer?"

"As I mentioned when we first met, you will be protecting scientific secrets that could have a global impact, once successful clinical trials are completed. We have a small team led by a Professor of Infectious Diseases working on these trials. It is essential that all aspects of the Professor's work are secure."

"Infectious diseases? What is he working on?"

"I think it best if we leave your knowledge base there at the moment Miss Bidebecker. The fewer people that know the full details, the better. We just need you to make everything ultra-secure from a cyber perspective. I need your security proposal within seven days and a plan of how you will implement it within the three-month window. Once I agree the plan, you will be paid another one million dollars. Once the plan is implemented you will be paid another two million dollars. If there are no breaches you will be paid the remainder of what we promised you."

She smiled. Stood up and walked out of the room with her closing words clearly showing she was in complete control. "Sounds reasonable."

As Alice sat in her mountainside apartment, taking in the wonderful view as darkness fell, she mused to herself. She had a feeling that she would need to have an exit plan if things got hairy. The NSA were undoubtedly trying to find her. That was the protocol. She was almost certainly breaking some US law or other and the Deepermeyers did not seem the sort of people to stay within the law if the money was right. This was going to be an interesting assignment.

*

Jacob picked up the phone to the Swiss passport control office.

"Lazlo. It's Jacob. A number of my team have passed through in the last twenty-four hours. The Americans will be asking for the CCTV. Make sure they get the edited version. Your money is in the usual place."

9

After another gloriously untroubled sleep, Alice met Clay and Shaun at the main entrance to the site to start the tour they had promised her. Clay came bounding up to her, full of smiles and enthusiasm.

"Miss Bidebecker. I hope you slept well?"

"Like a baby, thanks. How about you? Did you dream about all the money you are going to make?"

Clay's face displayed a cheeky, arrogant smirk. Shaun just looked at her, stony faced.

"Right Miss Bidebecker. We are going to walk you around the site and then take you into the technical suite. Please ask questions as we go around as I want to make sure you know what I want."

"OK, boss man."

They started at the main entrance to the site, accessible only from the cable car entrance and seemingly permanently guarded by two of Shaun's team. Alice noticed one of them had met her at the bottom of the cable car station the previous day. Cute. He winked at her. She looked away but logged it in the mental shag bank. *He might be worth a go*, she thought to herself.

Clay and Shaun explained more about the physical security and stressed this was not her concern.

They walked around the other buildings. There was the large accommodation block where Alice had her apartment, the leisure building where food could be obtained, numerous fitness things could be done and films could be watched at the state-of-the-art cinema. As they walked behind these buildings to the back of the site, Alice caught sight of three people going into another building. One was a member of Shaun's team, one was an older man with a full beard and a growing paunch, and the last was a younger, more slender man.

"Who is that?" she asked Clay.

"Ah, that is the Professor and his assistant George. They will be running the clinical trials."

"Can I meet them?"

"All in good time Miss Bidebecker. Like you, they have only just arrived and have a lot to do."

Alice watched them go into the building, which Clay later explained was the secure lab with a large accommodation block for the volunteers who would help in the clinical trials. He made it clear this was the building that would hold all the secrets and needed to be more secure than Fort Knox.

They finished the tour at her 'mission control', an extremely well-equipped technology suite.

"This is very impressive Clay. I will need quite a bit more stuff but this is a great start."

"I'm glad you approve. As I said yesterday, money is no object. We can't have anyone hacking our secrets."

"Like those troublesome rival pharmaceutical companies?"

"Especially them Miss Bidebecker and I'm not too keen on your old team getting any leverage."

Alice smiled. "Don't worry about them. I have just enhanced the latest encryption standards that they were testing when I left. They won't have a clue how to get around what I have done... goddam amateurs. I will make sure this is applied to all our cyber assets."

"Good. Good. You really are a diamond Miss Bidebecker. Could you send me the full specification of that encryption in a secure file? I have a feeling we may need to use that as a bit of leverage when the time comes to negotiate our drug deals with the US government."

"Yeh, no problem. I'll set up an ultra-secure area on the network where all the really secret stuff needs to be kept. I'll make sure the Professor saves his work to the same place."

"The Professor?... oh yes, that makes sense. Let me have the details and I will pass it on to him."

Clay and Shaun left Alice to start her work. As she started to develop her wish list, she pondered on the last thing Clay said. *Why was he so defensive when I mentioned the Professor's name?*

She carried on but there was something else that was niggling at her. When she saw them, there was something about the Professor and George's body language that didn't seem right.

*

Jon Ruganzi called Chad and Mahindra in for the first of many regular debriefings about Operation Hawk.

"Right. Any updates?"

"No," they both chorused.

"Shit. Are you telling me that we have access to the most sophisticated surveillance tools in the world and we can't find a missing analyst?"

Mahindra spoke. "The digital trace has given us nothing in the last twenty-four hours. We lost her at Innsbruck Airport and there has been no footprint since. She has gone completely dark. Her phone is dead, she hasn't used her email, social media, credit cards, online banking. Nothing."

"What about her passport?"

"She passed through passport control at Innsbruck Airport but nothing since."

"Come on Mahindra. Think outside the box. She is a fucking cyber expert. If she has gone rogue, she will have changed her identity. You need to look at people passing through the borders.

Cross-reference them with their digital histories and find an anomaly. She will be out there somewhere."

"What if she is still in Austria?"

"Well she might be but my bet is that she has crossed the border somewhere. Get onto it."

Mahindra scribbled down notes of what Jon had asked for. This was going to take some time but it was now obvious that no stone was to be left unturned.

"Chad. What have you got?"

"Again, nothing. There has been no movement at her flat. No visitors. No house sitters. Nothing. We also hit a complete blank with the CCTV around the park."

"For Christ's sake. OK, Chad, I need you to go to Innsbruck. If Mahindra keeps an eye on the digital trail, I need someone to follow the physical one, however much of a needle in a haystack it might be."

"OK boss. I'll make the arrangements."

Jon dismissed the meeting and steeled himself to make the difficult call to his boss, Dirk Landsley, who in turn would have to ring the President. If he didn't get results soon, he was going to be in a very difficult place. He couldn't believe that Alice was a traitor.

10

Brighton, England

He sat under the arches of the railway bridge, which took the mainline coastal train along the Sussex coast to places that he didn't know or had long since forgotten about, as his life spiralled out of control.

The familiar shakes began. The alcohol he had consumed a few hours ago was wearing off and he needed some more. The other homeless people that joined him in this daily hell of trying to keep warm and begging for money to get whatever fix got them through, were all sat around in various states of stupor. He shouted out in desperation, his speech still slurring.

"Oi, Lenny. Hash yuz got any a'cohol?"

"Wot? Wot you shaying Moley?"

"I said, hash yuz got any a'cohol?"

"Fuck off Moley. Get yur own."

He gave him the finger and shut his eyes, trying to make the pain go away. It didn't work. He tried to get himself up, slipping and sliding a few times before he made it. As he stood there unsteadily trying to get his brain to send the right signals to his legs, he noticed the silhouette of a man standing in the entrance to the arches. He was standing there, staring at them, saying nothing.

"Oi, Mister. Wot you want? Do ya hash any fooking money?"

The stranger didn't speak, just stood there looking at them.

Moley started toward him. As he got closer the man turned to leave, but left something on the floor. By the time Moley got to where he was standing, he was out of sight. He looked down at the floor and couldn't believe his eyes. The man had left a roll of £20 notes.

Moley snuffled it into one of the raggedy pockets of the latest coat he had found in some bin, before any of the others noticed. He cracked a drunken smile. Maybe tonight was going to be a good night after all.

11

The Professor and George sat in the new state-of-the-art lab that the Deepermeyers had promised them.

"I am sorry George. I couldn't let them kill you. We are just going to have to do what they want and try to find a way out of this hell."

"I know Prof. I guess I didn't really fancy a bullet in my head but do you really think they are ever going to let us go?"

The Professor looked at George with an expression of pain that only came from the heartrending effect of true love.

"We have to keep the faith."

"Come on Prof, don't be so naïve. As soon as we do what they want they are going to kill us. We have to escape."

"Look around George. We are up a fricking mountain with only one way in and one way out. How are we getting out? Are we suddenly going to learn to fly?"

"We have to find a way."

"Look, we have no means of communicating with the outside world and no way of getting off this mountain. Let's just start doing what they have asked for and see what happens."

"OK Prof. What do we need to do?"

"Well, they have brought over all our files, clinical samples, the stockpile of the virus we have been using for tests, a small stock of the ingredients for the last compound we used and the records of our trial patients. This is enough to prepare the next level of clinical trials but we need them to supply around twenty to twenty-five trial patients if we are going to be able to complete the next set of tests. We have to see whether we can start replicating those stunning results with a wider group."

"How will they do that? We are up a mountain. Not exactly your walk-in clinic."

"I don't know but Jacob told me to write down everything we want and right now, more trial patients is what we need."

*

Later that evening, Alice sat in the bar after a very nice meal. The Deepermeyers were certainly holding to their promise that everything would be provided for. They had at least got some decent chefs in.

The bar was reasonably quiet. It seemed to Alice that the people staying on the site were, not surprisingly, kept to a bare minimum but there did seem to be an on-site team of caterers, cleaners and maintenance people, some of whom were sitting over the other side of the bar chatting away and seemingly happy to be there.

As she got engrossed in filling up the music playlist on her new phone, she was suddenly aware of a presence standing over her. She looked up.

"Mr Hardacre. What can I do for you?"

"Mind if I join you?"

"Yes, I do mind actually and I would appreciate it if you looked at my face when you speak to me, rather than staring at my tits."

He ignored her bravado and sat down. Alice looked at the arrogant smirk on his face with some displeasure. So befitting of a man of his type, she thought.

"What do you want?"

"You are a very attractive girl, Miss Bidebecker."

"I know. What the fuck has that got to do with you?"

"Well, let's just say that many women have very much enjoyed my company in the past."

Alice couldn't believe what was coming out of his mouth. Did he really think she was going to shag him at the drop of a hat? An arrogant, old and quite frankly butt-ugly misogynist.

"Fuck off old man. I am not interested."

William Hardacre stood up with the smug, arrogant smirk still fixed on his face. As he walked away, he left Alice with no doubt where he thought the power lay in their relationship.

"I do hope your potty mouth doesn't get you in trouble Miss Bidebecker. You really don't want to make an enemy of me."

12

The following morning, Alice met up with Clay and Jacob Deepermeyer, relieved that the perv William Hardacre was not at the meeting. She had been handling dickheads like him all her life but she was wary of his reputation. She knew people like him didn't get to where they got to and make all the billions they make without getting what they want.

She sat down at the conference table and gave them a short report.

"Right, here is the high-level plan and the items that I will need to implement it. We need a military-grade satellite dish to implement the anti-satellite surveillance. I don't know how you will get it but it is what we need if you want me to stop you being seen from space."

Clay responded. "Don't worry about that Miss Bidebecker. We have our contacts. You shall get what you need."

"OK, I also need some upgraded kit for the servers, network, firewalls and new readers for all internal doors to implement my proposed triple-level entrance security. If you want key buildings completely locked down, we need to implement DNA, iris and fingerprint readers. You can decide which buildings need all three, the Professor's lab I presume, and which need just one, such as the leisure building. I will configure it so all movements are tracked."

"Sounds good. We will get this ordered for you. Anything else?"

"Yes. The current network is internal to this site. There are no routes out to the internet, no email, no video conferencing. What are you expecting for this? Are the staff allowed to use the internet because, as you know, at its basic level it is not secure? Are you expecting fully encrypted access to all these things so they can't be traced back here and if so, who for?"

Clay and Jacob were clearly impressed with the detail she was covering and seemed to keep a pleasant, conciliatory manner as they interacted with Alice.

"Thank you for checking. This is an important point. The staff on site must not be able to use the internet, email or make phone calls whilst they are here. Everything must be locked down and any staff or visitors must surrender their phones to Shaun's team on arrival. The only exceptions are myself and Clay, Mr Hardacre, Shaun and yourself. You can access all these features with the encrypted phone we gave you but you must use your new identity. We need encrypted access to the internet and email. We do need secure video conferencing. I want this to be untraceable though. Can you do that?"

"Of course. I guessed this would be the case. Why are the Professor and his assistant not being given the same access rights?"

Suddenly Jacob's mood went from pleasant and conciliatory to firm and slightly confrontational.

"He does not need it. He is to focus solely on the clinical trials. We will get all he needs. He will not have this access under any circumstances."

Alice held her hands up in a mock 'sorry I asked' pose.

"O... K... I hear you loud and clear."

As they wound up the meeting, Jacob's reaction began to firm up what Alice had suspected. The Professor was being controlled. She would have to find a way to speak to him and find out just what the hell was going on there.

*

Jon Ruganzi was with Mahindra in the conference room, dialled into a video conference with Chad who was on his flight to Innsbruck.

"Right. Updates please. Mahindra?"

"I have obtained the list of all females crossing the Austrian borders on the day they arrived in Innsbruck and the following day."

"How many names?"

"Well, if you remember your geography, you will know that Austria has borders with eight countries. I have over a thousand names crossing passport control during that period. I will start trawling through them but it is not going to be quick. They definitely picked the right country to disappear in."

"Shit. Any digital footprint?"

"None. She has gone completely dark. I am sorry to say it, but it seems like she is betraying the US."

Jon rubbed his eyes. The stress was really beginning to tell.

"Chad. Anything?"

"No, I have kept an eye on the physical surveillance around her flat but there has been nothing. None of her neighbours saw anything and said she just kept herself to herself. Nobody thought she had been acting strangely before she left."

"This is too much. We are in a major shitstorm here. We are supposed to be able to find anyone, anywhere. Why the fuck can't we find her?"

"I am sorry Sir. You have to remember she was one of our team. She knows the drill. If anyone can avoid surveillance, it's Alice. If her motivation was to disappear, then she is going to do it."

He slammed his fist on the table, making Mahindra jump.

"For fuck's sake, this is ridiculous."

Chad and Mahindra said nothing. They just let Jon stew. They knew his head could be on the line if he didn't make some progress. After a moment, he spoke again.

"OK, both of you keep going with what you are working on. Don't work on anything else. Chad, get straight onto Innsbruck Airport security when you arrive. I want that CCTV secured and re-examined. There must be something we can use. Dial in same time tomorrow."

*

A while after their meeting with Alice, Clay and Jacob met up with William Hardacre. Clay started the informal meeting.

"William, we have the preliminary requirements from Miss Bidebecker. We will order the stuff she needs and we should be on target to be completely secure within a couple of weeks."

William looked at them both with a concerned expression.

"What is the matter William?"

"That girl is trouble."

"Why do you say that? Did she reject your advances?"

Clay had meant the comment in jest but he could tell from William's face that he had touched a nerve.

"Fuck me, she did. What the hell are you playing at, trying to nail her? You are old enough to be her father."

"Don't lecture me on what I can and can't do. She is a bitch and can't be trusted."

"We are paying ten million dollars for her loyalty."

"Don't be naïve Clay. You have given her completely free access to the outside world. How do you know she is not betraying us to her NSA buddies right now? You are relying on her to do our security, which means she can create any vulnerabilities she likes and we wouldn't know. She does not seem to be the type of person that can be bought off. It was a mistake to use her."

"Look William, stop feeling sore because you didn't get laid and focus on the job in hand. She is absolutely vital to us achieving what we need to do here and is going to help us make billions of dollars. You need to be cool with her role here and stop trying to satisfy your sexual perversions."

William stared back, stony faced. Clay continued.

"What I need you to do is prepare the ground with your government and start getting the people in we discussed for the clinical trial. The Professor told us that he has enough supplies to complete the next trial, so we need those people within a couple of months. Can you do that or shall we just end our little relationship?"

William sat quietly simmering. He didn't like working with these people. He never trusted the Americans but this deal would make him even richer and he knew he had to bide his time. He had not become rich and successful by constantly walking away from a challenge. He decided in that moment that he would have to keep an eye on the 'bitch' himself.

"Well, don't blame me when I am proved right but, whatever. I am laying the ground in the UK government. Despite the unfortunate incident with my pathetic excuse for a son, I still have strong influence in the Cabinet. When the time is right, I can rely on a few people to bend the will of the PM. As for the people, I already have my man scouting for candidates. We will be ready."

"OK William, thank you. Jacob, do we have our American network set up to find our trial patients?"

"Yes, we do Clay. I have supplied details to Miss Bidebecker and we should start getting applications in any time soon."

"Good. Good. Gentlemen, I think we are on our way."

They all stood up to leave. As Clay shook William's hand, he fixed him with a firm stare.

"Have a good evening William and try and control yourself around the staff."

13

Ellie Baker was sitting in the canteen of the packaging company that she had worked for since she left school, eating a poor excuse for a club sandwich. Six years of hard graft and not much to show for it. Stuck in the arse end of nowhere a few miles outside Phoenix in Arizona. She really needed to change her life.

She was idling through her various social media accounts when she noticed an interesting post forwarded by her friend, Rachel.

A progressive pharmaceutical company is seeking volunteers to be involved in some top-secret clinical trials that could change the world. Give us 3 months of your life. We will pay you $40,000 and put you up in our beautiful scenic location in Europe. All your needs will be catered for during this period. All we need is you and your absolute discretion. Interested? Follow this link to register...

"Shit me! Forty thousand dollars for three months. Christ, I don't earn that in a year."

Others starting looking at her, wondering why she was talking to herself. She shut up and clicked on the link.

She typed in the few personal details they asked for and clicked 'submit'. A few minutes passed and a message came back.

Thank you for your interest in our clinical trials. If you wish to proceed to the next stage, we need you to follow this link. You will be required to scan your fingerprint and iris as part of the security process to gain access to the next layer of information.

47

Ellie decided to move to the toilets and hide herself in one of the cubicles. People would definitely know she was up to something if she started scanning her eyes in the middle of the canteen.

She clicked on the link. She was asked to go through a series of security scans. The fingerprint and iris scans were done. A picture of her face had to be taken, passport style. She filled in some more personal details and clicked on the 'complete' button.

The screen whirred away for a few minutes. Another message popped up.

Thank you. The registration process is complete. You are booked on a flight to Innsbruck. If you do not wish to pursue this please click here. If you wish to secure your flight please click here.

Ellie looked at the details. The flight was in three weeks' time. She put her hand on her mouth. What should she do? A few minutes went by before she made the decision.

She clicked to accept the flight.

As she left the cubicle and looked at herself in the mirror, she had a sudden pulse of nervous excitement. Was this going to be the first step in a new life? She got back to her computer terminal and started writing her resignation letter. She would give it to them at the end of her last shift. She didn't feel like she owed them any notice.

She printed it out, put in an envelope and shoved it in her bag. She leant back on her chair with a contented smile and thought about how she was going to spend the money.

*

Alice sat in the technology suite, working on the security configuration she had agreed with Clay and Jacob. They had ordered all the kit she needed but it would take a few days to arrive. In the meantime, she was setting up the secure email, telephony, internet access and conferencing they had asked for. As she idled away, she opened up the new bank account. The balance was $3 million. They had paid her as promised.

Her dreams of what she would spend the money on were interrupted by a message popping into the secure portal she had set up for the US clinical trial applications.

The first application was in. Ellie Baker. A little younger than Alice. Her credentials checked out. Alice had worked hard on developing the security protocols for the application process. This woman was on the level.

And, Alice thought, looking at the woman's profile picture, she wasn't exactly hard on the eyes.

Not now, Alice told herself.

All the same, there was something in the other woman's eyes that held Alice, made her linger a little longer. What did people call this? Bi-curious? Her relationships with men always seemed to be about the sex but she had often admired other women without ever having the courage to explore her feelings further.

She tried to put it out of her mind and cleared Ellie's application, forwarding it to Jacob.

14

The sun was setting over the beautiful spring vista that they could see from their apartment. The snow cover was beginning to leave the lower parts of the mountain and the low sun was creating a rich colour scheme that was a joy to behold, but George wasn't looking at it. He was pacing the floor.

"I can't do this Prof. I can't just stay here waiting to die."

"You have to calm down George. There is nothing we can do. Not at the moment."

"For God's sake Prof, we have to do something. We are dead men walking."

"Look George, Jacob told me that they are getting the trial patients in to the site within the next couple of weeks. They are not going to kill us while they need us to work on this cure."

"But what if the next trial doesn't work? It was only six patients. What if we don't recreate the results with this next batch?"

"Then we do more tests. Adapt the compound. Review the UMF level to see if that is a factor. There are lots of options."

"And you think they will be patient?"

The Professor looked at George with a sense of pity. He knew he was right but he had to remain strong for both of them. He would have to manage the Deepermeyers' expectations as best he could. He knew their lives depended on it. He stood up and hugged George.

"Come on. Sit down and have a drink. I promise I will get us out of this. Somewhere. Somehow."

George mellowed a bit and sat down but a minute later, his anxiety was back.

"My parents. Shit Prof, I hadn't thought about them. I usually speak to them at least once a week and I was gonna have lunch with them on Sunday. They will be frantic with worry. I have to let them know I'm OK."

"They are not going to let you do that George."

The tears started to flow. The Professor held him close.

"I will speak to Jacob and see what I can do. I am sure they don't want your parents badgering the police about your disappearance."

"Surely the university has already done that?"

"Well, I guess so but I will try to convince him that it would reduce the risks of people trying to find you."

*

The Professor met up with Jacob the next morning over breakfast.

"We need to get a message to George's parents to say he is OK. They will be frantic with worry."

"Impossible. I told you, no contact with the outside world while you are running these trials."

"So, we are prisoners?"

"No. I just need you to focus on what we are paying you for. I would hope that ten million dollars each should compensate you for the inconvenience."

"How can we trust you? You haven't given us any access to check your so-called promises."

"Don't you worry about that. We will make the payments. You just have to get the trials going."

"OK, but you really need to think about the fuss they are going to make in the US when they realise he has gone. I am sure the university has already started making waves about our disappearance."

Jacob shovelled another pancake into his mouth and stared at the Professor.

"OK, maybe you are right. Get his parents' email address and I will organise a message to say he is working away in Europe for a couple of years. I'll message the university as well. I wouldn't want any meddling CIA types to make our work here that much harder."

The Professor left the table and set off to start his day in the lab, musing on what Jacob had just said. *Hmm... a couple of years. Maybe we have longer than I thought.*

*

Jacob strode into the technology suite with an air of importance that really didn't impress Alice one bit.

"What can I do for you Mr Deepermeyer? You aren't going to try to shag me as well are you?"

Jacob smirked at the barb. So, William had tried it on with her.

"No, my dear. You're really not my type."

Alice smiled inwardly. She wanted to make sure she kept the upper hand with these men.

"Good. What do you need?"

"I want you to send a secure, untraceable message to George's parents and the University of Minnesota, letting them know that he and the Professor are safe and working on a project in Europe. I have done the words and here are the email details. I trust you can do that without it breaching our security."

"That is what you are paying me for."

"Good. Send it straight away please."

As he left, Alice logged onto the secure email that she had set up for the management team and typed out the text he had written. The message was basic with a 'sorry we had to leave at short notice' line.

Jesus, this is cold. I am sure his parents will know this is not from George. Oh well. Do as you're told Alice.

She sent the email and opened up the network management tool that would alert her to any attacks. Nobody would get through. She was too good. Her new encryption was the best anyone had ever designed. She smiled at the thought of her old NSA pals getting involved in the hunt for the Professor and dealing with cyber security that they thought they understood.

She wondered whether they had yet made the connection between her disappearance and the Professor's. *Maybe not.* But she was sure that someone would be looking for the Professor and George, sooner rather than later.

*

Mary and Theodore Mankley sat on their porch reading the morning papers when the familiar ping of an email coming in broke their concentration from consuming the day's news.

Theodore picked up his smartphone and opened the email.

"Huh. Strange. It is a message from George. Says he is in Europe. Working for... for two years! What is he playing at?"

"Let me see that?"

Mary put her hand to her mouth in shock.

"How could he do that? Just leave like that without coming to see us. Email him back and tell him to come back here and explain himself."

Theodore went to reply.

"I can't reply. It won't let me."

*

The Executive Assistant to the Dean of the University of Minnesota was trawling through the hundreds of emails that had come in overnight.

After a while she came across an email from an anonymous email address. She almost deleted it without reading it, as they

53

had all been warned about malicious emails, but something in the text on the preview pane caught her eye. It was a message from Professor Jenkins and his assistant George. She opened up the full email. They were in Europe working on a new project and apologised for their sudden departure.

How curious, she thought. *I had better get this to the Dean straight away.*

15

Reading, England

It was getting late but Clark was still sitting in his technology-rich 'man cave' poring over the numerous news feeds he had flowing from several terminals. He was still obsessed. He still needed to get justice for his father. He had helped crack one of the UK's biggest conspiracies without ever being identified. He was a master hacker but all his hard work on finding the evidence to blow the conspiracy wide open had failed to nail the one man he so desperately wanted to bring to justice. The injustice still burned inside him and he constantly watched and searched for anything that would give him the opportunity to get this man a second time.

One of his terminals pinged. A message from Proton, the online hacking community that he had been a member of for as long as he could remember. A place of anonymity where like-minded hackers shared their skills and helped each other out to get wherever they wanted to go in the cyber world. No names, no identities, nobody knew where each other was in the real world. As a result of his unfortunate surname... Kent, he went by the tag of Krypto.

SNAPDEVIL: Anyone online?

KRYPTO: Yo, Snap. How's it hanging?

SNAPDEVIL: Good. Hearing some rumours that the NSA have lost one of their best

KRYPTO: Where did you get that from?

SNAPDEVIL: From Blowfish. He seems to have the inside track on the CIA and NSA

KRYPTO: Interesting. What is the vibe?

SNAPDEVIL: Seems like it triggered a high-level national security incident, authorised by el Presidente

KRYPTO: Must be some heavy shit

SNAPDEVIL: Rumours are that it is their best senior analyst. A cyber genius

KRYPTO: Sounds juicy. Keep me updated

A message interrupted their conversation

HARLEQUIN HAS JOINED THE CHAT.

KRYPTO: Yo, Harlequin. Snap was just updating me on some juicy gossip

HARLEQUIN: Cool. Do tell

KRYPTO: Snap has heard from Blowfish that the NSA has lost one of their best analysts

The cursor blinked on the screen. There was no response.

KRYPTO: You still there Harlequin?

HARLEQUIN: Uh, yeh, sorry. Something's come up. I need to go. Speak soon

HARLEQUIN HAS LEFT THE CHAT.

KRYPTO: What the fuck was that all about?

SNAPDEVIL: Dunno. Weird.

They chatted some more but once he was offline, staring at the news feeds again, Clark couldn't take his mind off what had just happened. Why had Harlequin been so weird when they mentioned the missing analyst?

16

Alice woke up with a start. Her sleep had been troubled. The chat on Proton the previous night had completely floored her. How had her cyber friends found out so quickly? The NSA was supposed to be secure. How would someone know she had disappeared?

She got out of bed and made a coffee but nothing would shift the uncharacteristic doubt that was now consuming her. She had been a member of Proton for years, learning many of the skills that she applied to her job at the NSA from this group of cyber friends. It was the purest self-sustaining relationship you could wish for.

As she turned it over in her head, she kept trying to talk herself down.

They don't know it is me and there is no way they will find out if I don't tell them.

But, the devil on her shoulder kept bringing the doubts back.

How did they find out? Is Blowfish in the NSA? Could they be someone in her old team? Sitting next to her? David? Chad? Jez? Mahindra?

*

Jon and Mahindra sat in the NSA offices for their morning debrief. Chad had been in Austria overnight and had dialled in. Jon started the meeting with a tone that had exasperation written all over it.

"Morning, please tell me you two have got somewhere in the last twenty-four hours."

"Yes," they both chorused.

"Thank fuck for that. Mahindra. You first."

"Well the good news is that there has been a bank transfer to Alice's bank paying off the eighty-thousand dollar mortgage on her flat. The bad news is that when I try to trace the origin of the payment, there is a form of ghosting encryption present. Every time I try a trace it ghosts it back to my IP address."

"Ghosting encryption? Do you mean the ghosting encryption that we have been working on?"

Mahindra shuffled a bit nervously in her seat. "Don't you mean the ghosting encryption that Alice was working on?"

Jon pursed his lips, clearly unimpressed by this belligerent attitude that seemed to have consumed Mahindra since Alice's disappearance.

Mahindra carried on, trying to ignore the look of disapproval.

"Anyway, yes, I am convinced this has the hallmarks of the latest NSA encryption standards."

"Hold on. Why can't we just counter these standards if we wrote them?"

"Because she has enhanced them. Our double-layer cypher encryption is present, as are the high security IP location counter measures that we apply to all top-secret communications, but she has added some form of ghosting protocol that bounces the IP search back to the originator's computer. I have to say, it is fricking brilliant and at the moment I have no idea how she has done it."

Jon rubbed his face in frustration.

"Chad, what do you think?"

"Sounds like Alice's work to me. Mahindra and I can work on breaking the encryption but it's likely to take some time."

Jon was torn. This did at least confirm she was alive but alarmingly suggested she was betraying the US.

"What have you got Chad?"

"Well, two things. Although this country is backwards when it comes to surveillance, with limited CCTV, traffic cameras and satellite coverage beyond the airport, I did manage to get all the CCTV of Alice's arrival. The man she met was wearing dark glasses, which reduced the effectiveness of the facial recognition software we use, but he did have a distinctive scar on his left cheek."

"Yes, and?"

"I did a new composite, removing the glasses and guessing at his eye shape and colour. We got an eighty-two per cent hit on one man."

"Who?"

"A guy called Shaun Lester. British. Ex-special forces but known to us and the British Security Services as a category two risk. He seems to run a gun for hire business out of the UK and has popped up all round the world, using several different aliases. No one has ever been able to get anything on him but the people he associates with are high on our watch list. His presence with Alice is a definite red flag."

"Anything else?"

"Yes, I reviewed the CCTV for several days around Alice's arrival and found that he was at the airport earlier that day. He met some guys in a Hummer and a large transit lorry. They were loading some long cargo boxes."

"Any hits on the facial recognition?"

"No, we don't have anything on either of them but I have added their faces to our records as unsubs."

"This is good, Chad. Any trace on the number plates of the vehicles?"

"Unfortunately, nothing. As I said, they don't have CCTV or traffic cameras beyond the airport. They could have gone anywhere. I did check the passport control lists that Mahindra was looking at but no Shaun Lester has passed any of the borders."

"Hmm, if this thing looks and sounds like what we fear, he will be using a new identity. Mahindra, I presume you haven't found anything on your passport control search for Alice?"

"No."

"Chad, is that it?"

"Actually no. There is one more thing which is a bit strange. I was checking the CIA alert logs around the time of Alice's disappearance and I noticed that the local PD in Minnesota had escalated a report of a missing Professor from the university. Apparently, he and his assistant disappeared from campus and no one has seen or heard from them since. The university was concerned because he has been working on some highly sensitive infectious disease studies. When they realised he was gone, they checked his lab. All his research, clinical supplies, patient records and testing equipment have gone."

"Do you think it is connected?"

"I don't know but I think it is worth looking into."

"Good, do that and see if there is anything else you can get from Austria before you come back. Both of you carry on with what you are doing and let's meet each morning. Don't wait though if you have something significant. I am relieved we can give Dirk something to tell the President but we need to keep onto this."

17

Alice sat in the bar after another decent meal, a vodka and lime helping to settle her strangely addled mind. She had been completely cool with all her recent decisions but the last forty-eight hours had been weird.

She couldn't shake the feeling that the Professor was somehow here under duress. She had still not seen him or his assistant to talk to. Maybe they were just busy.

She was puzzled by the weird feelings she had when she saw the picture of that Ellie person. What was that all about? And the discussion on Proton about her disappearance. Just what the hell was going on?

She was trying to ignore it but all these events had led to a feeling deep down in her gut that something wasn't right about this situation. Had she made a terrible mistake?

She was jerked out of her self-persecution by a notification on her phone. The guys were back on Proton. Her hand hovered over the screen, trying to decide what to do. Eventually she knew she had to scratch that itch.

*

Clark was sitting in his usual place of an evening, preoccupied with his latest project. He was trying to hack into the phone of the man he desperately wanted to bring to justice. His efforts to find something when he hacked his email had proved fruitless.

There was nothing incriminating in his business emails, which meant he had to be using some other secure communications tool to do his illicit business. Clark suspected he was doing it through an app on his phone. He had to hack it to find the secrets and use the GPS to find out where he was going. He knew the one person on Proton who could help him. They were always the 'go to' person for phone hacks. Harlequin.

He logged onto Proton.

KRYPTO: Yo, Harlequin are you on line

The cursor flashed. No response.

KRYPTO: Yo, Snap are you online

SNAPDEVIL: Yo dude, always. They still not responding

KRYPTO: No and need help

SNAPDEVIL: Why?

KRYPTO: Phone hack on the H bastard

SNAPDEVIL: Ah, still after that dude then?

KRYPTO: Always. Will not let this rest

Suddenly a message flashed up. HARLEQUIN HAS JOINED THE CHAT.

KRYPTO: Yo, Harlequin. Good to hear from you. RU OK?

HARLEQUIN: Yeh, fine. Just got myself into some stuff

KRYPTO: Can we help? You seemed a bit weird the other night

HARLEQUIN: No, it's fine. I can handle it. Will let you know if I need anything

KRYPTO: OK. Need your help

HARLEQUIN: What?

KRYPTO: Phone hack. Can you send me your script?

HARLEQUIN: Yeh, give me a few minutes. I leave it on the site. Laters

KRYPTO: Legend. Laters

HARLEQUIN HAS LEFT THE CHAT.

KRYPTO: Harley seems back on track

SNAPDEVIL: Yeh, I am sure they will tell us if they need help

Clark left the chat and searched for Harlequin's script. Within a few minutes it was up on the ultra-secure shared site they all used to share hacking scripts and tools.

He opened it. The hack into the phone carriers' network was a piece of cake. He found the credentials for the phone he wanted to hack. He ran the script.

Within a few minutes the management tool that Harlequin had created to track the hack's progress popped up on Clark's screen.

It was live. He checked the GPS. The person he was after was in Switzerland.

18

Jon Ruganzi called Mahindra and Chad in for the morning meeting. He had a haunted look, like the weight of the world was on his shoulders.

"Welcome back Chad. Please tell me we have achieved something in the last twenty-four hours."

"There has been one interesting development around that missing Professor. The university received an apparent correspondence from him saying that he was sorry he had left in such a hurry but he was now working on a new project in Europe for a couple of years."

"What do you mean 'apparent correspondence'? Is it a fake?"

Chad smiled at Jon. He knew he needed a boost and he was about to deliver it.

"The email was from an anonymous email box, so hard to verify, but I have found something."

"What? Stop pissing me about Chad. I am really not in the mood."

"I tried to trace the origin of the email and encountered the same encryption that Mahindra found on the bank transfer."

"Eh? So that means…"

"Yes, Alice's disappearance is connected with the Professor's. She sent the email. Now, whether it is designed to throw people off the scent or it's a fake is unclear, but Alice is somehow involved in covering up his disappearance."

"What about the other person? The assistant?"

"His parents received a similar email from the same source."

"Hmm, this is good. Add this intel to the Operation Hawk file. We need to get down to Minnesota to investigate the Professor's disappearance. Mahindra, do you want to go?"

"Yes, no problem."

"Good, what have you found in the last twenty-four?"

"I have received CCTV from six of the eight countries that they could have crossed into. I have the seventy-two-hour period after Alice landed at Innsbruck, from each of their border checkpoints. I ran facial recognition on Alice and 'Shaun' but nothing has come up. My trawl of the passport records is also hopeless. There are just too many names."

"OK, which countries are we waiting for?

"Germany and Switzerland."

"OK, I will speak to Dirk. Hopefully he can get the President to apply some diplomatic pressure. My gut tells me they have moved out of Austria and we need to find where they went, before the trail goes cold."

Jon had clearly perked up and brought the meeting to a close.

*

William Hardacre sat in the conference room and dialled his contact.

"Gavin, it's William. How are things progressing?"

"Good, boss. My people have been scouting around. They reckon they can get twenty or so."

"Excellent. Can you get them rounded up within the next two weeks? I can't let the Yanks get an upper hand."

"Yeh, I reckon we can do that? Presume we are still going overland?"

"We are going to have to. We have a better chance of evading the authorities by road. A plane is too easily traced."

"OK boss, I will make the arrangements."

As William put the phone down, Clay and Jacob walked into the room.

"William. How y'all today?"

"I'm fine Jacob. I was just organising things from my end. They will be here within three weeks."

"Good, the American end is progressing nicely. We should be ready to start within the month."

"Well, I am going back to the UK. I want to make sure this all happens and I need to do some more groundwork with my government contacts. I don't want any delays when we hit them with it."

"OK, sounds good. Let us know when you are due back."

*

The Professor and George sat in the bar, having a drink after another nice meal. In his last chat with Jacob he had insisted they had more freedom within the site. If they were going to play this game, he demanded that they felt less like prisoners. Jacob had been surprisingly accommodating. He had put up a bit of resistance about getting a message to George's parents but seemed to mellow once the Professor had outlined the benefits of keeping them sweet. He wasn't naïve enough to think he had somehow got the upper hand, but anything he could do to stop George stressing about their situation was for the best.

As they sat and chatted, they noticed a young woman coming toward them, slim and curvy with nice shoulder-length mousy brown hair and a very pretty, fresh face. They had seen her around, talking to the Deepermeyers, but didn't know who she was. She bounded up to them like an excitable puppy, hand outstretched.

"Hi, I'm Alice. It's great to finally meet you."

The offer of the handshake was ignored by both of them. George gave her a frosty response.

"What do you want?"

Alice drew her hand away and sat down.

"OK, not sure what the hostility is all about but, whatever, just trying to be nice."

"We don't need you to be nice. Just leave us alone."

*

Alice was shocked by the reaction but wondered whether it confirmed her suspicions about the Professor and his assistant. As she was about to respond to their harsh words, a voice came from behind her.

"Miss Bidebecker. Can I have a word?"

Alice looked round. It was Jacob. She grimaced at the Professor and George. Her attempts at getting to know them were clearly going to have to wait another day. She stood up and walked over to him.

"What do you want? I was trying to make friends," she said with a heavy sarcastic tone on the word 'friends'.

"You don't need to be friends with them. They are being paid top dollar to do a job just like you. Anyway, I want to know how your work is going and get an update on the American applications."

Alice sighed and sat down.

"The security config is almost done. Your secure email, telephony and conferencing is up and running. The network and anti-surveillance will be fully operational when the new kit arrives tomorrow."

"Good, and the applications?"

"I sent you the first one that came in. She checks out. I have another thirteen that have come in today that I need to vet."

"Well get on with it, instead of wasting your time trying to make friends. I want these applicants cleared and on that plane in three weeks."

She stared him down as he got up and walked away. Clay had been delightful but Jacob was a piece of work.

"Give it time. Give it time Alice," she muttered under her breath.

As she stopped brooding, she turned around. George and the Professor were gone.

19

Several days had passed and Jon Ruganzi was on the brink. The trail had gone cold. Mahindra had been to the university in Minnesota and found nothing. The Professor and his assistant had disappeared off campus without anyone seeing anything. The CCTV gave no clues. Nothing unusual had happened around the time of their disappearance. No strange visitors. Nothing.

Chad and Mahindra had failed to crack the encryption. He told them to carry on but he worried that they were not capable enough to counter what he now accepted as the undeniable truth. Alice was brilliant. The best he had and somehow, he had allowed her to slip through his fingers.

Germany and Switzerland had provided their border control CCTV but there were no hits on the facial recognition. Jon was no nearer finding where they had gone but could at least be sure they were still in Austria. The needle was still well and truly in the haystack.

*

Alice sat in the technology suite. The Deepermeyers had delivered the military grade satellite dish she asked for and her anti-satellite surveillance was configured and operational. Anyone trying to see them from space would be met with the equivalent of a satellite black spot. The enhanced network and firewall components were installed, all backed up by her 'super strength' encryption. She was proud of what she had achieved. No one would ever find them in the cyber world. She was the best, and the best was what she had delivered. She stood up and looked at herself in the mirror.

So, time to tell the Deepermeyers that I have delivered on their requirements and pocket another two million dollars.

She went to their offices and knocked on the door.

"Come in."

Jacob and Clay were both present. Jacob took the lead.

"Ahh, Miss Bidebecker, just the person we wanted to see."

"Oh, really. Why?"

Jacob fixed her with a firm stare. She stared back.

"Mr Hardacre is worried about you. He thinks you can't be trusted."

"Where is the sex pest, anyway?"

"He is back in the UK dealing with our business."

"Well, I'm not sure what he bases that on. I have just finished the implementation of the cyber security and anti-surveillance requirements you asked for. No one is going to find you in the cyber world. Is that the actions of someone that can't be trusted?"

"Is that why you are here?"

"Yes, I thought you would want to know and I think that means you owe me another two million dollars."

Clay tried to take the tension out of the situation.

"Oh, that's great news Miss Bidebecker. Hold on one minute."

Clay tapped away at the keyboard.

"It's done."

Alice tapped away at her phone. The balance was just under $5 million.

"Good, have a nice day."

She walked out before either of them could say any more. As she walked back to her apartment, her concerns about Jacob were growing. He seemed irritated by her presence and if William Hardacre was winding him up, just because she had refused to sleep with the disgusting pig, this was not going to make her life any easier. *Thank God for Clay*, she thought to herself.

*

A few minutes after Alice had left the room, Clay went on the attack.

"Just what the fuck was that all about Jacob?"

"Get some balls little brother. I'm tending to agree with William. I don't like her and I'm not convinced we should be trusting her with all our secrets."

"Are you out of your mind? Without her skills, we would be exposed to the world. Do you really want to give any of our rivals the merest hint of what we are doing? We would be totally exposed to every cyber-attack under the sun. And have you forgotten the potential revenues when we deliver a cure for the common cold? It's billions and billions of dollars Jacob."

"Don't patronise me, you piece of shit. I'm well aware what is at stake here, which is why I'm being cautious about her motivations. Do you really think she has just switched off her loyalty to the US government?"

"She seems pretty chilled to me. Happy to be here."

"Well, I'm sorry Clay, but you are being naïve and I'm not going to take any risks. We have our insurance policy to protect us against Miss Bidebecker. I think it's about time we put it in place.

20

Alice sat in her apartment watching the sun set, pondering the juxtaposition of such a beautiful place being tainted by greedy bastards with questionable motives, hidden away like some Bond villains in their mountain lair. She was holding her own but every day seemed to bring something else that made her question her decision to take this 'job'.

She went back to the one place that always gave her solace. Proton. Snapdevil, Krypto and Blowfish were online.

KRYPTO: Yo, Harlequin. How ya doing?

HARLEQUIN: Fine. What's the goss?

BLOWFISH: That NSA analyst is still missing. Hearing she is alive though. Traitor status

SNAPDEVIL: How do you know this Blowfish? Surely that is classified info?

BLOWFISH: Hey, come on guys. You know our code. No names. No pack drill

HARLEQUIN: Do ya have an inside source?

BLOWFISH: Yeh, something like that

KRYPTO: What's the vibe? What are they worried about?

BLOWFISH: Apparently, she is their best. Worried she is selling cyber secrets to rogue states

HARLEQUIN: I'm sure that's not it

BLOWFISH: Why do you think that?

HARLEQUIN: Dunno, maybe we should give her the benefit of the doubt

There was a pause in the chat. Like some uncomfortable moment in a normal conversation. Krypto broke the silence.

KRYPTO: How is your odd situ Harley?

HARLEQUIN: Oh fine, under control

SNAPDEVIL: You know we are here if you need help

HARLEQUIN: Yeh no stress. How is your phone hack Krypto?

KRYPTO: Working OK. Got the GPS, so tracking where he is, but having trouble hacking into his apps. Anyone heard of Zephyr?

BLOWFISH: Yeh, that is a non-prop app. Strictly dark web stuff. Used for ultra-secure communication. Is this man you're after a crook?

KRYPTO: Too bloody right. I need to take him down but he is a slippery bastard. Do you have a hack for it?

BLOWFISH: No, never actually looked at it. Shall we have a little competition to see who can break it first?

SNAPDEVIL: Game on Blow

KRYPTO: Yeh, sad acts. Eat my dust

HARLEQUIN: On it

BLOWFISH: What do the kids say? LOL!

Alice logged off and reflected on the conversation. Who the hell was Blowfish? Whoever it was, they were right that their code was fundamental to the trust of Proton. No one ever asked the 'who and where' question. Never. But there was something about Blowfish that unnerved her. How could they have such immediate access to classified information? Either someone in her old team was leaking information or Blowfish worked for the NSA.

*

Clark sat in his man cave and searched for information about this Zephyr app on the dark web. He was going to win this little hackers' competition. As he started to trawl the dark web his mind wandered to Harlequin's reaction to Blowfish talking about that analyst. Why were they so defensive? Maybe Harlequin was female and was doing the whole 'girl power' thing or maybe it was something else. He knew that little brain worm would sit and fester.

*

Blowfish poured himself a coffee. It had been a long few days and the pressure was on at work. He needed some sleep but the interaction with Harlequin had bothered him. All these guys were normally so straight. No drama, just good ole hackers' bantz, but Harley seemed genuinely put out by what he had said. Did they know more than were letting on? He had his contacts. No reason why they couldn't have the same connections. After all, their world was all about the information. He would see how future chat went. Something about Harlequin was niggling his conspiracy radar.

21

'Moley' tried to open his eyes. The spring nights were still cold and his body was chilled to the bone. His head was pounding and his joints were stiff. He needed a drink.

As he tried to orientate himself, he saw the familiar figures of his homeless mates that bedded down under the railway siding night after night, laid out like elephant seals on the beach. It was light but he had no idea what time it was. As he tried to force himself into a sitting position, he saw it. The same silhouette he had seen the other day. The shape of a man. The man that had left all that money.

He was suddenly awake and frantic. He needed more money. He needed more drink. He tried to move without waking the other men. He stumbled toward the man. He expected him to move at any minute, but he didn't. He just stood there. He got closer.

"Oi, Mister. Hash yu got money?"

The man stared at him. He said nothing.

Moley was now in his face and started poking him.

"Oi, Mister. Gish us some fooking money."

The man reached into his pocket and got out a £20 note. He stuffed it in Moley's pocket.

Moley was just about to utter a sort of 'thank you', when he felt a sharp scratch on his neck. His world went black and he fell to the floor.

Moley's head was pounding more than usual but he was warm and dry. Where was he?

He opened his eyes. He was behind bars but not in a police cell. He stood up and looked out. He was in a massive warehouse with multiple 'cells' strewn out across the large expanse of space. He could see other people lying on the beds in each cell.

"Oi. Where am I? Come here yoose bastards."

There were a few murmurs from other cells.

"Oi. Oi! Let me outa here."

Suddenly, a face appeared.

"Can you keep it down please? People are trying to sleep."

"You wot! Fooking let me outa here."

"All in good time. Name please."

"Wot?"

"Name please."

"People call me Moley."

"Real name."

"Moley."

"Mr Moley. Unless you cooperate, you will not get out of this cell."

"I need a drink."

"Real name. PLEASE!"

"Simon Mole."

"See, that wasn't too hard now was it? Addictions?"

"Wot?"

"Addictions. What do you take while you sleep rough?"

"I don't do drugs. A'cohol. Just booze."

"Good, that will make your recovery much easier so we can get you ready for your little journey."

"Wot journey?"

"Just relax Mr Mole. We will give you some medicine for the

withdrawals, lots of nice food and a warm, dry place to sleep. That must be better than the streets?"

"Fook off."

The man walked away. Moley started to shake. He desperately needed a drink.

22

William Hardacre sat in his Mayfair offices, waiting for Henry White-Taylor to turn up. His PA buzzed. He had arrived.

"Henry, good to see you. How is the government these days?"

"Hmm, tolerable. Since your stupid son lost his head, we have had to put up with Jeffrey and you know what a boring incorruptible bastard he is."

"Well, Henry that is why I have you."

"Yes, thanks for the girls the other night. I do like an Asian with big tits. They are so polite and willing. Made me cum like an express train."

"Spare me the details Henry. I need to talk to you about this new venture I am involved in."

"Of course. What can I do?"

"We are working on a scientific breakthrough that will make us billions of pounds. We are just doing some clinical trials but should be ready to go within a few months."

"OK, what do you need?"

"There will come a point when our group make representation to the US and UK governments. We will be demanding a significant amount of money to release preliminary details of what we are selling. When our demands arrive in Cabinet, you need to influence the discussion."

"You will need more than me."

"I know. I am working on it. Charles, Heather and John are

being 'influenced' to see our point of view and I have others in the pipeline. But, I need you to lead them."

"Fine, give me the nod. I assume my cut will be the usual percentage?"

"Of course, as long as you deliver. Watch out for Plutus."

"What?"

"Plutus. It is the name of our organisation."

"Oh, I see. No problem."

With that Henry departed and William smiled to himself. If only he could find a way to corner this market for himself. Beat those bastard Yanks. He picked up the phone.

"Gavin. What is the progress?"

"We have twenty-two in the holding area. We just need to dry them out and we're ready to go."

"Good, good. Let me know when you are planning to leave as I want to get back to Switzerland. I want to keep an eye on this personally."

*

Chad was sitting at home. Alice's enhancements to their cyber encryption were genius. He could see what it did but could not work out how to crack it. Mahindra was no further forward. Jon was relying on them to sort this but he worried they would never do it. He had to take his mind off this nightmare and started watching re-runs of *Friends*. Why couldn't he be as chilled as Joey?

*

Jon Ruganzi was preparing his weekly briefing for the Director of Intelligence. The news was not good. No progress had been made and the leads had gone cold. Alice's face stared at him from the incident board in his office, haunting his every waking moment.

His only saving grace was that Operation Hawk had dropped down the DoI's priorities due to a credible threat of terrorism around Langley. He was thankful for small mercies and decided to keep his head down.

*

Another day had passed and Alice was once again sitting in the bar. Her security and anti-surveillance configuration were up and running. There had been no attacks and no breaches. The problem was she was bored, and the boredom led her mind to obsess about whether she had put herself in a really stupid situation. She kept checking her new bank account. The money was still there but every interaction with Jacob Deepermeyer made her more and more nervous about what would actually happen to her when this little venture was completed.

She knew she was drinking too much but what else was there to do? So far, she had downed three straight vodkas and sat alone at the back of the bar with a fourth. She loaded up the music on her phone, put the earbuds in and shut her eyes. Trying to shut out the constant whirring of her psyche.

A few minutes later she sensed that someone was close. She was just about to tell them to 'fuck off', expecting it to be William Hardacre or one of the other misogynistic bastards, when she saw it was one of the guards in Shaun's team. The one that had winked at her. Twice.

She took out the earbuds.

"Hi, I'm Jake. Can I join you?"

Alice pursed her lips. Maybe it was the drink, and her addled mind, but she suddenly felt like talking.

"Yes, army boy. What can I do for you?"

He was talking but he wasn't making eye contact. Like most men that met Alice his eyes were focused on one thing… or two if you wanted to be precise about it.

"Fucking hell. Men. What is it about men and tits?"

Jake looked flustered and quickly averted his eyes.

"Oh fuck, sorry... erm... it's just... erm..."

Alice stood up, grabbed his arm and dragged him out of the bar toward her apartment.

"Come on big boy. Let's see if we can't give you a closer look at these puppies."

23

George was up early, like most days, staring out at the mountain landscape as the sun began to rise. The Professor was still asleep, snoring loudly.

He pondered what was going on with the woman that attempted to speak to them the other evening. She seemed like she wanted to engage with them.

George got back into bed and tried to get back to sleep, the question of what to do about the woman raging round his brain.

*

Alice woke up. She had a mild hangover. She bolted up and remembered what had happened last night. She was completely naked but Jake had gone. She smiled to herself.

Hmm, a shag and go type of guy. I like your style.

The sex had been functional and just the release she needed but the demons soon invaded her brain.

She tried to shake her increasing fear about her situation. She decided all she could do for now was to keep her head down and get all the US patients cleared to start the trials and on the plane. As she thought about the trial patients, her heart gave an unexpected flutter. She stopped and smiled to herself. What on earth was that all about? Why was she so excited at the prospect of meeting that Ellie person?

*

Jon Ruganzi sat down in his office with Chad and Mahindra for what had now become a weekly review of Operation Hawk. The stress was clearly telling on Jon. The dark rings under his eyes told Chad and Mahindra he hadn't been sleeping and he was more irritable each time they met.

"Guys, please tell me we have made some progress."

Chad and Mahindra did the uncomfortable shuffle in their chairs that Jon was sick of seeing.

"Come on guys, you are supposed to be the elite fucking team in the NSA. You must have something for me. Just because the threats at Langley are focusing Dirk's time does not mean we are off the hook."

Chad spoke first.

"I am sorry Jon. Mahindra and I have been going over and over the encryption on these messages Alice sent but we just can't work out how to counter it. She must have been developing this in secret. We can't find any notes on our network that might explain whether she was working on this while she was still here."

"Is there anyone else in the team that can help?"

"I don't think so. No one else has been working on this type of thing."

"Crap, crap, crap. What about the CCTV, the vehicles they were using, passport control, the university? There must be something."

Mahindra spoke. "There is one thing Jon, about the CCTV supplied by the Swiss passport control office."

"What?"

"I got our techs to recheck all the footage we received from all eight countries to see if there were any anomalies in the recordings."

"And?"

"The one from the Swiss has been edited. The frame ratios are out. Someone has edited frames out of the recordings."

"What does that mean?"

"I think it means someone doesn't want us to see certain parts of their CCTV, which means it is a pretty good bet that Alice and Shaun crossed the border there."

Jon was suddenly excited.

"Has it given us any more leads?"

"Well, maybe. If we assume they crossed into Switzerland, it reduced the people we needed to review going through passport control down to 133 women and 127 men."

"And, any conclusions?"

"Well, there was someone crossing the border called Shaun Griffiths. We ran the picture scanned from his passport against the mocked-up facial recognition that Chad did and we got a seventy-seven per cent hit."

"That's good enough for me. They are in Switzerland. I just know it."

Chad and Mahindra relaxed a bit, glad that Jon at least seemed re-energised by what they might have found. He went into command mode.

"Right, here's what we need to do. Keep trawling through the females and find Alice. She will be there somewhere. Get onto our opposite numbers in their security services and discuss getting access to their satellite imagery. We can make a decent guess at which way they travelled. Let's see if we can get a track on any of their vehicles during the period after they landed."

"OK boss," they choroused.

Jon dismissed the meeting and picked up the phone to Dirk. He hoped this latest bit of intel might just save his job.

24

Another nice meal had been consumed and as Alice walked out of the restaurant, she spotted the Deepermeyers over the opposite side of the room, deep in conversation. She put down her tray and diverted toward them.

"I want a night out in the local village. You did say that was part of the deal."

Clay looked at her with a kind, welcoming expression. "Of course, Miss Bidebecker. No problem."

Jacob's interaction was, as usual, less friendly. "You need to be escorted by one of Shaun's team."

"I'll go with Jake."

"Oh, on first name terms, are we?

She smiled at Jacob sarcastically.

"Is that a problem?"

*

The arrangements were made and Alice and Jake went out for the evening in the small village of Boden, a short drive away from the bottom of the cable car station. As they sat in the bar, Jake tried to make light conversation.

"This is nice. Our first proper date."

"Don't flatter yourself big boy. I just needed to get out of there and you seemed like the best worst option of your little band of army boys."

"You didn't think that when we were going at it last night."

"I used you for sex Jake. Nothing more. I needed the stress release."

"Ooh, savage. So how big are they actually?"

Alice slapped his face.

"Sorry, as we are apparently treating each other as sex objects, I thought I would discuss your best assets. I mean they are spectacular."

"Why are all men such losers?"

Alice took a swig of drink and stared off into the distance.

Jake grabbed her hand.

"OK, Alice, I am sorry. I didn't mean to be a bastard. I really like you. The sex was great and you are so sexy..."

He defended himself from another slap.

"... not just because of your great rack. You have the most amazing eyes, your hair is beautiful and you have a cute nose."

"Does this crap normally work?"

He smiled. The cheeky smile that had convinced Alice to bed him last night. She put her head in her hands.

"Jesus. What am I doing here?"

"I thought you were the cyber expert?"

"For God's sake Jake, I know who I am. I just don't know why I have been so stupid."

"Why do you say that?"

She didn't know what to do. Could she trust him?

"Just forget it. What is the deal with your group? How did you come to work for Shaun?"

"I am ex-special forces, had to retire due to a knee injury. People who were managing my exit put me in touch with Shaun. He looks after his own."

"How long have you worked for him?"

"This is my first assignment."

"And what do you think you are here for?"

"To provide physical security for this science thing they are doing up there. Some big secret project."

"Are you being paid well?"

"Better than being on the dole, I can tell you."

"Do you feel safe?"

"Safe?"

"Yeh, are you worried about what will happen when this is all over?"

"No, Shaun says we will go onto the next assignment. It's just security. We do the job and move on."

Alice took another sip of her drink. She was trying not to crack up.

"Is everything alright? Why are you asking about being safe?"

Alice was deep in thought.

"Alice?"

She looked at him, fixing him with a firm, defiant look.

"Because Jake, I am pretty sure the Deepermeyers are going to kill me when this is all over."

25

Moley woke to the smell of cooked breakfast. His head was still pounding but the smell of the food was amazing. He hadn't drunk alcohol for almost two days. The shakes came and went but this morning was like his senses had suddenly been rebooted. He could murder a bottle of whisky but the food seemed like an equal pull on his desires. All of a sudden there was lots of noise as their cells were opened and people were streaming out toward the food. Moley noticed a number of his 'mates'. Where the hell were they? Was this some kind of extreme soup kitchen? Was it Christmas?

Moley followed the small crowd of about twenty or so people toward the area where a full English breakfast was being served. As they hungrily devoured the food, a man stood at the end of their table and started to speak.

"Ladies and gentlemen. I hope you have enjoyed our hospitality—"

"Fooking prison," Moley shouted.

"No, not prison. We locked you up to protect you from yourselves. We have been drying you out, given you warm, dry accommodation, showers and fresh clothes, to prepare you for what we need you to do."

There was lots of murmuring between the sounds of breakfast plates being wiped clean.

"In a few hours, you will be loaded onto coaches to go to Switzerland. You will be helping with some exciting scientific trials and will each be paid five thousand pounds."

"Where the fuck is Switzerland?" one shouted.

"Where's the booze?" another shouted.

"Five fucking grand will get you all the booze you need," shouted another as the collective group laughed at the wisecracks.

Moley just sat there. A full belly but totally bemused.

*

A few hours later the man who had given the big speech was making the final preparations for the trip. He would soon have them all packed off on the journey, backed up by the lovely batch of fake passports Mr Hardacre had organised. He checked his bank account. The money was there. Show time.

*

Ellie arrived in Miami for her flight to Innsbruck. As she moved into the departure lounge, a woman approached her.

"Miss Baker?"

"Oh, yes."

The woman was tapping away on her tablet. She turned it around. All of the credentials that Ellie had registered with were on the screen.

"Can you just put your finger on the pad please, so we can verify your identity?"

"Err, yes OK."

The scan was accepted.

"Excellent Miss Baker, please can you join the group of people sitting in the seats over there."

Ellie walked over to a group of about thirty people, all ages and ethnicities. She said hello to a few and sat down.

What a strange group of people, she thought to herself. *I guess the promise of forty thousand dollars attracts all sorts.* She sat and waited for the flight to be called.

26

Clark was reviewing the GPS history on the phone he was tracking. It had moved from Switzerland and was now back in the UK. In central London. His hunting ground.

He pinged the phone operating system. Still nothing. The bloody Zephyr app was still stopping him accessing any of the activity on the phone. He logged onto Proton.

KRYPTO: Yo, Snap, Blowfish. Any progress on Zephyr? I'm still a lame arse

SNAPDEVIL: Oh, you poor sweet amateurs. Snap has delivered once again

BLOWFISH: No shit Snap. Have you cracked it?

SNAPDEVIL: Of course, but it is not all good news dudes

KRYPTO: Why?

SNAPDEVIL: The app is clearly for peeps that don't want any footprint

BLOWFISH: Why? What have you found?

SNAPDEVIL: Every action on the app is immediately deleted after it happens

KRYPTO: Eh? It must leave some footprint

SNAPDEVIL: No, this is clever stuff. Every email, text, phone call, post that is sent is followed by a complete cyber wipe. Every bit, every byte is wiped from the phone memory

KRYPTO: There must be some way of tracking the activities

SNAPDEVIL: I haven't worked out how to do that yet. We need Harley on this one

KRYPTO: Shit! I need to know what this man is doing

BLOWFISH: Sounds like military grade shit

KRYPTO: Is this NSA or CIA then, as you seem so well acquainted

BLOWFISH: No, not directly but I have heard about this type of thing

KRYPTO: I am gonna ping Harley. I need to get this man

*

Alice couldn't shake the complete sense of dread that was now pervading her every waking hour. She had done what she was trained to do. Analysed the situation and every scenario led her to one conclusion. This situation did not stack up.

Jake had been no help, so she decided to test the water. She went up to see the Deepermeyers. As she walked in, she cursed to herself. Jacob was the only one in.

"And what can I do for you Miss Bidebecker?"

"Where's Clay?"

"He's out."

"Oh. Well, look. I want more freedom. I want to go off the site more, do some hiking, hire a bike, go swimming, something different to this mundane existence."

Jacob raised his voice.

"The amount of money we are paying should make this bearable. Your every fucking whim is catered for up here. Free food, free accommodation, any personal supplies you need. Why the fuck isn't that enough?"

Alice stared him down. She couldn't abide big shouty men.

"I can walk out of here you know, and then where would you be?"

Jacob smiled at her. The arrogant smile that seemed to be a permanent fixture every time Alice challenged him.

"You really think we are going to let you just walk out of here?"

The menace in his voice was all too real but he soon regained his composure.

"The thing is Miss Bidebecker, we are not amateurs. We know what we are doing and we know what you can do to us. Which is why we have an insurance policy."

Alice was trying to remain calm but she was beginning to feel like she was on the back foot. *What did he mean, 'an insurance policy'?*

Jacob turned on the large computer screen in their office. Alice couldn't believe her eyes.

27

Alice sat in her apartment. Tears were streaming down her face. In that moment, every negative thought that had been playing through her mind, had suddenly taken on a frightening reality.

She was looking at the hard copy printout of what Jacob Deepermeyer had put on the screen. A mocked-up newspaper front page.

ALICE BIDEBECKER IDENTIFIED AS NSA TRAITOR
Selling U.S. cyber secrets to rogue states

He had the story ready to go to all the US media outlets, at a snap of his fingers, the moment she tried to leave the site or attempted to betray them. If this story broke, she could never work in the US ever again. She would be a marked person, high on the US most wanted list.

She paced the room. This was a disaster. She had lost control of the situation. She stared out of the window, willing the beautiful mountain views to give her some inspiration. She needed a plan and quick.

As she stood and agonised, her computer pinged. It was a Proton message from Krypto. He needed her help with the phone hack. "Sorry Krypto. Not right now."

*

Another day had almost gone and the Professor was beavering away in the lab, preparing for the trial patients. George could not believe how focused he was, like he was just having a normal day at work. George was hungry and wanted to finish for the day.

"Professor, can we go and eat?"

There was no response.

"Professor!"

"Oh, what? Yes, you go. I will be a while yet."

George just stood there, dismissed like some lowly lab rat. He walked out.

As he reached the restaurant his mood was getting worse, but as he lined up to select his meal, he noticed the woman from the other day, already sitting down and tucking in.

He got his food and walked over to her table, put his tray down and sat across from her.

She looked up. Disinterested. She didn't speak.

"I'm sorry if I was rude the other night."

She chewed on a piece of meat and stared at him, sizing him up.

"Apology accepted."

"I'm George by the way."

"I know. I'm Alice."

"Look, I was rude to you because I assumed you were one of them."

"One of them?"

"The management types. The people that are keeping us here against our will."

Alice was playing it cool. This is what she suspected and what she had been trying to talk to them about the other night before Jacob deliberately interrupted them.

"Can't you just leave when you want to?"

"No. We are prisoners."

There was an uncomfortable pause while Alice decided what to say next.

"How did you get here?"

"I don't know. We were abducted from our university labs and woke up here."

"Do you think they will kill you when they have finished with you?"

"Yes."

Alice nodded. Her stomach was churning up inside. This was further confirmation. She couldn't believe how quickly this had all unravelled. She was trying not to show any fear because she desperately needed to fully understand what was going on.

"Well, that doesn't sound good for you George."

"Why the fuck are you being so obtuse?"

"Obtuse? Big word. Do you even know if you can trust me?"

"I don't but after I saw you the other night and thought about what you tried to do... I guess I hoped you were in the same position."

"Thanks George, do you always hope for bad things to happen to people?"

"No, no, of course not. I am a nice pers—"

Alice laughed.

"Stop it, I am just baiting you. The truth is I am fucking terrified. I was not abducted but came here on the promise of ten million dollars. My stupid greed didn't see this for what it is. A date with death. I may have nearly five million dollars in my new bank account but I don't expect to be alive to spend it. I am trying to pretend that I am completely chilled and enjoying my conversation with you because we are being watched by Clay and Jacob."

George started to look round.

"Don't look round. We need them to think we are just having a nice chat."

George stopped himself and started shovelling the curry into his mouth.

"What can we do?"

95

"I don't know, but if I know you are with me, we can work something out."

George smiled.

Alice finished her food and got up. As she left, she whispered to George.

"We will talk again. Try not to worry."

*

Alice was back in her apartment, her mind racing with everything that had happened in the last crazy twenty-four hours. Despite her rising terror, having George on her side somehow made this all a bit bearable.

She picked up her phone. It gave her unlimited access to the outside world, but who could she call? Any suggestion that she was betraying the Deepermeyers would prompt them to release the news story. She couldn't contact the NSA. Surely, she had well and truly burnt those bridges. No parents, no siblings, no friends that would take a call like this. The loneliness once again consumed her. She tried to stifle the tears.

Eventually she logged on to Proton to try to take her mind off everything, catching up on the guys' attempts to crack the Zephyr app.

Snap had made some progress but the programme was uber clever. Alice knew she could crack it, if she could only concentrate, but nothing was working. She did a quick workaround and messaged Krypto.

Krypto, this tech is very clever. Don't have time to investigate fully but have added Snap's hack to my management software and overlaid it with a mirroring hack. This will only allow you to watch what he is doing in live time. Will not record his actions or resolve the cyber wipe. Will take me much longer to work out how to do that. Soz. Hope this helps for now.

28

Jake was guarding the lower cable car station with Gav. They had been told to remain alert as they were expecting the first batch of trial patients but his mind couldn't shake what Alice had said to him a few nights ago.

The noise of the cable car coming down from the main site bolted him out of his daze. It was Shaun. They both stood to attention.

"At ease men. Just checking in. We are expecting the first batch of visitors within a few hours. Please get them through, quickly and efficiently."

"Yes Sir," they chorused.

Shaun stopped and stared at Jake. Mean and intimidating.

"Is there something else Sir?" Jake asked nervously.

"I hear you have been getting your end away?"

"Um, err, yes Sir?"

"Was she good?"

"Err, yes Sir. Very good."

"Do you think she would shag me?"

Jake didn't know what to say.

"Soldier. I asked you a question?"

"Err, I really don't know Sir."

"Oh, you don't think I am good enough for her… or are you just trying to keep all the pussy to yourself?"

Jake was using all his training to try and maintain a calm demeanour but inside he was bricking it. As his brain tried to process what to do next, Shaun started laughing and slapped him gently on the cheek.

"You should have seen your face. I thought you were going to wet yourself soldier."

Jake heaved a sigh of relief and cracked an uncomfortable smile.

"But, seriously watch yourself. The Deepermeyers think she is trouble. You need to tell us anything she says in your… pillow talk."

"Of course, Sir, fully understand."

Shaun got back on the cable car. Jake looked at Gav and puffed out his cheeks.

Maybe Alice was right, he thought to himself.

*

Just after 6 p.m., Jake and Gav were alerted to a car pulling up to the cable car station. They were locked and loaded but soon relaxed when they saw who it was.

"Gentlemen, good to see you alert and ready for action."

"Yes Sir, always Sir."

"Are the Deepermeyers in?"

"Yes Sir."

"Good, my coach of trial volunteers should be here within the hour. Make sure they are sent up without delay."

"Of course, Sir."

*

Clark was logged on as usual after a quick meal and his usual caffeine fix. There was a message from Harlequin on Proton. Harley had done a workaround on the Zephyr app. Clark ran the programme. It connected to the phone he was tracking. The mirroring tool came up. He was sending a text.

Gavin, I am here. I will clear you at the bottom cable car station with the security team. Get them up here as soon as they arrive.

Quickly followed by another.

Clay, Jacob. I am…

Just as he was reading the second text, the management software went dead. He tapped away at the keyboard. Nothing changed. The screen was in limbo. He clicked on the GPS tab. The phone was not showing on the GPS tracker.

What the hell just happened?

Clark looked back at the GPS history. The phone had travelled from London to Austria, almost certainly by plane, and then followed a road from Innsbruck into Switzerland. The GPS had dropped out at the bottom of a mountain range about one mile above a small village called Boden. He checked back to the GPS location of the last reading he had in Switzerland. The GPS location history was not there.

Eh, how can that be? He was in Switzerland before and I had a fix on his location. Now it is gone. That does not make any sense.

He logged onto Proton to message Harley. They would know what to do.

*

Alice sat in the technology suite after an early meal. Jacob had told her that the British trial volunteers were on their way and she needed to get her scanning equipment ready, as none of them had gone through the same process as the American volunteers. He refused to answer when she asked why they were different. They had done extensive vetting on all the American applicants. She was curious as to why the British were different, especially with their extensive security requirements. Once again, something about this wasn't right.

She was almost ready when she noticed a message from Krypto. He was asking how the GPS element of the phone hack she had provided could suddenly stop working.

She read it a few times and her heart began to sink. She mouthed the answer to herself.

It would only stop working if my anti-satellite surveillance was in operation.

She stared at the screen.

Shit! Who is Krypto following and how have they come into my anti-surveillance zone?

Alice was in no doubt. The only way her GPS hack would not work was if it encountered her anti-surveillance. It was like a fingerprint. Unmistakable. One of a kind.

Alice's mind was racing. First Blowfish and now Krypto. Why did these people, who she had been cyber friends with for as long as she could remember, suddenly seem to be close to her real life?

Her growing panic was broken by a message. The British volunteers were here.

29

Clay, Jacob, William Hardacre, Alice, the Professor and George convened in the large meeting room. They settled down while a procession of people filtered in and each found a place to sit. Nineteen men and three women. As they shuffled in, looking restless and jumpy, everyone turned to William with a look of astonishment that simply said... what the fuck is this?

They were confronted with a group of people that could only be described as 'down and outs'. Their clothes seemed quite new but there was no disguising the hard lives that were shown in their faces and general demeanour. Someone was trying to 'polish a turd'. No amount of new clothes and quick showers could disguise where these people had come from.

Jacob broke the sense of shock that was pervading the room.

"William. Can I have a word outside?"

They walked outside, leaving the two sides of the audience staring at each other in sheer amazement.

"What the fuck is that bunch of tramps doing here?"

"They are your British volunteers Jacob. What the fuck do you think they are?"

"We need normal functioning people, not drop-outs and drunks. What the hell are you thinking?"

"They are human beings Jacob. We have dried them out and they are ready."

"What did you do? Drag them out of the gutter? Are they even here legally?"

"Legally! Ha, that is rich coming from you. They all have passports that have just passed three passport control checks. There are as legal as anything else you are doing here."

"Jesus William, you are taking too many risks. When we expose ourselves to our respective governments, we need no trails that they can follow, other than the ones we want them to follow."

William slapped him gently on the cheek.

"Jacob, Jacob. You worry too much. No one is going to track this bunch of losers. Trust me. They are as disposable as a box of tissues."

They re-entered the room and the crowd were getting restless, murmuring away.

"I need a drink," shouted one.

"Yeh, where's the five fucking grand you promised, so we can buy some bloody drink. I'm having the DTs over here."

William stood up, trying to take command of a situation that had everyone else in the room absolutely perplexed.

"Gentlemen, ladies, we just need to do your security scans, get you checked into your accommodation, and then tonight's drinks are on me."

There was a big cheer from the audience. Jacob looked at Clay and shook his head. William was completely taking the piss but they had to let it run for now.

William told Alice to get her software scanning set up quickly at the end of the room, clearly worried the natives were going to rebel. He organised a line and Alice started scanning their fingerprints and irises, whilst taking a DNA swab. All three were logged onto the system to allow them to get into the scientific block where the trials would be held and their accommodation was located. She processed them quickly and efficiently, trying to ignore the obvious smells of BO, alcohol and various bodily functions which were not being masked by cheap soap and cheap clothes.

By 10 p.m. all the volunteers had been allocated their rooms and were now consuming large amounts of alcohol in the bar.

Jacob watched the scene with distaste.

"What the hell do you think you are doing William?"

"They are all drunks Jacob. We dried them out for the trip over but you will get no co-operation from them if you deny them their vices."

"You had better know what you are doing."

"Oh, I do Jacob. Don't you worry about that."

*

The Professor and George were also watching the scene unfold.

"Jesus, George, what the hell am I supposed to do with this lot?"

"They are just enjoying themselves Prof. Don't worry about it."

The Professor looked at George perplexed.

"You have changed your tune. I thought everything about this was freaking you out."

"It is, but I am taking your advice and trying to chill a bit. Also, I spoke to that girl, Alice. I think she is alright. Seems to be in the same position as us and is going to help us get out of here."

The Professor studied George's face. Something had changed.

"Oh?" he replied, trying not to show his concern.

George smiled back. The first smile the Professor had seen since he had been here. Something had changed.

"You do realise that if all these people are alcoholics the trial data is going to be compromised. Their blood alcohol levels will skew the results. I can't see how we can use these as representative."

"Why do you think they are alcoholics?"

"Oh, for God's sake George. Look at them. That man has dragged a load of down and outs off the streets of the UK and landed them here. I think it is a pretty good bet that they are all addicted to something."

George stood up, put his arm round the Professor and said, "It will be fine, you worry too much", then walked over to the bar to get a drink.

The Professor watched him. Something had changed.

30

In the accommodation block where the UK volunteers had been staying, the morning was the predictable carnage. Lots of hangovers, lots of abuse directed at anyone who tried to get them out of bed and a constant request for more alcohol.

The Professor was not impressed.

"George, I am going to see Jacob about this. These people are impossible to work with."

George went to say something but the Professor left before he could get the words out.

He flew into Jacob and Clay's office. Jacob was the only one there.

"Professor. Come in please."

"What the hell do you think you are doing landing me with a bunch of drunks? I can't work with them."

"Look Professor. I am sorry. Mr Hardacre promised us volunteers from the UK to work alongside the ones coming from the US. I didn't realise he was going to land us with a load of drop-outs. Is there nothing you can do with them?"

"They will work as human trialists but they are all drunk from last night and completely uncooperative. We need people that are compliant to make the trials work. If they get pissed every night, the results will not be representative. They need to go."

"The US volunteers are due around noon today. Leave it with me. I will sort it out."

"Thank you."

Jacob called William into the office and found Clay. He wanted his brother to be here for this.

"William, you have failed us. The Professor has just been to see me and can't work with the bunch of drop-outs you have landed us with. They are all pissed up and refusing to move. Not the sort of people we need to help this trial."

William stared him down.

"You Yanks are arrogant bastards. You think you know it all. I have supplied you with a batch of untraceable people, off the grid, that nobody cares about. What have you done? Put a fucking message out on social media that anybody can find. Leaving a trail, getting people that will be missed, that can be tracked. It is not me that has failed. It is you."

Both sides looked at each other, not breaking eye contact, seeing who had the biggest balls for the fight. Jacob gave a firm response.

"I want them gone William. All of them. NOW!"

William stormed out.

Jacob looked at Clay.

"We don't need him. He is a liability. We need to cut the UK out of our plans. Make sure he leaves the site and revoke all his security privileges. I don't want to see him ever again."

*

An hour later, Jacob and Clay watched as the motley crew of UK volunteers were 'persuaded' to leave the site and get back on their coach by all of Shaun's team, who pointed their semi-automatic rifles at anyone who tried to fight back. William was nowhere to be seen.

As the last person got on the bus, Jacob called Shaun to one side.

"Get rid of them Shaun and make sure Mr Hardacre is off the site and can't get back in."

"Yes Sir. Leave it with me."

The coach drove away from the bottom cable car station, closely followed by two of Shaun's men in the Hummer.

*

Just after midday, a coach arrived with forty-three trial volunteers from the US. They were invited into the same room that had been the scene of the UK volunteers' debacle. Everything was more civilised and compliant, with all the people checked off by Alice, their previous scans verified and validated. William was still nowhere to be seen.

Alice worked her way round the room, introducing herself. But then she found herself shaking hands with Ellie Baker. The woman's photograph hadn't done her justice. Her eyes were even more penetrating in real life, and her skin was soft to the touch.

"Hi, Ellie. I'm Al… I mean Jasmine."

"Well, which is it?" Ellie asked, her voice gently teasing.

"Jasmine," Alice said, hoping that her slip would be forgotten. "How was your journey?"

"I still don't really know what I'm doing here. But the money is so good, I guess that…" She trailed off.

"You'll be fine," Alice said. Then, without thinking, "Maybe I could show you around – are you free for a drink later?" She could have kicked herself. That was not what she should be asking. She should be treating all these people equally.

"That would be lovely Jasmine. Thank you."

*

As the US volunteers settled in, Jacob was still buzzing around.

"Shaun. Where is Mr Hardacre?"

"He is gone. All his stuff is out of his room. Gav said he checked him out of the bottom cable car station about an hour ago."

107

"Good. Have you revoked his security detail?"

"Yes Sir."

"Excellent. Good riddance to bad rubbish."

*

Clark had not heard anything from Harlequin. He had been keeping an eye on the GPS tracker on and off all day but nothing was changing. It was still not transmitting any information.

As he was about to give it up as a bad job, he checked one more time and suddenly realised that the software was working again. The phone was visible and moving away from the place where he had lost the signal, toward the main road leading to Austria. He watched it, captivated. Suddenly the Zephyr hack pinged into life. He was sending a text.

Gavin. We have a problem. The Yanks have betrayed us. All our volunteers have been chucked off the site. I am on my way back to the UK. I won't let these bastards get away with this. I need to implement plan B. My Trojan horse.

Clark was excited. Something was going down and he intended to find out what.

31

Erica Mole was in Brighton. Ever since her brother Simon had fallen out with their parents over his drinking and left the family home, she made the pilgrimage from her home in Edinburgh a couple of times a year to check how he was.

His descent into full-blown alcoholism had been heartbreaking. He left in a fit of pique, angry at their parents' constant criticism of his lifestyle, but he had no plan. No job, no money and nowhere to live. He became another homeless statistic very quickly. Erica tried to help him, bringing him food and clothes, putting him in touch with the homeless charities but, every time she looked for him, he was back living rough underneath the same railway arches in Brighton.

As she made the demoralising trek toward the arches, she hoped for something different, something better for Simon. As she turned the corner and looked into the dark, dingy cavern she got a shock. The place was almost empty. Normally there would be twenty to thirty men strewn around the space but all she could see were two figures, lying on the floor.

She moved tentatively toward them, always on her guard. These men were volatile and could lash out at any moment. She got to one, who was half asleep. She risked nudging him.

"Hmph, wo, gerroff me."

"Please mister, I'm looking for Moley. Have you seen him?"

"Wo, who are ya? Gis some money."

"I will give you some money if you tell me where Moley is."

The man tried to sit up, eyes glazed, trying to focus. Erica tried to ignore the smell of urine, mixed with alcohol.

"Where is Moley?" she repeated, trying to get some sort of coherent response.

"Gone. All gone. Man. Big bus."

His eyes started to close again and his upper body slumped back to its starting position.

Erica nudged him, trying to stir him back to some sort of life.

"Wake up. Wake up. What do you mean they've all gone?"

Her efforts were hopeless. The man was, once again, dead to the world. She stuffed a £20 note into his pocket and walked away.

Erica walked the two miles back into the centre of town and found the police station. After a short wait, a neighbourhood officer invited her into the interview room adjacent to the station's front desk.

"Hi, I'm PC Sharon Baines. I understand you want to report a missing person?"

"Yes, I'm Erica Mole. My brother Simon Mole is missing."

"Has he been missing for more than twenty-four hours?"

"Well, yes, I think so. He's homeless. I come down from Scotland a couple of times a year to see how he is. He is usually under the railway arches. I have just been there and another homeless guy said he had left with a load of others."

The PC put on a sympathetic but ultimately unconvincing face.

"Um, I am sorry Miss Mole but this doesn't sound like a missing person if your brother is a transient."

"A what?"

"A transient. Someone who moves around. Has no fixed abode."

"I am telling you he is missing. You may not give a shit about him, just because he is a down and out, but I do and I can tell you that he is not where he normally should be."

"I assure you madam, we do care about all our citizens but

our procedures for assessing the level of risk around your brother do not meet any sort of priority level. He is just as likely to turn up there tomorrow as he is to be ten miles away, drinking himself unconsciousness in the next seaside town."

Erica tried to calm her rage.

"I spoke to another homeless guy and he said he had left with a load of others."

"Oh, and that is such a reliable source of information."

Erica was ready to punch this woman's lights out but thought maybe assaulting a police officer was not a good move.

"Do you have something against the homeless?"

"No."

"Then why won't you help?"

"Look, I am sorry if you think I'm being unhelpful but nothing you have told me at the moment suggests your brother meets the criteria to be a missing person. My suggestion is you contact the local homeless charity, as they have a much better handle on who is sleeping rough in the town and where they might be."

Erica stood up and stormed out.

She knew where to go. She had been to the local homeless charity many times and they were certainly more helpful than that idiot of a police officer. Their offices were only a ten-minute walk away, where she met a man she had spoken to before about Simon.

"Ah, hello, Miss... Miss..."

"Mole, Erica Mole."

"Ah yes, sorry I couldn't remember your name. Simon's sister."

"Yes, that's right."

"What can I do for you?"

"Simon is missing. I went to the arches and another homeless guy said he had left, with a load of others."

The support worker suddenly looked very concerned.

"You had better come with me."

He invited her into one of the small side rooms.

"Do you want a cup of tea?"

"No. No. What is wrong? Has something happened to Simon?"

"I am sorry to tell you this Erica, but we are really concerned about the homeless community that lived under the arches."

"Lived! Why are you using the past tense?"

"Sorry, poor choice of phrase. We don't know what happened but about a week ago one of our street wardens, who regularly check up on our homeless community, found the arches completely empty. There are usually twenty to thirty homeless people that congregate there, including Simon, but they were all gone."

"So, the guy I spoke to was right?"

"Well possibly. Our warden has checked every day since and none of the regulars have returned. The guy you saw was probably a new one who has just found the space."

"I have just been to the police and they didn't want to know."

"Hmm, I'm not surprised, we get very little support from them."

"There must be something we can do."

"Erica, let me take this on. I will contact the police about the whole group that usually dossed there. They might be more interested if we go to them about a larger group."

"I'm not sure. The police officer I spoke to seemed to think Simon would just turn up or had buggered off to the next seaside town."

"They don't know much about homeless people, do they? They tend not to stray from their usual area unless someone like us moves them elsewhere. They don't just get on a bus and go to the next town. If they are not in Brighton, something has happened to them."

Erica thanked him and left the building. She had booked overnight accommodation in a B&B. She headed there, worried out of her mind.

32

The Professor was in the large meeting room, ready to brief the US volunteers about the trial.

"A much more civilised bunch," he whispered to George. As the general murmuring in the room reduced to a level where the Professor felt he could be heard, he launched into his welcome speech.

"Ladies and gentlemen. Can I have your attention please?... Thank you. My name is Professor Carlton Jenkins and this is my assistant George Mankley. We will be running the clinical trials you have signed up to."

There were lots of attentive, agreeable nods from the audience.

"We hope you have settled in to this lovely location and your accommodation is OK."

A voice came from the back of the room.

"It's very nice Professor but why all the military security? Why are we up a darned great mountain in the middle of Switzerland with no ability to contact the outside world?"

"Well my role is purely scientific but as I understand it, from the people that are paying the bills, the work we are doing here requires the utmost secrecy. They are not prepared to let our work leak out or be compromised before we can complete successful trials. I believe you are being paid well for your time and this should compensate you for any inconvenience."

George was surprised how 'on message' the Professor was. It was almost as though he had been brainwashed into believing the Deepermeyers' mantra, despite the obvious threats to their lives moving forward. His face must have given some hint to his feelings as another member of the audience piped up.

"Your assistant doesn't seem convinced by what you are saying. Is there something wrong? Something we should know?"

The Professor turned to look at George, concern all over his face. George snapped out of his daydream.

"Oh, er, no nothing's wrong. The Professor is quite right. The gentlemen running this trial need your absolute discretion. This work is potentially groundbreaking."

They could sense the mood of the room was changing and not for the better. The questions from the audience continued.

"What are these trials trying to cure?"

The Professor took back the floor.

"I can't tell you that. It is part of the contract you have signed that you are not able to discuss any aspects of this trial, contact anybody outside whilst you are here or be told the full details of the research."

The general dissatisfied murmuring seemed to grow. The Professor pushed on.

"Look, ladies and gentlemen. I am here to explain what will happen during the trial but if anyone is uncomfortable with moving forward, I am sure the Deepermeyers will be happy to discuss your concerns. If anyone doesn't want to stay for this briefing, you are free to go."

The Professor let the murmuring play out, people talking to each other trying to judge the pack mentality. As the murmuring subsided, nobody had moved. The Professor smiled inwardly. *Money does talk*, he thought to himself.

"OK. So, we are going to run three cycles of the trials. You will be split into three groups. The first group will be infected with the virus... and, before anyone worries, it is not life threatening. It is something your bodies will be more than capable of dealing with. This group will be given the new trial medicine within twelve hours of the virus being given to you. George and I will be monitoring the effectiveness of the medicine in terms of how quickly the virus is eradicated from your bodies. The second group will be infected with the virus but be given traditional medicines to measure the comparisons between this and the new medicine. The control group, the last group, will not be infected directly with the virus but there is every chance that normal cross contamination will occur. If you do become infected in this first trial, you will not be given any medicine. We will monitor how the body deals with eradicating the virus through natural means. Each cycle will last two weeks to allow your bodies to recover from whatever infections might occur. We will start the next trial at the beginning of the following two weeks and you will be in a different group for this and the final trial. During the infection periods, you will be asked to remain in the accommodation to minimise infection to the other staff on site. All your meals will be brought over. We will let you know on an individual basis when you can use the wider site. OK, any questions?"

The mood of the room seemed more compliant but questions did flow.

"Professor. Can you give us some idea of how we are going to feel once infected?"

"Yes, I expect you to have 'flu like' symptoms."

"And how quickly do you expect the virus to leave our bodies if the medicine works?"

"Previous trials have shown a complete removal of the virus within twenty-four hours."

There were lots of impressed nods.

"Can we pull out at any point?"

"Yes, but I guess payments will be reduced."

As the questions died down and the mood seemed to remain civil, the Professor closed the session down.

"OK, ladies and gentlemen, the trials will start at nine a.m. on Monday. Give yourself some time to settle in and enjoy a nice relaxing weekend. I will meet you in the trial labs on Monday."

Alice was halfway through her day. The US trial volunteers were all in and settled. The security was holding. No cyber-attacks. No breaches. She was happy that they were basically invisible. The threats from Jacob Deepermeyer still played on her mind, as did the interactions with Krypto and Blowfish, but what was really distracting her was Ellie.

They had a brief drink in the bar the previous night and seemed to click instantly. Ellie had been charming, funny and... Alice could hardly bring herself to say it... so sexy. The physical contact had been fleeting but when Ellie touched her, it was like a bolt of electricity coursing through her body. Alice had never had feelings like this. She kept telling herself to remain professional but there was something about Ellie that was completely consuming her.

*

Erica Mole was on a train back to Edinburgh. She had spoken to the manager from the homeless charity. He had been to the police and they agreed to investigate. She didn't hold out much hope. Something had happened to Simon and she was determined to find out what.

33

Clark had finished another day at work and went straight into 'mission control'. He hadn't heard from Harley but he finally had a scent. The man he had been after for nearly three years was in his sights. He was going to get him this time. *William Hardacre.*

The GPS was still working and the live view of his phone was giving him something to watch. The texts were confusing, abstract but with his web skills it would give him something to go on. He started to write up the key points on his whiteboard.

Switzerland – GPS drops out near Boden – has stayed somewhere for several days at a time

Clay and Jacob – American?

Gavin – volunteers – what for? Where did they get them? Illegals?

Betrayed by Americans? – Plan B – Trojan horse – he has an insider – for what?

Clark sat and pondered. How could he begin to make sense of this? He started with Clay and Jacob. He searched the conventional web, using their names as a combination, separately and with the word 'American' in the search criteria. He clicked on a few links and examined the results.

Baseball players – **Clay** *and* **Jacob** *Truman, Boston Red Sox*

Jacob *Marshall – CEO of Minstrel* **Clay** *Company, Indiana*

Senator **Jacob Clay,** *New York State*

Map of **Clay** *Lane,* **Jacob's** *Ladder, South Dakota*

Clark started to rationalise out loud.

"Hmm, knowing Hardacre, the Senator is a good bet but his message said Clay and Jacob, not Jacob Clay. Two people, not one. I can't see the baseball players being a thing. The others are just nonsense. Shit, this is frustrating."

As he sat there trying to work out what to do next the Zephyr app popped up on the hack management screen. He was texting again.

Shaun, can I count on you? How many of your team are in on our plan?

A text came back fairly quickly.

The three guys that have been with me for the longest time are solid. I can't rely on Jake and Gav at the moment. They are new to the team. I need more time. Four of us can work this.

William Hardacre texted right back.

Good. I want that formula. Let me know when you have a plan. I will come back and pick it up personally.

The texts stopped and Clark looked at the now empty screens as the frustrating cyber wipe instantly removed each message, but he wrote down the key word on the board – *formula*. What the hell was he up to now?

34

Jake had just finished his shift and needed a drink. He wondered whether Alice was around and up for some more 'friends with benefits'. As he walked into the bar she was just leaving with a slim, good-looking girl with medium-length blonde hair and a great arse. They didn't see him and went on their way. *Oh well,* he thought to himself, *an empty bed again tonight.*

*

Alice walked back to her accommodation block with Ellie. A second night of drinks, fantastic conversation and a growing attraction to Ellie had almost distracted Alice from all the other demons that were raging in her head.

As they reached the outside door to Alice's apartment, they both stopped, an awkward silence hanging between them. Ellie broke the tension.

"Can I come in for... coffee?"

Alice's heart was doing somersaults. "No Ellie, I don't think that would be a good idea. I'm supposed to be doing a job here, not fraternising with the patients. We have to keep this strictly professional."

Ellie pouted. "That's a shame. I didn't read anything in the paperwork that said we couldn't have fun."

Alice looked down at the floor. Every bit of her psyche

was screaming at her to invite Ellie in but she had to keep the boundaries clear.

"Please Ellie. I love your company but let's just leave it for now."

Ellie leant in toward Alice, seemingly trying to kiss her. Alice moved away.

"No Ellie, I'm sorry. We can't do this."

Alice quickly opened the door to her apartment and went inside, leaving Ellie standing there. Rejected and confused.

*

Alice paced around the room. *What have I done?*

Her feelings for Ellie were new, confusing, like nothing she had ever experienced. Was this... *love?* Was this what it felt like? Her relationships with men had been fun, full of lust and great sex, but she never had an emotional connection like the one she was feeling right now.

She walked up to her apartment door. Stopped. Listened. *Was she still out there?*

Alice stepped away from the door, walked to the feature window that framed the fantastic view, the snow on the higher levels still illuminating the mountains in the fading light. She stared out for a while, not really looking at anything.

Suddenly, she turned and ran to her apartment door, wrenching it open.

Ellie was gone.

35

Mahindra grabbed Chad and knocked on Jon's door.

"Come in."

She tried to contain her excitement but launched straight in.

"Jon, I think I have found Alice."

"What? Where?"

"Well, I started to focus on the hundred or so women passing the Swiss passport control. I used the scanned passport images against our facial recognition and got a hit, of sorts."

"What do you mean 'of sorts'?"

"Well, it's Alice but it's not Alice."

"Mahindra, stop talking in riddles. Have you found her or not?"

"We had a sixty-six per cent match against a person called Jasmine Bakerfield. Now, a sixty-six per cent match is not that conclusive so I got our techs to look at it. The image seems to be of Alice but it has been deliberately tampered with to cheat the facial recognition. It is not that sophisticated, anyone with a photo editor could do it, but they did have some knowledge of how facial recognition works when they edited it. They have changed facial features just enough to not cause an issue when a passport control officer was comparing the picture to the actual face but it is enough to reduce the facial recognition match. But, look at it. That is Alice."

Chad and Jon looked at all the images Mahindra was showing them.

"Well done Mahindra. That is Alice alright, facial recognition or no facial recognition. With the hit on Shaun, I am confident we can update the intel on Operation Hawk. They crossed into Switzerland."

*

Erica Mole was home but still frantic. She contacted the police that covered the Brighton area. The investigation had been given a unique reference number but a detective team had not yet been assigned. *Shit! This is impossible. Where are you Simon?*

*

Alice sat in the bar, waiting, hoping that Ellie would appear. She had been tormenting herself for the way she had treated her. She needed to see her, to explain. At this point, Ellie was potentially the only person that could keep her sane.

As she scanned the room, she saw George approaching. He seemed more relaxed than during their first two interactions.

"Hi George. How's it going?"

"Well, we have started the trials today. The group are all OK and nicely quarantined in their living quarters."

"Quarantined?"

"Yeh, they have to stay in the building during the infection period, to avoid wider contamination to the other staff. All their food is delivered to the building."

"What? I didn't know that. Can't I see…"

"Oh, you have a 'friend'. You are a quick operator Alice. Go girl. Who is it?"

Alice looked a bit sheepish. She didn't like her private life being aired to all and sundry.

"Come on Alice, spill!"

She smiled. George seemed harmless.

"OK, OK, its Ellie Baker."

"Hmm, nice girl but not my type of course."

"Oh, are you gay?"

"Isn't it obvious? I thought us gays could always spot kindred spirits."

"Actually, I'm… err, I don't know what I am… but my gaydar has always been a bit rubbish. Are you and the Professor…"

"Yes, actually. He's quite the stud for an old man."

They laughed but as the merriment waned, they both realised that not much had changed in the general peril stakes. Alice decided to probe for information, hoping that anything she could glean from George might help her rationalise the situation.

"What is this big secret cure then George?"

"I'm not sure I should tell you. We've all had to sign confidentiality clauses stating that we won't divulge any of the details. They are paranoid about this getting out."

"I know but they wouldn't tell me when I asked."

"I thought you had access to everything being the IT geek?"

"Well, yes, in theory, but you and the Professor haven't used the ultra-secure part of the network to store any electronic files, so I can't snoop even if I wanted to."

"Ah yes, the Professor does like his paper records. Doesn't seem to trust the technology."

"So?"

"Don't Alice, you'll get me in trouble."

Alice had to smile at George's reluctance to 'break the law' despite her growing concerns about the Deepermeyers' intentions. She pushed on, probing for more.

"OK George, I won't push it but tell me, how long have we got before things get hairy?"

"Well, initially we are running three, two-week trials. We need a week or so to consolidate the results and I would expect us to need to run a second or third trial."

"So, a minimum of six to seven weeks."

"Well, for the first trial, yes."

"Come on George, do you really expect them to be patient? They will expect instant results. These men are greedy bastards. They will want to make money as soon as they can."

"I can't see how. If this trial isn't conclusive, we need another batch of clinical trialists."

"Do the Deepermeyers know that?"

George looked pensive.

"Um, I don't know. The Professor has been the one speaking to them. I just do what I am told."

"Shit George, that's not much of a plan. We need an exit plan within six weeks. Trust me."

They both took a slug of their drinks and got lost in their own thoughts. George broke the silence.

"What's your exit plan then Alice?"

She was just about to speak when she spotted Jake heading in their direction. She lowered her voice.

"I'm working on it but part of my plan is walking over here."

George turned around and quickly glanced back at Alice with an approving look. She smiled.

"I don't think he swings your way," she whispered.

George put on a pouty, disappointed face. Jake reached the table.

"Hi Alice, can I join you?"

She looked at George. He gave a subtle nod.

"Of course, soldier boy. This is George."

"Oh yes, hi, we met when you first arrived. You are working with the Professor?"

"Yes."

"So, Alice, who was that girl you were with last night? She had a great arse."

"Jesus, you don't change. Jealous, are we?"

"Jealous? Of what?"

"I am sure you can work it out."

Jake looked at her, confused. Alice let it play through his little mind. She guessed he wasn't the sharpest tool in the box but she thought he would get it eventually. After a short pause he reacted.

"Oh, you and her... um... you know, did the dirty."

"Does that turn you on Jake?"

"Um, er, well, I guess. I can't say I have ever experienced that."

"Calm yourself soldier boy. Nothing happened. We're just friends."

George was cracking up, trying to stifle a laugh. Alice was precious. She was clearly very good at winding up men like Jake. He decided to join in.

"Do you not like the gays then Jake?"

"God, no. It's fine. These days it's just... normal I guess."

Alice and George couldn't hold it in any longer and absolutely cracked up. Jake looked at them both. He put on an embarrassed face.

"Ha, ha, you got me. Very good."

*

It was late as he sat in Jacob's office.

"How is it going?"

"Good, you were right about her. She is plotting a way to get out of here. I'll let you know as soon as I find out what she is up to."

36

Clark logged into Proton. Snap and Blowfish were online.

KRYPTO: Evenin, anyone heard from Harley

BLOWFISH: Nada

SNAPDEVIL: Nein

KRYPTO: They did me a part hack on the phone issue. I can see what the dude is up to but it still gets wiped immediately. Was hoping they would have cracked the whole thing by now

BLOWFISH: There's something strange about Harley

SNAPDEVIL: Why do you say that dude?

BLOWFISH: They reacted strangely when I was talking about that analyst

KRYPTO: Yeh, to be fair, they were odd when we first mentioned that story

SNAPDEVIL: Yeh agree. They said they were into something heavy. Maybe they is a bit distracted

BLOWFISH: Dunno, something ain't right. Do you think they know something about the analyst?

KRYPTO: Thought you were the insider on this story

BLOWFISH: Nah, not really, just picked up the story from contacts. Haven't heard much else

KRYPTO: I messaged them three times over the last few days. Nothing

SNAPDEVIL: Maybe they is in trouble

KRYPTO: They said they would tell us. Get our help

BLOWFISH: There is another possibility

SNAPDEVIL: Wot?

BLOWFISH: Have you ever considered that Harley is a female? Could they be the missing analyst?

KRYPTO: FM, really?

BLOWFISH: Why not? I know we don't do the identity thing but hackers come from all backgrounds. This missing analyst is supposed to be one of the best cyber analysts in the world. Think about the stuff that Harley provides to our community. They know some serious shit. Some stuff that we are not so good at. Why couldn't they be NSA and still indulge in our community?

SNAPDEVIL: Jesus. That would be a major head fuck if that's true

KRYPTO: Difficult to deal with. We can't break our code

BLOWFISH: I know

Clark sat staring at the latest chat. Could Blowfish be right? Was there a possibility that the missing analyst was somehow connected to their little community? Harley was undoubtedly a talented hacker but would they... she?... really be part of their group if she worked for the NSA? *It might explain their recent weird behaviour,* he thought to himself.

He let the thought fester and went back to watching the phone hack, desperate for William Hardacre to do something. Something that would let Clark nail him, once and for all.

*

Chad logged off from Proton. He had been Blowfish on Proton for nearly five years and he had never suspected that Alice, the spiky, shit-hot analyst that had sat across the desk from him for nearly a year, could be a member of their hackers' community. He had been agonising over whether to test out his theory on Krypto and Snap because it went against their code. They had been OK and had not dismissed his mad idea.

He grabbed a beer out of the fridge and sat staring at his screen. Harlequin. What was it about that name that was now niggling his conspiracy radar?

He slugged most of his beer. He was just about to get another one out of the fridge when it hit him. He found the pictures of the previous year's office party. It had been a fancy-dress party. Chad found what he was looking for.

A picture of Alice as the Batman villain, Dr Harley Quinn.

37

They were a few days into the trial and the Professor was worried.

"George, I am really concerned about the results from the main test group. They are not exhibiting the same pattern of results as our last batch of six."

"Are you surprised?"

"Yes, I am a bit. The results of those six were so consistent, so incredibly pure. The science just worked."

"I did warn you not to get your hopes up."

"Look George, I am the scientist and will judge what is right and wrong. I don't deal in hope. The scientific outcomes of those six was like nothing I have ever seen. I don't understand why only three of the batch of fourteen are exhibiting the same results. Did you mix the formula exactly as we had it before?"

"Yes, absolutely."

The Professor turned away and started reviewing the test results for the hundredth time. Distracted, searching for the answers, no longer engaging with George.

*

Erica Mole was now making daily calls to the police and to the homeless charity. She was not going to let this lie. Simon had not turned up back under the arches or anywhere else in Brighton. She couldn't shake the gut-wrenching feeling that he was no longer alive. Somebody had hurt her brother. Killed him maybe and no one seemed to care.

*

Chad and Mahindra joined Jon for their weekly review of Operation Hawk. Jon was in better spirits as progress had been made, but Chad didn't know what to do about his suspicions that Alice was Harlequin. What could they do with it anyway? She was still ignoring all attempts at contact with him, Krypto or Snap. He agonised over whether that very fact confirmed her guilt. He decided to keep it to himself and focus on what they could confirm.

"OK team. What is the update?"

Chad launched in.

"We have liaised with the Swiss about their satellite coverage and got some hits on the vehicles that Shaun and Alice got into at Innsbruck Airport. They definitely travelled into Switzerland from Austria. We had some pings on the few roadside cameras they have along the main route from the border into a large mountainous area. We lost the trail but this confirms the work Mahindra has done on the passport pictures and fixes their location to a broad geographical area."

"That is great news Chad, but why do you think we can fix the broad area?"

"Because the vehicle would have pinged cameras further along the main route across Switzerland. It didn't, meaning it must have stopped in this broad area."

Jon and Mahindra studied the map. It was an area of about fifty square miles dominated by high peaks and small villages running along the valley.

Jon rubbed his face.

"It's good – it still feels like needle in a haystack time, but at least the haystack just got a bit smaller."

38

William Hardacre sat in his plush Mayfair office with Henry White-Taylor and Julian Watkins.

"Gentlemen, welcome. Henry, this is Julian Watkins, the CEO of Westbrook Pharmaceuticals. Julian, I am sure you know Sir Henry White-Taylor, the Secretary of State for Health and Social Care."

"Yes of course, nice to meet you Sir Henry."

"Likewise. So, what's all this about William?"

"We have a problem with the Yanks. They have cut me out of their deal over some piffling trial volunteers. They didn't like what I supplied."

"What did you supply?" asked Henry.

"Let's just say, I found some people that no one would miss. The Yanks didn't like the fact that most of them liked a drink or two. Said they 'weren't compliant enough', stupid bastards."

"So, what happened William?"

"They kicked them all off the site and told me to leave too."

"It's unlike you to be so passive."

"Well gentlemen, that is because I have a plan B and I need you both to be part of it."

They both nodded their approval.

"So, Henry. The group I was part of will not now be making representation to the UK government as I had expected. In fact, I suspect without me they will just concentrate on the US government."

"OK, but what do you need me to do now?"

"Well, there will come a point when the government will be asked to licence the formula that is being developed in Switzerland and Julian's company will be the sole producer and distributor in the UK. I need you to make sure that licence is granted."

"Alright, seems pretty straight forward. You won't need as many ministers on side as for your original plan."

"I know. Good, isn't it?"

Julian cut across the mutual appreciation society that seemed to be William and Sir Henry's relationship.

"William, you haven't actually told me what I am selling. What is this formula?"

"All in good time Julian. All you need to know is that it will make us billions of pounds. This is THE scientific breakthrough of the century and I am not going to let the Yanks win."

"OK, I am going to trust you on this but how are you going to get this formula to me and how am I going to know how to make the compound."

"I have an inside man. Now that I am not there, he is going to steal the formula and all the scientific notes."

"What, just like that?"

"Well, no, the place is locked up like a nun's knickers but he is part of the security team. He will find a way."

"How long will this take?"

"They are doing the trials now, so the formula is being administered. They just need to find a way of getting it."

"OK, I will get my development team on standby but without the full information, I am not going to be able to produce anything."

"Don't you worry Julian. I won't fail. No one gets away with treating me like that."

Sir Henry and Julian left and William got on the phone. His call was answered immediately.

"Yes, boss man."

"Shaun, I have the UK end ready. When will this be done?"

"I am going to speak to my team tonight. We can get in the building no problem, as all my team have clearance, but only the Professor and his assistant can get in the test lab. That is going to be the problem as that is almost certainly where the details will be."

"You need to make this happen Shaun. I won't be beaten by those bastards."

"I know. I will work something out."

*

Clark was just walking back into his man cave when he noticed the phone hack software was running. William was on the phone. Clark rushed up to the screen, but it was too late. William had disconnected and the cyber wipe had cleared all trace of the call.

Shit, this is impossible. I can't be watching this twenty-four hours a day. Come on Harley. Where are you? I need you to fix this.

He sat staring at his screen. He wondered whether Blowfish was right. Could Harley really be that missing analyst? It would at least explain why they were not their usual reliable hacking genius. What had Blowfish said? 'One of the best cyber analysts in the world.' It was certainly feasible but was not helping Clark work out what the hell William Hardacre was up to.

He needed some therapy. He knew Snap would be online.

KRYPTO: Snap, this phone hack is driving me crazy

SNAPDEVIL: Wassup dude?

KRYPTO: The GPS is working again, your hack gives me access to Zephyr and Harley's hack at least allows me to see what he is doing but the cyber wipe means I have to be watching it constantly

SNAPDEVIL: Soz mate, that tech is some serious shit. I couldn't work out how to counter the cyber wipe

KRYPTO: I've only got snippets to go on. He was in Switzerland and for some reason the GPS dropped out for a time but came back on when he started to move out of the country. I have some words from his texts. Two names, Clay and Jacob, reference to a formula, a discussion with a Gavin about being betrayed and something about volunteers. Any ideas?

SNAPDEVIL: The GPS will just be a lack of coverage, though must be remote as eyes are everywhere these days. Formula and volunteers suggest some sort of medical trials. Doesn't Hardacre have the licence on betrayal so no surprises there

KRYPTO: Hmm, good thoughts. Medical trials to make money. Sounds right up H's street. Looks like he was near a mountain range so may explain GPS. Can you do a trawl on the names Clay and Jacob as a pair. Americans. He is, or was, working with them

SNAPDEVIL: No probs dude. Will find your dodgy Yanks. I promise

Clark logged off and pondered the conversation with Snap. Medical trials. An interesting possibility. How could he find out more? He needed more clues from Hardacre's phone activity. He resigned himself to watching the hack software. Boring, but his only real option.

39

The Professor had been summoned to see Clay and Jacob for a progress update.

"How's it going Professor?"

"Well, early days but the formula has only produced a hundred per cent success rate in three out of the fourteen people in that trial group."

Jacob looked at Clay with concern.

"That is not good Professor. That is a significant reduction in success to your previous trial. What have you done?"

"Nothing different. George assures me that the formula was manufactured in exactly the same way as for the alpha trial. I don't yet know why the results are so different. I will continue to look at all the scientific markers of the trial patients to see if I can find some reason but, in reality, we just need to keep testing it and maybe tweak the components to see if that makes a difference."

"How long is this going to take?"

The Professor looked at Clay and Jacob. For the first time he saw a look of desperation on their faces. He already knew he was in deep shit but he had hoped that they would give him the time to do the job properly.

"Look gentlemen, this will take as long as it takes. I plan to run three two-week trials, rotating the current groups around to ensure all are tested with the new formula. That will give us some clear beta test results but we will need more people to test this on. We need at least a year."

Jacob exploded.

"Look Professor, maybe we didn't make ourselves clear. We are not patient men and every day you delay is costing us money. Make it work with these trialists. We don't have time to get any more people in. Now, I suggest you get back to work and sort this out."

The Professor stood up and left the office. As he walked back into the lab, the ashen look on his face was hard to disguise. George picked up on it immediately.

"What's the matter Prof?"

"I have just seen Clay and Jacob. They are not happy. You are right. We are in deep trouble. They seem to want instant results from this bunch of trial patients. I don't know what to do."

"How long have we got?"

"I really don't know George, but they are expecting the impossible."

*

Shaun had posted Jake and Gav on the lower cable car station to keep them out of the way. He gathered the other three men in his team, Scotty, John and Maverick, in the hut by the top cable car station.

"Right lads. I have spoken to Mr Hardacre and we need to kick in with plan B. As you know he has fallen out with the Yanks and wants this thing all for himself."

Maverick spoke first. "If he is committed boss, we will be loyal to whoever pays the most."

"Trust me, he will pay. He is desperate to beat the Yanks."

"Do we know what they are doing in there?"

"It's a big scientific thing. Some cure or other. Big business. Big money. Mr H can definitely afford to buy our loyalty."

Scotty and John nodded their approval. Maverick pushed on.

"What about Jake and Gav?"

"They are not in this. They are too new. I know they are good lads but I don't know whether I can trust them yet. Please keep this to yourselves."

"OK. What's the plan?"

"Well, we need to get the formula and any scientific notes they have about it. I am pretty sure they are storing these in their test lab, which only the Professor and his assistant have access to. Mav, John, can you go and do a security sweep in the lab building and see if there is any way we can get in there. That American bint has put multiple security layers on the access doors. I am pretty sure we can't get in there unless our fingerprint, iris and DNA scans are logged against the main door into that lab. Do a recce and check our options."

"OK boss, will do."

"Let's meet back here in an hour's time. Jake and Gav will be on shift at the bottom for another three hours so they shouldn't disturb us. Scotty, can you stay on security detail here please."

They all bumped fists and went their separate ways.

Maverick and John walked over to the lab building where all the trials were taking place and the volunteers were staying. Their fingerprint and iris scans got them into the main building and they started to walk through the corridors toward the main labs.

As they got closer to the inner test lab that Shaun had mentioned, they noticed the Professor was inside, hunched over rafts of paperwork and periodically looking into a microscope. He looked decidedly agitated. They walked past the window toward the door. The door had the same iris and fingerprint scanners that were on the front door but, Shaun was right, this one had the DNA scanner. Suddenly a voice came from behind them.

"What the hell are you doing?"

They looked round. It was the Professor's assistant. Maverick took the lead, as always.

"Sir, we are doing a security sweep. I hope that is OK with you?"

"No actually, it is not OK. During the trials we need to minimise any additional bodies in here. There is a risk of cross infection and our trial data may be compromised. Now get out."

The door to the lab opened.

"George. What is going on here? What is all this noise about?"

"Sorry Professor, I was just telling these guys to leave the building."

The Professor looked at the hard, grizzled faces of the two members of the security team. The type of alpha males that instantly got his heckles rising.

"Yes, yes, George is right. You should not be in here during the trials. Please leave immediately or I will have to report this transgression to the Deepermeyers."

Maverick and John held their hands up in mock surrender.

"Hey don't sweat it Dumbledore. We're outa here."

With that they turned around and walked away, cracking up at their 'hilarious' joke.

They reconvened in the hut. Shaun was keen to get the updates.

"So, guys, what did you suss out?"

Maverick responded.

"You were right. Their inner lab has the extra DNA scanning security on it. I reckon it is a good bet they are storing all the good stuff in there but I assume we don't have access. We didn't get time to scan our credentials to see if they worked because the Prof and his assistant got all menstrual on us."

"What happened?"

"We told them we were doing a security check but they got all antsy about us being in there during the trials. Something about cross infection."

"Hmm, what are our options then?"

"We can probably bash our way in when they are not around but it's not that subtle and we would need to do it at night when no one is in the labs. With all those trial people sleeping in there at the moment, it really isn't an option."

"I like the direct route but what else?"

"Can we convince that Alice bint to give us access?"

Shaun smiled. "Well Jake has been shagging her but I don't want to bring him into this. Can't any of you get in her pants?"

Scotty piped up. "I thought she was a lesbo. She was with that fit American girl with the cracking arse the other day."

"Fuck me, I would like to watch that," said John.

Shaun interjected. "Put your dicks back in your pants. Maybe she isn't the best option but I don't want to dismiss it. Any other ideas?"

Maverick spoke. "Why don't we just go old school and force them to give us everything at gun point?"

Shaun laughed and patted Maverick on the cheek. "You know Mav, I knew there was a reason I fucking liked you."

40

It was late afternoon and Alice had gone back to her apartment, the daily security checks done and nothing much else for her to do. As she fiddled with her phone, there was a gentle knock on the door.

She opened it and her heart leapt.

"Ellie! I have missed you so much."

She manhandled her into the apartment.

Ellie stood looking at Alice, with a perplexed look on her face. "Are you sure? I thought we had to keep to these artificial professional boundaries you put up the other night."

Alice checked herself. Ellie was right. What was she thinking?

"Oh, err…, yeh, sorry about being weird the other night. I do like you Ellie and I have missed you terribly… but you are right to remind me… we have to keep a professional distance."

They stood staring at each other, trying to read the body language. An awkwardness hung in the air. All of a sudden Ellie moved toward Alice, grabbed her neck and kissed her passionately.

Alice let it happen, her hands by her side, not responding but not resisting. Ellie drew away and smiled. "Fuck boundaries," she said.

Alice stepped away and sat down, licking her lips, the taste of the kiss fresh and new. She looked up at Ellie.

"We just can't do this Ellie."

"Why?"

Alice started to cry. Ellie came toward her, grabbing her face in her hands. "What is wrong Jasmine? Tell me."

"Stop calling me that."

"What?"

"Jasmine."

"Why?"

"Because it's not my name."

Ellie looked at Alice, confused and a little bit hurt. "What? I don't understand. Why would you give me a false name?"

"Because… I can't tell you Ellie. There is some serious shit going on here and I don't want you to get involved. Just leave it… please."

Alice gazed into those beautiful eyes that had so attracted her to Ellie when she first saw her picture. Ellie's whole facial expression had changed to something that seemed to show pity for Alice. After another few awkward moments, Ellie broke the deadlock.

"OK, I don't know what's going on here but I will do what you ask and leave it alone… for now. Just one thing."

"What?"

"Tell me your real name."

"Alice. It's Alice."

Ellie had left shortly after. Alice knew she couldn't keep living a lie, but she had only touched the surface of the truth with Ellie. The kiss had thrilled and confused her in equal measure and every new, exciting feeling she was getting from being with Ellie was just adding to the list of fucked up things that were competing for room in her head.

She lay down and closed her eyes, hoping that the demons would go away.

*

Jon Ruganzi met up with Chad and Mahindra. They were meeting a bit more frequently now that things seemed to be moving forward. "Any updates?" he said with just a hint of passive aggression.

Mahindra launched in. "Yes, Chad and I have been using our military satellites to scan the broad area that Chad thinks the vehicle might have stopped in. We have a slight anomaly in one area. It seems to be a black spot. We can't get a read on the terrain or any detail around it. It seems to be like a blanket over one of the high mountain ranges."

"Is that unusual?"

"Well, not necessarily. We do sometimes have satellite black spots but that is usually because there is some form of military installation where anti-surveillance measures are in place."

"Are we aware of any military installations in that area?"

"No, and we have spoken to the Swiss FIS. They say the only thing in that area is an old spa retreat but they didn't think anyone was running it anymore."

"Can we get them to do a physical recce?"

"No, they were prepared to answer our questions but stopped short of doing our bidding. I think the good diplomatic relations between our countries only extends so far."

John sat and pondered. "Could one of you go and do a visit, off the record, see what we can find?"

Chad responded. "I'll go."

"Good, do it but keep this low profile. I don't want Dirk to know just yet. The recent intel we have given him has kept him off our backs for now but I would like to be a bit more certain about this before we divulge anything else."

"OK, I will get booked on a flight."

"Excellent. Now, have you got anywhere with cracking this encryption?"

They both looked uncomfortable. "No," they replied in unison.

"Fuck me you two. Where's your pride? Are you really going to let that traitress bitch beat you?"

41

Alice sat in her usual place in the bar, drinking too much once again. The place was fairly empty as usual, with the large space only disturbed by a couple of the trial patients milling around. Alice looked for Ellie, desperately hoping they could speak again but she was nowhere to be seen. Alice popped her headphones on and set the music going on her phone. She closed her eyes.

Alice wasn't sure how long it had been and whether she had actually dropped off to sleep, but she suddenly came to. Someone had touched her arm. Ellie's beautiful face looked back at her. Alice bolted up, getting tangled in the headphones as she tried to sit up. Ellie laughed, a laugh that tore at Alice's heart.

"Ellie, hi. Sorry, I was miles away."

"You are beautiful Jas– sorry, Alice."

"Why are you being so nice to me?"

"What a strange question. Are people not normally nice to you?"

"Actually no. I dunno, I seem to attract weirdos or people that just want to put me down."

"Oh thanks!"

"No, not you Ellie. You're... you're different. I've never felt the things I feel when I'm with you. It's weird and scary."

"So, you haven't been with a woman before?"

"Err, no."

"Well, there's your problem. In my experience, men are generally a waste of space. They don't get what a woman really wants."

"Yeh, I guess."

There was another uncomfortable pause. Alice broke it. "Look, I'm sorry about earlier and yesterday and…"

"Alice, stop beating yourself up about this. I can see this is all new to you. I really like you and it would be great to spend as much time with you as I can, whilst we are on this crazy adventure. And, when you are ready to tell me what is worrying you about this situation, I'm ready to listen."

Alice stifled back the tears. Every time she was with Ellie, her heart felt like it would explode. She composed herself and moved the conversation onto what was happening with Ellie. She had to get a grip on what was going down. More than anything she needed to validate what George had said the other night.

"What happened in there Ellie?"

"We were split into three groups. I was in the group that was getting the new magic formula. They infected me with whatever thing they are trying to cure and then gave me the medicine twelve hours later."

"Why did they let you out?"

"That fricking formula worked. I felt a bit weird after they infected me, but within a few hours of having the formula I was completely fine. Don't know what they are trying to cure but whatever that formula contains it's amazing."

The feeling of dread that seemed ever present in the pit of Alice's stomach was not helped by what Ellie had just said. If they really had a magic formula to cure some disease or other, they would make millions of dollars if they could get it out to market. Actually, check that she thought. *Billions of dollars.*

Alice tried to shake the fear and focus back on Ellie. "What happens next?"

"I think we go back into the second trial phase shortly. I should be in a different group this time. I guess I won't be able to see you for a little while."

Alice saw the mischievous look on Ellie's face. *Can I really go there?* she thought to herself.

After more drinks than they probably should have had, they found themselves back at Alice's apartment door. They looked at each other. The kiss was soft and passionate and this time Alice didn't hold back, embracing Ellie and holding her as if her life depended on it.

As they drew away from each other, Alice fumbled for the door handle and dragged Ellie into her apartment.

42

Erica Mole woke up and the gut-tightening feeling that something bad had happened to Simon hit her almost immediately. She checked her phone. No messages from anyone. She wondered whether it was time to involve their parents. They had abandoned him once. Would they do it again?

*

The Professor sat in their apartment drinking coffee and taking in the view. It was still early.

"Can't sleep Prof?" said George.

"You know George, I had kind of sorted my head out about this situation. I thought we would be safe while they needed us to do these trials but I can't believe how naïve I have been. They seem to be expecting miracles."

"I did say they wouldn't be patient."

"I know but what still bothers me is why they think we can just deliver a cure overnight. They have never spoken to me in any detail about the work we were doing in Minnesota. What are they basing their optimism on?"

"You said they had they surveillance on us the whole time. The disturbances in the office. You remember, you were convinced they were watching everything we were doing."

"I dunno. There is something off about that. If they had spy cameras or something, then they would see and hear what we had been discussing but unless they had access to all our physical and electronic files, they would be basing their decisions on our conversations only. They don't seem the sort to invest all this money and create this massive, frankly highly criminal enterprise without some detail behind their decision. It just doesn't make sense."

"If they have been in our labs, surely they could look at the physical files and maybe they hacked the electronic files. We wouldn't know, would we?"

"I don't know George. I just don't know. There is something about this whole situation that I am just not seeing and it's driving me crazy."

George tried to move the conversation in a different direction.

"What are we going to do about the trials? We are never going to deliver what they want in six weeks."

"Um, well, the only thing we can do is change our approach. We need to infect all forty-three volunteers with the virus and have no control group. We just need to go full pelt with seeing how this formula works on the whole community. Thereafter we need to up the proportion of Manuka. I am sure the concentration of that compound is the key. If we can test this quickly in several batches, and increase the UMF level each time, we should get some improvement in results."

"But, what about the volunteers? Trial protocol does not recommend infecting people with the same virus over and over. Surely it will skew the results?"

"I think we are way past protocols. This is our only chance."

They both stared out of the window, downing their second coffee of the morning, lost in their own thoughts. George broke the awkward silence.

"I'll speak to Alice again. She is working on a plan to get out of here and we need to be part of it."

The Professor looked at George with a mix of love and admiration.

"Thank you, George. What would I do without you?"

*

Alice stirred. The lovely spring sun was just appearing over the mountains. She adjusted her position. Warm and comfortable. There was movement on the other side of the bed. Ellie. She smiled to herself. She had done it. She had countered her inhibitions, all her doubts and taken it to the next level. Quickly, passionately, sensually.

The joy of making that step was quickly muddled with the familiar feeling of dread that returned to her mind every time she remembered where she was. She tried to stifle the tears that welled as a surge of emotion consumed her, but it wasn't enough. Ellie woke up.

Ellie pulled herself up, leaning on her elbows, her face fixed with concentration, expectant.

"OK babe. I said I would leave it but now you have to tell me what is going on."

Alice tried to control her sobs.

"I'm a traitor Ellie. I left my job at the NSA because the men running this little venture offered me ten million dollars to work for them, but now they are threatening to expose me as a traitor unless I comply."

"WHAT! Ten million, and I thought forty thousand was good."

"The problem is they are criminals. They abducted the Professor and his assistant against their will because of whatever science cure they were working on. They are forcing them to run these trials and prove the cure works. They promised them millions of dollars as well but I don't believe they will ever pay it."

"Have they not paid you then?"

"Well yes, I have almost five million dollars in a new bank account they set up under my false identity."

"What! Just go then. Move the money somewhere else and go live on an island where no one can find you."

"I can't. We are basically prisoners here. They are threatening to leak a fake news story about me if I betray them and all our movements are restricted. The one time I was allowed out, I had to be escorted by one of the soldiers. When this is all over, I just don't think they are going to let me go. They are going to kill me, Ellie."

Ellie stared at Alice's face. The anguish and terror were suddenly very real. She tried to take it all in.

"Do you think MY life is in danger?"

Alice started crying again. She hugged Ellie.

"Ellie, I don't know. I'm so sorry to get you involved in this."

"It's not your fault. I was the one that applied to get away from my shit life."

"It is my fault. I security cleared you because you are so hot and I needed someone."

Ellie pulled away from the hug and looked at Alice.

"Look babe, no one forced me to come here. I could have refused after you cleared me, but I didn't. Like you, I wanted the money, so stop beating yourself up and let's work out what the hell we can do about this situation."

"I'm sorry Ellie but we are all in real danger. We are only alive because they need us but, as soon as we are dispensable, they are going to clean us up as loose ends. I'm sure of it."

"Jesus, you are full of the joys of spring."

"Ellie, you must believe me. No one is safe. We have to find a way to get out of here."

43

Clark was watching William Hardacre's phone, hoping, waiting for something to happen. Suddenly, a text message.

Julian, plans in Switzerland progressing. Aim to have the formula and all the clinical notes within three to six weeks. Can you get your clinical teams ready? I want this mass produced and ready to licence within one month. Sir Henry is going to sort the licence.

Clark scribbled down the key points. Julian? Switzerland. Again. Formula. Clinical notes. Mass produced and licenced. All within the next few months. The game was definitely on.

Clark looked at his dad's picture with a frisson of excitement. He knew that sometimes his dad's picture became lost in the vista of technology that was strewn across the man cave, a loyal, uncomplaining picture frame that got knocked about and dusty. But, Clark never forgot. When he needed to, he talked to the picture, reminding himself of the mandate for pursuing businessmen like William Hardacre who had killed his father with their greed and contempt for human life. Tonight was no different.

"Dad, I have him in my sights again. This time I won't fail."

Clark raised his coffee cup up to the picture in a 'cheers' motion. As he downed the latest in a long line of caffeine hits, he reflected on what he had scribbled down.

Bloody hell, Snap is right. This is some sort of medical scam. They are developing something in Switzerland that Hardacre clearly thinks he can make big money from. He must have fallen out with the Americans and is now trying to steal it for himself.

Clark sat and pondered. The little grey cells were buzzing. He continued his internal monologue.

Who is Julian? Must be some medical link. The producer of whatever Hardacre is stealing? A pharmaceutical company?

Clark started tapping away searching for UK pharmaceutical companies with a senior exec called Julian. It didn't take long.

Shit me. Julian Watkins, CEO of Westbrook Pharmaceuticals. That must be it!

Clark searched their website. Big enough to do what Hardacre wanted and clearly corrupt enough to deal with scumbags like him. He hadn't written the other name down but it stuck in his memory. *Sir Henry.*

Now Clark knew he had the right trail. The only Sir Henry that made sense was Sir Henry White-Taylor, the Secretary of State for Health and the minister that would oversee the licensing of new drugs.

Clark looked at his computer screen and flared his hands out from the top of his head. Mind-blowing.

He messaged Snap and told him to look for pharmaceutical links with Clay and Jacob. That clearly gave Snap some greater focus and he was back within the hour.

It was a bit difficult dude but the pharma focus helped and we have a winner. John Jacob Deepermeyer and Isaiah Clay Deepermeyer. Joint owners of Deepermeyer Pharmaceuticals!

Clark punched the air. He had it. Now he knew what this was all about.

44

The Professor gathered the forty-three trial patients in the conference room.

"OK, ladies and gentlemen. We are at the start of the second trial period and I just need to update you about a change in the testing protocol."

The people in the room immediately started to mutter to each other, the mood seemingly sceptical about the Professor's opening gambit.

"We are not going to split you into three groups this time. You will all be infected with the virus and given the test formula within twelve hours. We are keen to see how many of you respond in the same way as our alpha group."

A large, ruddy-faced man with a thick beard spoke out.

"Is that normal Professor? It seems strange to change your protocols so quickly."

The Professor cast a nervous glance at George but attempted to respond. "In truth, the first trial didn't give us the results we were expecting. Only three of the fourteen that were given the test formula responded in the same way as our alpha group. We need to test this immediately with a wider demographic to see if we need to make adjustments to the formula for later phases."

The man continued to challenge. "Is there something you're not telling us?"

"I don't know what you mean."

"You look troubled Professor. You shot a strange look at your assistant when you first answered my question. Are the money men hassling you to move this on faster?"

The Professor's gut was churning. He was desperately trying to hide his fears but clearly people were noticing. He tried to put on a confident facial expression.

"No, no, not at all sir. It is perfectly normal to change clinical trial protocols if test outcomes are not what were predicted. The 'money men' as you describe them are obviously keen to make progress... as am I, but we will do what we need to do."

The mood in the room seemed to calm a bit but the man wouldn't let it go.

"I'm sorry Professor, you are not convincing me and I also want to know why this trial is a secret. It's obvious to me what you are trying to cure."

A number of people looked at the man, captivated by what he had said. Many were thinking, *does he really know?*

"I told you at the start that a cure like this is big business and it's perfectly reasonable that the Deepermeyers take every precaution in protecting their secrets."

"It's the common cold. Isn't it? I was in the group that was infected with no medication. I have had a cold for the past week or so. You have found a formula that works on certain people... haven't you?"

The Professor knew he was losing the argument and losing the room. The man's eyes bore into him. He had to take a position. Truth or lies. He went for truth... of sorts.

"OK Sir, you are right. You are being infected with a strain of the rhinovirus that is responsible for the most common strains of the common cold. We have developed a formula that has delivered exciting results in a small number of trial patients, eradicating the virus from their system almost immediately after they take it. We were disappointed with the first trial, which is why we want to change the protocols to see how a wider group responds."

The mood was mixed. Some seemed to respond well to the honesty. Others seemed less convinced. The man carried on.

"Thank you for your honesty Professor. I'm sure many in the room can cope with knowing a bit more about this so-called secret project... unless we are compromising our safety by knowing more?"

This time there were a few gasps at the man's statement. The shift in mood was like a constantly changing light show. Dark, light, dark.

"Look, ladies and gentlemen. I understand that you have signed confidentiality agreements that forbid you from speaking about the trial once you leave. I'm sure the extra information I have given you makes no difference to that situation. Now, I'm sorry but we really must get on. If there is anyone that does not wish to participate in this trial, please let my assistant know and we will arrange for you to leave. Bear in mind that the Deepermeyers are unlikely to pay your fee unless you complete the trial."

There it was. The money question. Forty thousand dollars for three months' work was good in anyone's book and the Professor had played that card at the right time. As he left the room, there was lots of fevered chatter but no one approached George to say they wanted out.

*

Ellie refilled her coffee mug, contemplating just what had happened.

Jesus, Alice is right. There is something very wrong with this situation.

45

Alice sat in the technology suite, monitoring the security. Everything was still perfect. No attacks. It was as boring as hell and Ellie was back in the trials, incarcerated. She had opened up Proton several times over the last week but could not bring herself to respond.

Krypto had messaged her three times asking whether she had done any more work on the Zephyr cyber wipe problem. She hadn't. She just couldn't concentrate. Ellie had been distracting her but the real reason she couldn't respond to Krypto was the GPS issue. The person Krypto was tracking had been in her surveillance black spot. They had been on this site. Who the hell was he tracking?

She tried to ignore the growing fear of her private cyber world suddenly closing in on her, when things got a little bit worse. A message from Blowfish.

I need a private chat. I know it breaks our code but I think I know who you are.

Alice's mind was racing. She opened up the link to Proton. Her fingers hovered over the keyboard. What should she do? The message from Blowfish had completely floored her. How could they possibly know who she was, unless of course her suspicions about their NSA and CIA knowledge were right? Did they work within the inner sanctum of US intelligence?

She didn't know what to do. Could she really chat to Blowfish without freaking out? She was about to log off, too scared to seek the answers, when a message flashed up.

BLOWFISH: Alice?

The cursor blinked. She was frozen with fear.

BLOWFISH: Alice?

The cursor blinked. Her hands were like lead weights. She couldn't move.

BLOWFISH: Alice? I know it's you.

*

Chad stared at the screen.

HARLEQUIN HAS LEFT THE CHAT

Fucking hell. It's her. I was right. Harlequin is Alice. What the hell do I do with this?

He downed his now lukewarm coffee and stared into space. His head was exploding with the enormity of what he thought he had discovered. He couldn't focus. His brain was racing, overloaded. He eventually made a decision. He would not tell Jon. Not yet. He had to get on that plane to Switzerland. She was there. He was sure of it.

*

Alice was shaking. What the fuck had just happened? Why had Blowfish used her real name? They knew that broke every protocol in using Proton.

Her world was closing in on her. She had to get out of this shitstorm and soon. She emailed Clay and asked if she could go out again to the local village with George and Jake. She needed a way to have a private chat with both of them. Jake in particular was key to her emerging plan.

46

Erica Mole phoned her mother.

"Mum, it's Erica."

"Oh, hello. What do you want?"

"Civil as always I see. Simon is missing."

"He's been missing for a long time Erica."

"No, I mean really missing. I went down to Brighton to see him and he wasn't where he usually is."

"And you're surprised, why?"

"Look Mum, you may have given up on Simon but I haven't. He does not stray from his basic area. The homeless charity said a number of the regulars where Simon stays are also missing and another homeless guy said they had all left with a man in some vehicle or other."

"Just give it up, Erica."

"No Mum, I won't. I knew it was a mistake expecting any help from you. You let Dad drive him away and did nothing about it. Ironic that he followed my lead and took your name. You don't deserve his loyalty."

"Goodbye Erica."

Erica looked at her phone with disbelief. She knew she was pretty much on her own in terms of worrying about Simon but of her two pathetic parents she at least expected her mother to show some interest. How wrong she was.

She opened up her email. Should she try her father? She twiddled her hair, the thing she always did when she tried to focus on tough decisions. Her hands hovered over the keyboard. He was the main reason Simon was homeless. Could she really expect anything from him?

She typed out a short and cryptic email.

Dad, I need to speak to you. It's important. Call me. Erica

Erica was gobsmacked when her phone rang ten minutes later.

"Nice to see you are trying to completely wipe me out of your life, which begs the question why do you need to speak to me?"

"What do you mean?"

"Erica Mole. My surname not good enough for you anymore?"

"Sorry Dad, but you lost any pull on our lives when you drove Simon away. We both felt it was the right thing to do. Not that Mum gives a shit about either of us though. Maybe we should have found a nice new surname that wipes you both out of our lives."

"I'm very busy Erica. Did you just want to chat about what a crap father I am or did you actually have something to say?"

"Simon is missing."

Erica heard her father laughing.

"Jesus Erica, had you only just noticed?"

"Oh, piss off Dad. I have been down to Brighton off and on for the last couple of years to see how he is. He is homeless and pathetic but never strays from his basic area. The homeless charity and some of the other homeless men say that Simon and a number of others are missing."

"What do you expect me to do?"

"Do you know Dad, nothing. Really, nothing. I am sorry I bothered you."

*

Julian Watkins put the phone down. He had not expected that. His son was pretty much dead to him, a lost cause, a disappointment, but he still occasionally wondered where he was and what he was doing. Despite the hardships, the love for his children never left him.

He stared out of the window of his top floor corner office in the West End of London, the political hub of his successful company. Offices in his hometown of Edinburgh, a manufacturing facility in Bolton and a sales division in Birmingham completed his business property portfolio, but London was where the action was and the place that reminded him of why Erica's call had shaken him up. He got on the phone.

"William, it's Julian Watkins. Where did you get those UK trial volunteers from, that you were talking about the other day?"

"Mostly from Brighton. Why?"

"Oh, no reason. What happened to them?"

"That is not your problem to worry about Julian. They have been dealt with. I'll let you know when I need your end to kick in. Please be ready."

Julian put the phone down and put his hand to his face. He could barely bring himself to say what was now racing around his head.

What have I done? Am I working with a man that has killed my son?

*

For once Clark was right on it. He was watching the Zephyr hack screen hoping for something to happen when William Hardacre took a call. It was from Julian Watkins. He had been right about that connection. The call opened up a curious new angle. Julian was asking about UK volunteers, the ones that William had referred to in the fleeting parts of the text messages that Clark had managed to remember. Julian seemed concerned about what had happened to them. William's response was not unexpected. Clark sat back and wondered why Julian was so interested. He wrote it up on the growing incident board he was constructing at the end of his man cave. The plot was thickening and Clark was beginning to piece it all together.

47

Alice was pacing the room in her apartment. She could not get Blowfish out of her head. How had they found out who she was and more to the point, who the hell were they?

As she agonised what to do next, an email popped into her inbox. Clay had approved her going out again.

"Brilliant," she said to herself. She needed to get George and sort out their escape. There was no time to lose.

She grabbed her coat and phone and knocked on the door of George's apartment.

"Oh, hi Alice. What's happening?"

She grabbed George and pulled him into the corridor. "Come on, we have permission to go out. We can talk to Jake about the escape plan."

"OK, Prof's still in the labs and I don't think he has even noticed I have gone. Fuck it, let's get pissed and plot their downfall."

Alice looked at him curiously. Was George losing it or was he finally getting some backbone?

They walked to the top cable car station and saw Jake was waiting for them. As they got nearer, they realised one of the other guards was with him. As she got closer, she shot Jake with a 'what is he doing here?' look. He picked up on the vibe and just shrugged. The other guard spoke.

"Ah, here are the prisoners, ready for their night out."

Alice looked at him with disdain. "Prisoners?"

"Yes, two prisoners, two guards."

Alice looked at George. He just pulled a face. This was not what she had planned. She started walking toward the cable car station, her mind racing, trying to formulate a plan to deal with the situation.

They got to the bar in Boden and sat in a corner booth away from the main throng of noisy punters. Alice had formulated a plan for ditching this idiot.

"So, soldier boy. What's your name?"

"My friends call me Maverick."

Alice put her hand to her mouth to stifle a laugh. He wasn't impressed.

"What the fuck is so funny?"

"Well, I am sorry, but you are no Tom Cruise."

"That's not what the ladies think."

Alice smiled to herself. *Men, oh so predictable.*

"Are you a tit man, Maverick?"

"Oh, well, tits or arse. I'm not fussy."

"It's just you have been looking at mine for most of the time we have been together."

He was about to react but took a moment to compose what he thought was a sharp answer.

"Well, Jake told us how good they were."

Jake look horrified but Alice was cool. This was exactly where she wanted the conversation to go. She leant in toward Maverick.

"OK, soldier boy. Here's the deal. I want some privacy. Some time to speak to George and Jake without your sparkling presence. Go and chat up that group of girls over there and if you pull, I'll give you a flash of my tits."

He stared Alice down, sizing her up. After a minute he reacted. "OK. You're on."

As he walked away, Alice smiled to herself. Hook, line and sinker.

George was gobsmacked. "You are not really going to show him your tits are you?"

"Of course not. I just played on his oh so predictable male ego and chanced that his brains were below the waist."

George and Jake smirked, Jake a little bit relieved that Alice hadn't believed he had been mouthing off about their sex session.

"Right, we need to talk before he comes back. Basically, we need to escape. Get off that mountain as soon as possible. Everything is going wrong and I don't believe it will be too long before we are dealt with."

Jake looked confused. "Dealt with?"

"Yes Jake, dealt with. I told you before that your little security job is not what you think it is. The Deepermeyers are criminals and will stop at nothing to get what they want. Once the Prof and George give them what they want, we will all be killed. I am sure of it."

"I don't know Alice. I haven't heard anything about what you are accusing them of."

"How long have you been with the team Jake?"

"A few months. I told you that. This is my first job with Shaun."

"Exactly, you are the new boy. You are not in the inner circle yet. You won't be party to their plans."

"I don't think you understand the soldier code Alice. We don't lie to each other."

"You are not in the army now Jake. You are part of a rogue guns-for-hire business. There is no honour in what Shaun is doing. Trust me. You are a small cog in this criminal enterprise. A worker ant. Nothing more."

Jake took a swig of his drink and looked over at Maverick, who was doing his best to ingratiate himself with a group of four women. Alice let him stew. She turned her attentions to George.

"What is going on at your end George?"

"You are right Alice. Things are getting difficult. The Deepermeyers were not impressed when the Prof told them that the latest trial had not gone well. He thinks we only have a limited time to sort this out. We got a load of aggro from the trial patients this morning when we told them that we were changing testing protocols to speed things up. They were really suspicious of our motives."

"See Jake. Listen to what George is saying. This is happening. This is real."

Jake looked at both of them. Troubled. His loyalties torn.

"What do you expect me to do about it?"

"You can help us escape. The cable car is the only way off that mountain. We need you to get us on it and out of there."

"I can't do that on my own. There is always at least one guard at the top and one at the bottom."

"OK, so who can you trust?"

"What? Do you really think another one of the team is really going to believe your hairbrained scheme?"

"Jake. Come on. How do you know you're not in danger? You have to have your own exit plan and if you need someone else to help you, we need to work out who that person is."

Jake looked over at Maverick again and back to Alice and George. "Gav. He is the only one."

"Good. Why do you think he is the one?"

"He is new and if you are right in what you are saying, he won't be in the inner circle. Shaun always puts us on shift together. There are large amounts of time when we are not with the rest of the team."

"This is great Jake. You need to talk to Gav."

Jake took another swig of his drink, agonising over what to do next.

"Christ Alice, if this goes wrong, I am done for. I will never work for Shaun again. I really don't know."

Alice grabbed his hand and gave him her most convincing smile.

"Look into your heart Jake. You know what I am saying makes sense."

Jake went quiet for a bit. Alice and George concentrated on getting pissed, whilst watching Maverick doing his best pulling techniques. He seemed to be making progress.

After another round of drinks, Jake seemed to come out of whatever haze he was in.

"Alright, I will talk to Gav but I can't guarantee anything. There is one other thing though."

"What?"

"Bloody hell, what am I doing? I shouldn't be telling you this."

"What?" George and Alice chorused in harmony.

"Oh shit… OK, the cable car isn't the only way off that mountain."

Alice was suddenly like a kid on Christmas Day. Manic. Impatient.

"You what! Spill!"

"There is a secret passage at the back of the site which leads to the other side of the mountain. It leads to a secret helipad that only the Deepermeyers use. They didn't even tell Mr Hardacre about it."

Alice was gobsmacked. Could this be an alternative plan? Where could she get a helicopter from? Her head was spinning with the possibilities.

"How well guarded is it?"

"It's not guarded at all because it has a bloody great steel door that covers the tunnel and it's always locked."

"Who has keys?"

"The Deepermeyers and I think Shaun."

"Can we get one somehow?"

"It would be difficult but I do know where Shaun normally keeps his keys."

Alice leapt up and kissed Jake.

"You fucking legend Jake. George, I think we have just found our way out of here."

*

165

Maverick saw the kiss. He had pulled and was going to spend the night with a fit blonde local with curves in all the right places. He needed Jake to cover for him. He ambled back to the table.

"Well Missy, I have scored and will be having some great sex, several times over if I get my way, so I look forward to seeing those tits very soon."

He turned to Jake.

"Is she trying to shag you again Jakey boy? You wanna watch her. She doesn't seem fussy and you don't know where she has been."

Maverick looked at Alice. She wasn't biting. He leant in to whisper in Jake's ear.

"Listen mate. I need you to cover for me. I could be away for some while. You can do that for me, can't you?"

"Yes Mav, no problem."

*

Alice was back in her apartment. Jake's revelation had changed everything. There was only one way she could get a helicopter. She would have to stop this madness and put herself at the mercy of her old team, or was this the moment to find out who Blowfish was?

*

He sat in Jacob's office. "So, what's the update?"

"She is plotting her escape."

"Oh really. Well, maybe we will let her play her silly little espionage games but, when the time is right, we will remind her who is in control here."

They both laughed.

"Keep up the good work son."

48

Clay and Jacob were in their offices, downing the first coffees of the day.

"So, what did you get from last night Jacob?"

"He confirmed that she is plotting to get out of here. She has clearly worked out that we are not going to let her leave this place with all our secrets."

"I'm not happy with this. This was not what we agreed. I keep telling you she is critical to what we are trying to achieve here. We knew she was intelligent and your behaviour has just led her to conclusions I didn't want her to get to at this point."

"Have you lost the backbone for this? Did you really think we could afford to let any of these people live once the cure was delivered? If any of our competitors get wind of this our billion-dollar nest egg will be blown out of the water. We can't risk any exposure. As for Miss Bidebecker, she is important to us... as collateral in our negotiations with the US government, especially now she has given us that kick-ass encryption. That will give us extra leverage when we approach the US administration. So, yes, we need to keep her sweet but, if she tries to escape, she will have to be dealt with."

"I don't know Jacob, this is all getting out of hand far too quickly. We have hardly begun the trial work. Do you really think she is going to hang around while she thinks her life is in danger?"

"Don't forget our insurance policy. I'm sure she will think twice about doing anything rash when we have that at a push of a button."

"On your head be it. I just don't know why you couldn't keep her sweet. Can we rely on him to keep close to her and find out what else she is plotting?"

"Oh yes, he seems to have her complete trust."

The conversation trailed off and they both refilled their coffee cups, Clay troubled by his brother's apparent gung-ho attitude. He decided to hit Jacob with the other thing that was giving him sleepless nights.

"What about William?"

"What about him?"

"Have we heard anything from him?"

"Why would we?"

"Jesus Jacob, am I the only one worrying about all the fucked-up situations you are creating round here?"

"What do you mean?"

"Well, apart from Miss Bidebecker and the trial patients getting suspicious about you forcing the Professor to accelerate his testing regime, you seem to be under the false illusion that William is going to take your betrayal on the chin."

Jacob glared at his brother. "You are pathetic. If William Hardacre comes back, Shaun's team have been told to kill him. Simple as that. So, you can be the pathetic worrying cry baby and I'll get on with making the hard decisions."

Clay got up and walked out of the room. Jacob shook his head and poured another cup of coffee.

*

The Professor and George sat in the test lab. They had the preliminary results of the second round of trials.

"Right George, can I check that all the volunteers were infected and all were given the same formula we gave the alpha and beta trials?"

"Yes."

"Well, of the forty-three trialists, we had seven that exhibited the same recovery patterns as the alpha group."

"That still doesn't sound good."

The Professor gave George a look that said *'don't state the bleeding obvious'*. George decided not to say another word, letting the Professor deal with his own inner turmoil.

After the kind of intense focus that George had seen many times from the Professor, he spoke again, no eye contact, just words tumbling out of his mouth like a tap needing to drain the thoughts from his brain.

"There is one good thing George. The three from the beta trial that had the fast recovery process exhibited the same results in this trial. We need to look at their blood work. There is something in their DNA that makes them responsive to the cure. We need to find some markers and compare them with the six from the alpha trial. There must be something we are missing."

"OK, I will get onto it. What else should we do?"

"Let's re-infect the four patients that exhibited the fast recovery results and see if they match these three in terms of a consistent pattern. For all the others, we need to monitor their recovery rates but I am tempted to mix up an enhanced batch of the formula, with a greater concentration of Manuka. We need to see if a greater UMF level reduces the recovery time for those less responsive to the alpha compound."

"You want to administer that on top of the alpha compound?"

"Yes George. We don't have time to do anything else."

"What about the original three? What do we do with them?"

"Keep them here. We might need to take more blood to do the screening."

"OK, who are they again?"

"Err, James Moir, Elizabeth Franklin and Ellie Baker."

49

It was early evening and Alice needed some air. Everything was closing in on her but Jake had given her some hope of an escape. Although it was May, the altitude still meant every night was close to freezing. Most of the snow around the complex had long since gone, but the mountainsides remained white. As she walked out of the accommodation block, she wondered what would happen in the winter. The reality of the situation reminded her.

Come on Alice. Don't be stupid. They don't plan to be here in the winter.

She slipped round the back of the building. She wanted to find this secret passage. Jake had told her where it was but she wanted to see it for herself. Envision what it would be like to go through the door to safety, to leave this living hell.

She tried to look nonchalant as she headed toward the building where the trials were taking place. She so desperately wanted to go in and see Ellie but she needed to push on. She started to go around the right side of the building. The terrain was more uneven and her footing slipped a couple of times. She followed the line of the building, taking care at each step. As she got to the end of the side wall, the path she was on led out to a narrower path that hugged part of a mountain outcrop. As she approached the path, she stopped, frozen in fear. The first part of the path was next to a massive drop. If you fell from here there was only one outcome. The path was full of loose stones and debris, making it extremely dangerous and the light was fading. Now she knew why nobody came this way.

Alice calmed herself and took a step forward. Her foot slipped and she screamed. She adjusted her position and moved gingerly forward, doing the type of stiff walk you reserve for navigating icy paths, except this was not ice, it was loose, dangerous stones. She inched forward, hugging the outcrop and refusing to look down. After what seemed like an eternity, the path widened and she could see a large bush set back from the path. Jake had told her the door was behind the bush. She relaxed a bit as she could move away from the precipice. She went behind the bush. There it was. A massive steel door.

The light was now fading fast and she cursed herself for not being more prepared. No torch. She decided to get back to the complex as fast as she could. As she got to the narrow, dangerous path she suddenly heard voices from the other end of the track.

Shit! She stepped back behind the rock face and listened.

"What is it Mav?"

"Dunno, I thought I heard a scream."

"I didn't hear nothing. Shall we check it out?"

"Nah, I ain't risking my life. Not when the light is fading."

Alice couldn't believe it. Of all the people that were patrolling, it had to be Maverick. She waited and listened. Five minutes passed. The light was fading every minute but she couldn't be caught. Not here and not by Maverick. She started along the path, rigid with fear, every step feeling like wading through treacle. She emerged on the other side. No one was there. She started back toward the side of the trials building. She moved slowly along the uneven path, watching her step. As she got close to the end of the building her heart sank as a voice came from in front of her.

"So, Miss Bidebecker. Just what the fuck are you doing sneaking around?"

Alice couldn't believe it. Maverick. She tried to front it out.

"Just getting some air Mav. You know, to get away from your body odour."

He grabbed her by the throat and pushed her back against the side of the wall. The impact of the wall on the back of her head dazed Alice.

"Look you little bitch. We all know what you are up to but let me make this quite clear. You ain't getting off this mountain unless we say you can."

Alice's eyes were bulging with the pressure on her throat, but she tried to keep a defiant look on her face. Maverick's grip remained but his facial expression changed from anger to something else. Something sleazier. Alice was panicking. What was he going to do? She soon got her answer.

He grabbed the zip of her jacket with his spare hand. As the coat fell open, his eyes went to her full breasts that were well sculpted in the tight top she was wearing. Tears started to fill Alice's eyes. Why had she been so bolshie the other night? Mav was going to get his revenge. Her grabbed her right breast and started to grope it.

Alice tried to struggle out of his grip but he had his whole body-weight on her, stopping any purchase she could get with her arms or legs. He leaned his face to her ear and sneered out the words.

"Oh, Jake was right, they are spectacular. You promised me a flash but feeling them is so much better. You are making me so hard."

Alice tried to move her face away. She didn't want to look into this sleazy bastard's eyes. He was having none of it. He changed his focus to the other breast and pressed himself against her.

"Can you feel it bitch? This is what your lovely tits are doing to me. Maybe I'll get it out and you can finish me off."

Alice couldn't stop the tears. She was helpless. As she willed for the assault to end, she suddenly heard a voice.

"Mav, Mav, where are you?"

He stopped his assault and eased the pressure on her throat. He adjusted himself and walked off, looking back with a sinister smile that told Alice exactly where he thought the power now lay.

Alice slumped to the floor, pulled the coat round her and sobbed. Hard and loud. Whoever that was had just stopped it going any further but the damage was done. She felt cheap, dirty and violated.

*

Jake bumped into George as he was entering the bar area. They exchanged a knowing look, the type of look that said they knew something others didn't. They went to the bar and got a drink. As Jake was waiting, he looked round and saw Alice, slumped in the corner. She had five shot glasses lined up in front of her. They were all empty. She had her face in her hand and did not look good. Jake nudged George.

"What's up with her?"

"Dunno."

"She don't look good."

"Let's go and see if she is alright."

They both wandered over and put their drinks down on the table by Alice. She didn't look up. Jake leant over. As he went to touch her, she jumped and pulled herself away from his advances.

"Alice. What's wrong?"

No response.

"Alice?"

She eventually looked up. Her face was mottled and tear-stained. There was bruising around her neck.

"What the hell happened to you?"

After composing herself she eventually spoke.

"Maverick."

Jake looked at George. He raised his eyebrows.

"What did he do to you?"

"He assaulted me Jake. Your fucking buddy sexually assaulted me."

"He ain't my buddy Alice."

173

"Really? You seemed happy to cover for him the other night, which made him think he had the right to grope me up because he thought he won some stupid bet."

"Sorry Alice, but you did rile him up by promising to show him your tits."

"Oh, just fuck off Jake. A typical male response. If any of you could see past your dicks you might understand that women aren't sex objects to be used at your whim."

Jake backed away. Alice looked at George.

"Where's Ellie, George? I need her. Now."

"She's still in the trial."

Jake and George said no more as Alice stood up, unsteadily, and stormed out of the bar.

*

It was late as he sat in the office talking to Jacob.

"What's up?"

"We have a problem. She has been assaulted."

"What? By who?"

"Maverick."

"Why?"

"Not sure. They had some banter the other night and seems like he got the wrong idea."

"Jesus, we don't need this. We need to keep control of this situation, control of her. If we start giving her more reasons to escape, our plans are going to suffer."

"I know."

"OK, I'll talk to Shaun and get him to sort that jerk out. You need to keep a closer eye on her now."

"Will do."

*

Alice sat on the settee in her apartment staring out of the window. The view was still amazing but it had now become the symbol of her incarceration. She had showered three times but nothing could get rid of the stench of Maverick's unwanted attention.

Her phone was staring up at her. She could phone anyone in the world. She had internet and email access. She could contact anyone in the world. But, once again, in that moment, she realised how alone she was. No family, no friends she could rely on. Nobody that would take a call or read an email, that would get her out of this hellhole. What the hell had possessed her to do this, to be the very thing that the Deepermeyers were holding over her? Being labelled a traitor. Was it really about the money?

That thought reminded her and she logged into the bank account. She stared at the screen in disbelief. The balance on the account was zero. Millions of dollars had disappeared. Alice's world had just hit rock bottom.

50

Erica Mole went through her daily routine of calling the homeless charity and then the police. Still nothing. Still no sign of Simon. She looked at a family picture sitting on her desk. She placed it face down. She couldn't look at it. Her mother and father had failed her, failed Simon. She hoped they would have some compassion but she had been sadly let down. As she stared into space, feeling helpless, little did she know that in another part of the country her guardian angel was about to spread their wings.

*

Clark was back in 'mission control' poring over what was written on his white board. The conspiracy was now becoming clear. The Deepermeyers were developing some new medical cure or potion and Hardacre wanted it. He started researching drug revenues. The numbers he found made him gasp.

"Bloody hell. A breakthrough drug can be worth ten million dollars... a day!"

He wrote that on the board.

"Three point six billion dollars a year. Fuck me. Now I definitely know why Hardacre is involved."

Clark had done what he always did when he was plotting a conspiracy on his whiteboard. He had printed pictures of the main antagonists and placed them on the board. It helped him to visualise who he was dealing with. The picture of Julian Watkins stared at him.

"So, Mr Watkins. Are you a greedy bastard as well? Why would you work for a scumbag like Hardacre? Is it all about the money?"

He drank some coffee and ate three of his favourite Jaffa Cakes. Brain fuel.

"Why were you so concerned about those UK volunteers Julian?"

Clark decided to delve into Julian's life. There was a connection he was missing. He soon found the basics. Divorced from his wife Miriam, eighteen months ago. Two grown-up children, Erica and Simon. Erica was a mortgage adviser in a bank in Edinburgh but had curiously changed her surname to Mole around the time of the divorce. A quick check found this to be Miriam's maiden name.

"Hmm, an acrimonious split then and the children favouring the mother."

He looked for details of Simon Watkins or indeed Simon Mole. There was nothing recent. Simon had been completely off the grid for nearly two years.

He needed to find Erica. Could she explain what was going on?

*

Chad had been delayed getting to Switzerland but he was finally holed up in a pretty hotel in a small village within the broad area where they thought Alice had stopped. He was still convinced that she was Harlequin but she had refused to engage in any messaging since he had revealed his suspicions. He decided to try Krypto and Snap again. They had been receptive to his mad ideas about Alice.

BLOWFISH: Hey dudes. Need your counsel

SNAPDEVIL: Always dude

KRYPTO: Yup. What's up?

BLOWFISH: Still convinced that missing analyst is Harley. I tried to speak to them about it but they refused to engage. Has just made me more sure

SNAPDEVIL: We don't do this dude. You know it's against our code to pursue each other's identities

BLOWFISH: I know but I think she is in big trouble

KRYPTO: Hmm, ever since that story broke Harley has been acting weird and has stopped contacting me about the Zephyr hack. They would have normally sorted it by now

SNAPDEVIL: I dunno dudes. This all don't sit comfortably with me

BLOWFISH: If Harley is the missing analyst, she is in some serious shit

SNAPDEVIL: Why? What do you know?

BLOWFISH: Look, my contacts tell me the missing analyst's movements have been tracked. She left the NSA with no warning and met up with a British national who is a red flag to national security on both sides of the pond. She has been tracked to a mountainous area in Switzerland

KRYPTO: Switzerland!

BLOWFISH: Yeh. Why are you triggered by that?

KRYPTO: The phone hack. The person I have been following has been backwards and forwards to Switzerland. The GPS drops out when he is in certain areas. Where was she tracked to?

Chad was suddenly getting nervous. Was he revealing too much? Who was Krypto following and how the hell did he seem to be linked to Alice's disappearance? He decided to close the conversation down.

BLOWFISH: Dunno exactly. Just heard it was Switzerland

SNAPDEVIL: Big place. Must be a coincidence

KRYPTO: Yeh. Sure it is. Keep us up to date Blow with any developments

BLOWFISH: Will do. Laters

Chad was shocked. First his suspicions about Alice being Harley and now Krypto tracking someone in Switzerland. Snap was right. It was a big place, but something about this whole situation was niggling at Chad. The worst thing was he had to keep it to himself. Jon could not know about his cyber life. It was against the NSA protocols, although if he was right, it seemingly hadn't stopped Alice. He decided to get some food and would start touring the area tomorrow, looking for something that would confirm his suspicions about Alice. He would put the Krypto thing on the back burner but he knew that there might come a time when he would need his cyber friend.

*

Clark sat back in his chair, stunned by what had just happened. Was it really a big coincidence that Blowfish had tracked the analyst story to Switzerland, the very place that Hardacre had been holed up on and off for a few months? It was a big country but Clark's conspiracy radar always placed Hardacre with big stories and it seemed the missing NSA analyst was a big story. He was curious how Blowfish knew so much. He seemed to have access to national security information. The more he pondered it, the more he was convinced. Clark didn't believe in coincidences. Not when Hardacre was involved.

51

Several days had passed and the Professor was so focused on the trial it seemed he hardly noticed whether George was there or not, except when he wanted something.

"George, George, where are those blood results?"

George came out of the side room into the main lab where the Professor had all his trial data strewn across the desks, staring at them manically and very much playing up to the cliché of the mad Professor.

"They are here, Professor."

He grabbed them from George. They were the results from the seven successful trialists. The four new ones had repeated their successful recovery results with the latest round of tests.

"George, we have something. Look at the CRP tests of these seven and the alpha trial. All of them have normal C-reactive protein levels before infection, raised levels two hours after infection but normal levels within two hours of taking the remedy. This means we now have thirteen patients that are exhibiting consistent recovery patterns with CRP blood results to match. The people that are not responding to the remedy are still exhibiting high CRP levels days after infection."

"What does that mean?"

"I don't know yet, but something in the compound is successful in reducing CRP levels in certain patients. We need to apply the enhanced formula to see if recovery rates and CRP levels are affected by a more concentrated dose."

"What do we do with the seven successful patients?"

"To be honest, we can let them go. We have all their clinical notes and their blood work. They can't really help us anymore. I am sure they will be happy to get their money and go home. Just make sure we have their contact details in case we need to do any follow-up."

"OK Prof, will do."

George went back into the side room. He knew someone was going to be pleased that Ellie was about to be released from the trials.

*

The Professor walked in to see Clay and Jacob, nervous about how they would react to the latest trial data. Jacob launched straight in as soon as he entered the room.

"Professor. I do hope you have better news for us."

"Well, yes, some progress. We now have seven of the forty-three trialists exhibiting the same recovery patterns as the alpha trial. I have also identified a significant marker in their blood tests that shows consistent results across all thirteen successful trialists. We are going to enhance the formula to see if we can get better recovery rates and similar blood results from the remaining thirty-six trialists."

Jacob did not seem overly reassured.

"It's still not a high success percentage Professor. I really hope for your sake that the next trial is more successful."

The Professor tried to ignore the veiled threats.

"Oh, also, I am happy to release the seven successful trialists from the study. We have their clinical trial results, blood tests and contact numbers should we need to do any follow-up. They can't assist me anymore."

"OK Professor, get us the names and we will sort it."

Clay and Jacob let the Professor leave the room before they spoke again.

"You need to give him more time Jacob. It sounds like he is making some progress."

"I'll give him some time, but I have a plan B emerging in my head."

"Really? Does it involve violence and unpleasantness like most of your ideas?"

Jacob tried to ignore his brother's barbs.

"Actually little brother, no, it doesn't. Think about it. The Professor has a formula that has worked on thirteen people. He has a cure... just maybe not for as much of the population as we would like at this stage but... it's still a cure. I think it may be time to consider starting negotiations with the US government."

"And that's your plan? To try to sell a half-baked cure?"

"Clay, Clay, Clay, you really are a wet weekend. We need to package this up as a deal which will licence our drug in return for them getting their analyst and their encryption back, as well as a nice upfront fee... you know, to show goodwill."

"They'll never go for it."

"They will if I pitch it right. Just leave the negotiations to me and we'll have money rolling in real soon."

Clay, as with most interactions with his brother, had to walk away. He knew they were always on a fine line with the law but his brother seemed so blasé about it.

As he began to walk out of the office, he turned back to his brother. "What about the Prof's suggestion of letting these seven trialists go?"

"Oh, I think we can give them the illusion of being let go."

"What's that supposed to mean?"

"Don't you worry about it Clay. Leave it all in my hands."

52

Alice had completely shut down. Since the sexual assault and the disappearing money, the fight had gone out of her. She felt hopeless and helpless. At the start of this nightmare, she wouldn't have hesitated to confront Clay and Jacob about the money or got revenge for Maverick's crimes, but now she just wanted to hide away and keep her head down.

She continued to agonise over the message from Blowfish. Did they really know her identity? Could they help her get out of this hellhole? And what about her old team? Did they think she was a traitor? Would they help if she fell on their mercy?

Alice was blasted out of her mental torment by a knock on her apartment door. She froze. Who was it? She sat rigid with fear. Another knock. She moved nervously to the door.

"Who is it?"

"It's me babe."

Alice wrenched the door open and practically manhandled Ellie inside.

"What are you doing here?"

"I'm out of the trials babe. They don't need me anymore."

Alice hugged Ellie and started crying; long, loud convulsive sobs.

"Hey babe, what's wrong?"

It took a while for Alice to calm down but eventually she told Ellie all that had gone on.

"I'm so sorry that happened to you. Have you reported him to the boss men?"

"Of course not. They are the ones keeping me here against my will, no doubt condoning that bastard's behaviour and stealing the money they promised me. I am trapped Ellie and they are going to kill me."

Ellie stared at Alice, trying to process all she was saying.

"Why are they letting me go then? They have transferred the forty thousand dollars into our bank accounts and are taking us to the airport tomorrow morning."

"You're… you're leaving tomorrow?"

"Yes."

"You can't go. I don't understand. Why would they let you go?"

"Maybe they don't see us as a threat."

"But that doesn't make sense. They have threatened my life, threatened to expose me as a traitor and made it pretty clear I am not getting out of here unless they say so. You have seen all that I have seen. Why are they not treating you the same way?"

"I dunno babe, but if everything you say is true, we both need to get out of here. Come with me. Tomorrow."

"How would we do that? I am never going to be able to get past them without being noticed."

They both sat, in a firm comforting embrace, not wanting to let go of each other but no nearer working out how they could escape together. A while passed, Alice feeling better to have Ellie comforting her. As her mind cleared, she made a decision. She sat up and fixed Ellie with a firm stare.

"I've decided Ellie. You have to go tomorrow. Without me. I am not risking your life to save me."

"But babe…"

"No Ellie, I have made my mind up. There is no way we can get past the guards and sneak me on your transport out. I only have one option. I am going to have to fall on the mercy of my old team. They are the only ones with the manpower and resources to get me out of this hellhole."

Ellie gazed into Alice's eyes. She could see that a little bit of Alice's fire was back. She kissed her passionately, hungrily. Their clothes came off quickly. They made love, lost in the moment, trying to shut out the horror, hoping this was not the last time they would ever share these fantastic intimate moments.

*

The following morning after spending the whole night together, Ellie woke up to find Alice sitting by the bed watching her. She was holding an envelope.

"Hey babe. Watcha doin'?"

"Just watching you sleep. You are so beautiful Ellie. I love you."

"I love you too babe. What's that?"

"It's a letter. To my old boss. It contains all the details of where we are, the location of the secret helipad and a secure email address they can contact me on. I am going to put my life in their hands and hope they can see past my actions."

"OK, but how will you get it to them?"

"I need you to post it for me, as soon as you get to the airport."

"Of course! Why don't you just email it?"

"Although I've set up all the security in this place, I can't be a hundred per cent sure that they are not tracking what I am doing somehow. They seem more cyber savvy than I had expected. They may have some form of surveillance I am not party to. I can't risk it at the moment. This is the only safe way of getting the message out."

Ellie took the envelope and stuffed it in her bag. They both returned to Ellie's room and packed her stuff. A few hours later, Ellie and the other six were gathering by the top cable car station. Alice hugged her tightly and whispered in her ear.

"I will see you soon. I promise."

Alice watched as the cable car took them down to the bottom of the mountain, into a waiting minibus.

She walked back to her apartment, still confused as to why the Deepermeyers had let these seven people go.

*

Jake watched as the minibus left. Maverick was driving and Scotty was following them in the Hummer. He had that uneasy feeling again. He didn't want to believe any of what Alice had told him, but he knew she had no reason to lie. He decided it was time to speak to Gav.

"Gav mate. Why do you think we never get to do the escorting?"

"Whacha mean?"

"Well, haven't you noticed that Shaun always puts us on shift together? We never get to do anything other than guard these cable car stations and we are not with the rest of the team for long periods. We never go out in the Hummer, never escort people in or out of the complex. Don't you think that is odd?"

"No not really. We are the new boys. Shaun just probably relies on the other guys more because they have been here longer."

"I dunno. It's just that Alice..."

"Ah, I see. I wondered how long it would be before we got around to the American bint. What's she been filling your head with now? Mav says she is a right bitch."

"He sexually assaulted her Gav."

"Who? Mav?"

"Yes."

"And you believe her?"

"Why would she lie about something like that?"

"Jesus Jake, are your brains in your dick? She is manipulating you. Mav said she is plotting to escape from here."

"Where did he get that from?"

"Dunno, he was talking about it yesterday."

Jake decided to end the conversation. Gav was not the person he hoped he would be and now he worried that everything he had just said would get back to Shaun. He felt more than ever that Alice was right. Something was badly wrong with this whole arrangement.

53

Clark had that familiar tingle of excitement; the tingle that told him the trail was hot. He looked at his dad's picture.

"I am going to get him this time, Dad. Then you can finally rest in peace."

Clark was overwhelmed with the progress of the last few days. The conspiracy around Hardacre was clear and the involvement of Julian Watkins' firm cemented the theory that this was about a new wonder drug. The potential link to the missing NSA analyst was a curious one but the more Clark thought about it, the more it made sense.

If you want to protect your multi-billion-dollar secrets, who do you call?... The best cyber expert in the world, that's who!

Clark chewed it over.

It just makes sense. The Deepermeyers must have somehow persuaded her to work for them... but why would she betray the NSA?

Clark couldn't shake it. The link to the missing analyst just made more and more sense but the really shocking thing was Blowfish's assertion that she was Harlequin. Was the world really that small? It had to be a massive coincidence. He ate another Jaffa Cake and offloaded his thoughts to no one in particular.

"I don't believe in coincidences."

Clark wrote up the new developments on the whiteboard. As he did, he remembered the other major line of enquiry. Erica Mole. He had to find her. He was sure she held the key to explaining what was going on with her family and how they were mixed up in this conspiracy.

It didn't take Clark long to find contact details for Erica. He opened up his email, fingers poised, trying to think how to phrase his first contact with her. The memories of the last conspiracy he cracked came flooding back. He had freaked Anya Novak out when he first approached her but eventually, he had convinced her and her partner that their lives were in danger. This was a bit different. As far as he knew Erica's life was not in danger but there was something about her father that was odd. Odd and definitely a bit dodgy, if he had William Hardacre as a best buddy.

He stepped away from the computer and paced around the room. Eventually he decided what to write.

Dear Miss Mole,

You don't know me but I believe you hold the key to explaining a conspiracy that I believe I have uncovered. It involves your father Julian and maybe your brother Simon. I need to know why your father is involved with one of the leading scumbags in this country... William Hardacre. I also need to know why your brother is off the grid and why your father was concerned about some UK volunteers that William Hardacre was using for a medical trial. Is it possible that Simon is somehow connected to this conspiracy? Has he gone missing? Does he have a connection to Brighton?

I know this has probably freaked you out but if you want to be reassured about my intentions, reacquaint yourself with the 'cash for babies' scandal that Hardacre was involved in. I was the guardian angel that the press referred to. My anonymity is key but I hope this convinces you that I am a force for good.

Regards

Your guardian angel

Clark hit 'send'. How long would he have to wait this time?

*

Erica Mole had just arrived home from another day's work, which had been polluted by the constant worry about Simon. She poured herself a glass of wine and opened up her emails.

Amongst the usual junk was a message from a curious email address. It had a funny alias, not the sort she was used to. She almost deleted it, knowing that anything odd was usually a hacker trying to steal your identity or some other part of your personal life.

She stared at it, not knowing what to do. Eventually curiosity got the better of her.

The wine glass slipped out of her hand and smashed into several hundred pieces as it hit the tiled kitchen floor.

54

Ellie sat in the back seats of the minibus and got herself comfortable. They were told that their flights back to the US were going from Innsbruck Airport, meaning a three-hour trip was ahead of them.

They had navigated their way down from the high mountainous area where the lower cable car station had been and were now driving along the main road toward Austria. She looked behind and noticed that one of the guards was following them in a 'big-ass' army type vehicle. She was curious as to why they needed an escort.

After another twenty minutes or so, she was starting to nod off with the gentle motion of the minibus, when she suddenly felt the vehicle climbing. She stirred herself and realised they had got off the main road and were driving up a sharp incline, back toward the higher mountainous area.

She got out of her seat and walked to the front of the minibus to talk to the driver.

"Why have we got off the main road?"

"Oh, we had a report of an accident on the main road. Traffic is stacked back. We are just taking a detour to avoid it. Don't worry. Sit back down and enjoy the ride."

Ellie walked back to her seat. Not completely convinced that he was telling her the truth.

She got out her phone and texted Alice.

Missing you babe. Get out of there as soon as you can. See you real soon.

The minibus was still climbing. The road was getting narrower and the drops either side of the road would make even those most tolerant of heights get a bit of vertigo.

She tried to ignore her growing concern by thinking about what she was going to spend the money on. She found the bank details that the Professor's assistant had given her. She wanted to move the money to her main bank account as soon as possible. Based on everything Alice had told her, she didn't trust these people as far as she could throw them.

She typed the bank details in and waited for the screen to refresh. The minibus had levelled out and was moving along a slightly wider mountain road. The screen refreshed. Ellie couldn't believe her eyes. The balance was zero. She hit the refresh key. It must be a glitch. Maybe there was no signal this high up. The minibus suddenly turned into a small layby. The screen refreshed. There was a signal. She could see the bars on her phone. The balance was zero.

She looked up. She hadn't noticed the driver had got out. Everyone on the minibus was looking around wondering what was going on. One of them got up and went toward the door. As they tried to open it, they realised they were locked in. Panic began to spread. Suddenly there was a bang. The Hummer had crashed into the back of the minibus. There were screams from the people on the bus. Ellie opened up her messages. She needed to text Alice. There was another bang and soon Ellie realised what was happening. The Hummer was pushing them off the road and down the mountain.

*

Chad had been touring the area of Switzerland where he was sure Alice was for three days now and it still had a needle in the haystack vibe. He had tried to split the area up into sensible grid patterns to ensure he wasn't driving around aimlessly but so far, he had found nothing. There were just too many minor roads going off in every direction. He had stopped at a viewpoint that gave him a good panorama of the valley and a number of road systems that snaked their way up and down in several directions. The place was beautiful, but it meant nothing if he drew a blank. Jon had been on his back every day expecting an update, but Chad couldn't give him anything.

He sat and rubbed his face in frustration. As he refocused on the view, he suddenly saw something, driving along the main road in the valley. A Hummer. Could it be the Hummer they had on CCTV at Innsbruck Airport?

He got his binoculars out and followed its progress, desperately trying to map where it was going on his phone. It turned off the main road about half a mile further along and began to climb upwards. Chad lost sight of it but he quickly co-ordinated the information on his phone. Finally he had a lead.

*

Alice sat in the technology suite, doing her daily checks, when her phone beeped. A text from Ellie. She was on her way home. Alice began to tear up but she knew she had made the right decision in letting her go. She just had to hope her letter would be well received by Jon and they would get her out of this hellhole. She texted back. Twenty minutes later, she had not received a response. Curious. Maybe they were not in a signal area.

*

Erica Mole had phoned work to say she was sick. The shock of the email had completely floored her. She almost emailed straight back, urging this so-called 'guardian angel' to explain themselves, explain why they were intruding on her personal anguish. Instead she spent most of the day staring at the words, trying to reconcile what this person was saying. What did her father have to do with this? How did they know that Simon was in Brighton?

She remembered the 'cash for babies' scandal. How could she not? You had to have lived under a rock to miss the scandal of the Prime Minister stealing someone's baby and the conspiracy around the other poor women affected by it all. She remembered the focus on William Hardacre and how many commentators believed he was the mastermind behind the scandal but had ultimately survived by feeding his sons to the wolves. There was a lot of speculation about an uber geek who had apparently helped the poor woman at the centre of the scandal to uncover the conspiracy. He was described as her guardian angel. Could this really be the same person?

Erica couldn't decide what to do. The worse thing, the thing that was stopping her contacting this person was the gut-wrenching feeling that her father was acquainted with William Hardacre and was somehow involved in Simon's disappearance.

After wasting a whole day agonising over her next steps, she put her phone number in an email back to this person and simply typed '*call me*'.

*

Chad got back to his hotel and examined the map. He tried to follow the trail he thought the Hummer had taken. The road they had followed had a number of routes going off it, but one of them went high up the mountainside and was well within the satellite black spot that Mahindra had found. He tried not to get overexcited but he couldn't help feeling that he may just have found that needle.

55

The Professor and George were examining the latest results of the trials. They were breaking all the trial protocols by constantly re-infecting the patients and administering different doses of the so-called cure, before they had even recovered from the original infection. The Professor knew the scientific integrity was being compromised but he had to see if the enhanced formula was making any difference.

"What is this telling me George?"

"Well, the enhanced formula seems to only have worked with two more patients. They are exhibiting recovery patterns and CRP blood results closer to our group of thirteen."

"Shit, shit, shit! This isn't good enough. We need more. More success than that. They are not going to accept this."

The Professor put his head in his hands and started to cry.

George didn't know what to do. The stress was breaking the Professor.

"Come on Professor, let's go and get something to eat and drink. This problem will wait until tomorrow."

The look on the Professor's face, as he looked up at George, told him in no uncertain terms that it was absolutely the wrong thing to say. George got up and walked out of the lab, closely followed by an empty test tube that smashed against the window.

*

It had been nearly twenty-four hours since Alice had sent the text to Ellie. She knew that she must have reached the airport by now and posted the letter, so why hadn't she texted her back? She tried to stop the horrible thoughts that were threatening to invade her psyche. Ellie would text when she could. Wouldn't she?

*

Chad set off mid-morning to explore the route he thought the Hummer had taken. The sky was clear and electric blue, making the scenery even more picturesque but Chad was focused on one thing. Confirming his suspicions about Alice.

He soon found the road the Hummer had taken and began to climb. There were several smaller roads going off the one he was on, but from the mapping he had done the previous evening, he knew the road he wanted was further up. He began to climb higher, the basic rental car poorly equipped for the task as its engine seemed to moan with the strain of the incline. After about a mile, the road he wanted emerged from the right. He quickly turned and started to climb higher, not wanting the car to lose any momentum. The landscape was dominated by tall pine trees as far as the eye could see, gripping to sheer rock faces. Chad's gut told him this was exactly the sort of place someone would hole up in.

He climbed for another five minutes when the road suddenly levelled out. As he began to drive along the next piece of road, he looked to his left and thought he spotted some buildings, high up on the mountainside. He stopped in a convenient layby and got out his binoculars. He scanned the area. There did seem to be a number of buildings but they were too far away to make out much detail. He scanned to the right and realised there was a cable car wire running down from the mountain. He tracked it and realised it seemed to terminate somewhere close to where he was. He left the car and started to walk along the road. As he emerged around the corner, he suddenly stopped, jumping back behind a rocky outcrop that had been concealing what he was now looking at.

About one hundred metres away were two guards at a cable car station. With guns. He tried to stay hidden whilst training his binoculars on their faces. He was sure one of them was at Innsbruck Airport on the CCTV. One of the Unsubs. He got out his camera and zoomed in. He had to compare their pictures with what they had. He got out his phone and zoomed in as far as it would go, recording a short video of what he was looking at. He sent it to Jon.

Armed guards Jon. This has to be where Alice is. It's the old spa place.

56

The Professor sat across from Jacob and Clay, his body language telling them everything they needed to know. As usual, Jacob took the lead.

"What's the latest Professor?"

The Professor just looked at them. Trying to put on a defiant demeanour but ultimately failing.

"Professor?"

"You two are insane."

Jacob looked at Clay with an amused expression on his face.

"Name-calling Professor. I thought you were better than that."

"This can't be done. Not in the timescales you want."

Jacob fixed him with a firm, aggressive stare.

"Failure is not an option Professor. You work faster, you work longer hours, or..."

"What? You are going to kill me? How would you get your fucking cure then?"

"You are a dead man walking Professor. You are getting to the end of your usefulness. I am sure there are other scientists who would love to pick up your work and claim the glory."

The threats hung in the air between all the parties. The Professor stood up.

"This can't be done. We have only made small incremental improvements with the formula. We need more time and a different set of trial patients. If you want to keep me and George prisoners to force us to achieve your goals, this is the only way we will make progress. It's up to you. If you kill us, it will put you back several months. It's your choice."

The Professor started to walk out, hoping his impassioned speech would somehow land a blow. As he reached the door, Jacob piped up.

"Professor."

He turned around.

"We spoke to your assistant. He doesn't seem as pessimistic as you."

"What? When did you speak to him?"

"Oh, we like to keep in touch will all our staff. He seems pretty relaxed about the whole thing."

The Professor stormed out. He wasn't going to rise to their goading. They were playing mind games. Trying to drive a wedge between him and George. He was sure that George had never spoken to them.

As he walked back to the lab, events of the last couple of months started to play on his mind. George had been frantic soon after they arrived. Terrified of what would happen to them but, there had been a change in him. He was more relaxed since he had started to talk to Alice but had also become more distant. The Professor knew he had been treating him badly, the stress of the situation clouding his mood. The problem was the Professor was beginning to wonder about George. Was he still loyal or had the Deepermeyers somehow bought his betrayal?

As he walked back into the lab, he looked straight at George, trying to read him. George smiled.

"You alright Professor?"

The Professor grunted and walked into his office, the brief interaction suddenly confirming his greatest fear. George had been got at. It was the only explanation.

*

Clay and Jacob poured themselves another coffee, lost in their own thoughts. Jacob broke the silence.

"This is not good Clay. I think it is time for my plan B."

"What are you going to do?"

"I'm going to get Miss Bidebecker to send the US government an anonymous email, protected by her lovely new encryption. We will introduce them to the Plutus Group and start our negotiations."

"You really think they will respond? They must get hundreds of emails from lunatics and fantasists every day. Why would they take any notice of ours?"

"Because dear brother, as I said to you before, I plan to use Miss Bidebecker and the encryption as leverage. I also have a pretty good idea which economic buttons we can press related to this cure that will eventually have them eating out of our hands."

Clay seemed resigned to playing second fiddle to his brother's grand plan. He did what he always did. Left the room to get away from his brother's disapproval. Whilst Clay had set out on this project to make himself richer than he could ever have imagined, he had wanted to do it cleanly and professionally. It was now clear that his brother never had any intention of doing the same.

As Clay walked out, Jacob let out a less than subtle laugh, goading his brother for his lack of backbone. If he had a cat, he would have stroked it, like the Bond villain he aspired to be.

*

Alice was in the security room, checking the daily logs. All was clear. She kept trying to approach each day as a normal working day but she never achieved it. The constant fear that the Deepermeyers would deal with her at any moment, the escape plan, the secret helipad, her love for Ellie, were all battling for space in her head. Something needed to give or she was heading for a complete breakdown.

As she tried to calm herself, the door opened and Jacob walked in. Alice tried to seem composed but she could feel her body tensing in his presence. Was this it? Was this the moment?

"Miss Bidebecker. I need you to send this email to the US government. We have decided to start our negotiations."

Her spirit was broken but she tried to recapture the sassy bitch persona that she had arrived with.

"And why the fuck would I do anything else for you now? You have stolen all my fucking money you lying bastards."

Jacob looked at her, sporting an expression somewhere between amused and angry.

"For one of the NSA's brightest, you really are rather naïve. Did you really think we were going to pay you ten million dollars? You have taken eighty thousand dollars from us Miss Bidebecker for a couple of months' work. I am sure that is more than you earn in a year. Get used to the new order Miss Bidebecker."

"Or what?"

Jacob sneered at her. "Do I really need to answer that?"

After Jacob left the room, Alice let out a breath mixed with a howl. The tears began to flow.

She needed Ellie. She needed someone to calm her down. Why had she still not texted back? She paced around. Nothing was working. Jacob's email wording stared up at her, goading her. She knew that once that email was sent the clock was well and truly ticking.

She couldn't stop shaking but she knew she had to send the email. Whilst they needed her to do stuff, she had a chance. She found the address she knew would get the email to the right person and started to type it out.

As she began to write, she stopped in her tracks. The words hit her like a hammer. She couldn't believe what he was expecting her to write. What the hell did this mean?

57

Clark picked up the phone and dialled Erica Mole's number. She picked up almost immediately.

"Hello. Erica speaking."

"Miss Mole, it's…"

"Oh my God! It's you."

"Well yes, if you were expecting a call from your guardian angel."

Clark heard the faint sound of sobbing.

"Are you OK Miss Mole?"

"Are you for real? Because if this is some sick joke, you are the lowest of the low!"

"I am for real Miss Mole. Did you not read about me?"

"Yes, I did."

"Well, you should know that I am the real deal. I have made it my mission to bring down people like William Hardacre and for some reason your family popped up in my research."

"Why? Why do you do this?"

"My father. People like William Hardacre and his political cronies forced him to take his own life and I have made it my mission to expose these bastards and bring them to justice."

"Oh, I am sorry to hear that."

"So, what can you tell me Miss Mole? Am I onto something with your father and brother?"

He could hear her voice breaking but she soldiered on.

"I think you have found something. Simon was forced out

of the family home by my pathetic parents. He is an alcoholic and they just abandoned him. Didn't try to sort him out. Just discarded him. He went to Brighton. Homeless and hopeless. I visited him as often as I could but a few weeks ago he wasn't there. I spoke to the homeless charity who said that nearly twenty of their regulars had not been seen for several days. Another homeless guy said they got in a vehicle and hadn't come back. I just know something bad has happened to Simon."

There was a long pause as Clark's worst fears were realised. He didn't want to deliver bad news within the first minute of their call, but his gut told him that she was right.

"Hello. Are you still there?"

"Yes, yes, sorry Miss Mole, it's just…"

"What?"

"Look, I am sorry to tell you this but based on the information I have managed to glean from my investigation, I fear something has happened to Simon."

"What? Do you think he is dead?"

"I can't be sure, but based on what you have told me, it seems too coincidental for Simon not to have been one of the UK volunteers that William Hardacre was referring to. I am sorry to say, I think he dragged a load of people, like your brother Simon, off the street to be his guinea pigs."

"Guinea pigs?"

"Yes, Hardacre is involved in some new drug development in Switzerland. I am pretty sure they needed clinical trial patients and Hardacre decided to target the homeless, with, I am afraid, poor intentions."

"What do you mean?"

"In text messages and phone conversations he seemed to suggest that these people were untraceable. I can only assume his intentions were to get rid of them once they had done what he wanted. There was a message that said something about them being dealt with."

Clark could hear Erica crying. This was not what he wanted but she had confirmed a connection that seemed too strong not to fit his theories.

"Miss Mole. I am so sorry but I will do all I can to find out for sure what happened to Simon."

He heard a faint "OK" from the other end of the phone. Clark gave it a minute and tried to plough on.

"Miss Mole. Can we talk about your father?"

She suddenly seemed more animated.

"That shitbag. If we have to."

"Why would he be working for William Hardacre?"

"He is not a nice man and is ruthless when it comes to his business. I think he would probably fit in really well with William Hardacre. I am not surprised they are working together."

"The link is quite obvious to me. Hardacre is developing a drug and he wants your fathers' firm to manufacture it. The problem is he is playing a dangerous game because I think Hardacre is planning to steal the formula from the Americans."

"Oh, that sounds just like the type of thing my father would want to be involved in."

There was a short pause while they both reflected on what had been said. Erica broke the silence.

"Do you think my father had something to do with Simon's disappearance if he is working with Hardacre?"

"Do you know Miss Mole, there was something about the last phone call I listened to between them that made me think he didn't have any knowledge that Simon was involved in this. He seemed genuinely concerned about what had happened to the UK volunteers."

"Well, that would be a first. He hasn't given a shit about Simon for nearly five years so I don't know why he would start now."

Clark was stoked by what Erica had told him despite the obvious stress it was causing her.

"Miss Mole. What you have told me has given me more leads. I will take this forward and let you know what I find. I will give you closure as I know how important that is."

"Thank you. What is your name? I can't call you my guardian angel."

"My name's Clark."

"Thank you Clark. You have given me some hope and please stop calling me Miss Mole. It's Erica."

"OK Erica. I'll be in touch."

Clark got off the phone and immediately crafted an untraceable email to Mark Chesterfield, the Met Commissioner, who had ultimately delivered the drop on the last conspiracy he had found. He wanted to get the intel to someone he trusted to look into it. There was no time to lose.

58

The Oval Office, White House

Mike Charlington, the President's Chief of Staff, sat nervously outside the Oval Office waiting for the President to finish his monthly briefing by the Director of National Intelligence. He had just received a communication that they would want to see urgently. He considered disturbing their meeting but thought better of it.

Ten minutes later the door was opened and Mike was invited in. President David Caruso, Dirk Landsley, the Director of Intelligence and Janet Wallbrook, the Head of the CIA, were all present.

"Mike, what can I do for you?" said the President.

"I am sorry to disturb you Mr President, Sir, Ma'am but we have had an encrypted communication from an anonymous source, sent directly to the White House email system. It was escalated to me pretty quickly and I think you all need to read it."

Mike handed round hard copies of the email to all present. It read:

To the United States Government

We have your analyst and we have your encryption. The encryption that you can't counter because your analyst has made it better to protect OUR secrets. You really didn't appreciate her... did you?

But don't worry, we are patriots and business men. You can have them both back if you do two things:

Make a payment of $50 million to the bank details below... a sign of goodwill

Licence our new wonder drug for exclusive distribution in the US.

We will tell you more about the drug once the first payment is made. Please don't miss this opportunity to do a deal. You wouldn't want other countries to get your encryption? You wouldn't want anything to happen to your best analyst? You wouldn't want to miss out on an economic boost that could be worth upwards of $30 billion a year, once this drug is available?... Would you?

The Plutus Group

The President reacted first. "What the hell is this? Thirty billion dollars! Who is this Plutus Group and why on earth do they think we are going to give them fifty million dollars?"

Dirk shuffled nervously in his chair. The President was on him in seconds. "Something to say Dirk?"

"Mr President. I'm afraid this looks like a development around Operation Hawk."

"Operation Hawk?"

"Yes, our missing NSA analyst. The team have been working tirelessly to try to find her and they have encountered this enhanced encryption that the note refers to."

"Yes, I remember. Did you just give up looking for her?"

"No, we established she flew to Austria and was met by a guy known to us and British intelligence. This was a red flag and cemented Operation Hawk as a category one operation. We tried to trace their movements but found nothing initially."

"Initially? Have you found her now?"

"No, the operation is under constant scrutiny. My team believe they crossed the border into Switzerland. We had some decent matches on facial recognition and picked up a vehicle of interest on some of the Swiss traffic cameras. We also connected her disappearance to a missing Professor from Minnesota. She has no digital footprint and has left us with this tricky encryption issue."

"What do you mean?"

"As I said, the team encountered this improved encryption on some correspondence and digital transactions that were linked to her disappearance. To date they have not been able to work out what she has done to improve it."

"Are you telling me we don't know how to crack it?"

Dirk shuffled nervously in his chair.

"My team tried but they just couldn't—"

"Jesus Christ Dirk. What the hell are we paying you for? How can you let this happen?"

"I am sorry Mr President. We employed her because she was one of the best cyber security analysts I had ever come across. I didn't think she would ever betray the US like this."

"What about her vetting? Didn't it highlight anything? Anything that might suggest she was a flight risk?"

"No. I have been back over everything. We recruited her straight out of MIT. She got a Masters Degree in Cyber Security. In her finals, she got the highest score in the whole of the United States and was immediately recommended to us. We fast-tracked her through our graduate programme and started her as a junior analyst. She was so good, we moved her into the elite Senior Counter Intelligence Team within twelve months of her starting at the NSA. He father and mother both died within a few months of each other in her early days with the senior team but all the welfare support she had didn't raise any red flags. I have reviewed her psych analysis and she was completely normal. Everything she has done seems completely out of character."

"Is she there against her will? Would that explain it?"

"It appears not. The limited amount of CCTV we have on her seems to show her leaving her apartment willingly and going to the airport alone. At the other end she seems perfectly comfortable with the person she meets, this British guy I mentioned earlier."

The President turned away from the conversation and stared out of the window, moving his focus between the view and the email that was staring up at him. After a short pause, where no one felt comfortable breaking the awkward silence, the President turned back to the people in the room.

"This is a potential disaster. If this is her resurfacing, working willingly for this Plutus Group, this could be some serious shit."

Everyone looked at the President, not knowing what to say. He suddenly changed his focus away from Dirk.

"Janet, any input?"

"I haven't heard of this group and I will need to work with Dirk to pool our resources to see what we can find but, for what it is worth, Plutus is the Greek god of wealth."

"Oh great, so not only do we seem to have a new type of extortionist terrorist group, they also think they are fucking comedians."

The three guests in the President's office sat and looked each other, waiting for the President to direct their next move. He stood up and looked out of the window toward the rose garden, momentarily lost in his thoughts. After a few minutes he turned and spoke.

"Mike, thank you for bringing this to us, I think we have to treat this as a credible threat. They are trying to extort money from the US government and should be treated at the same level as other terrorist threats. Dirk, Janet, I want you to pool your best resources and give me a fuller evaluation of this Plutus Group and their demands within twenty-four hours. Organise with my outer office when you leave to come back for a face-to-face briefing. Also, Dirk, review everything you have on this Operation

Hawk. I want some results. Mike, keep this under wraps and let me know the minute we get any other communication from this group."

"Understood Mr President," they chorused as they stood up and left the office.

The President sat down in his chair and stewed on this new development.

"My God," he said to the empty room, "what is this madness?"

59

It was late and George went back to the lab, looking for the Professor. As he reached the door, he saw the Professor slumped over his desk. He ran in and grabbed him.

"Professor. Professor, are you alright?"

The Professor stirred. He had been asleep on his desk. There was an empty whisky bottle on the floor.

"Oh, Professor, what have you done to yourself?"

The Professor tried to sit up, unsteadily, only staying upright due to George's attentions. He looked at George and smiled.

"Shjorge, I love shoo, you na. You do knose that don't yus?"

"Yes Professor. Now let's get you to bed."

As George manhandled the Professor out of the lab and back to the accommodation block, he kept trying to speak, slurred nonsense.

"Ish madnish Shjorge. Can't be done. 'Slike eating an efelant. Can't be done."

George got the Professor into bed, and went back to the lab to find whatever had sent him over the edge.

He re-examined the carnage in the lab, created by the Professor's impromptu drinking session. As he rooted through the paperwork on the desk, he found what he was looking for.

Shit, the latest clinical trial results are worse. Patients that were showing positive signs similar to our successful thirteen trialists have gone backwards. Jesus Christ. No wonder he turned to the bottle.

George went back to his apartment. He had a lot to think about.

*

Alice sat on the sofa in her apartment, watching the sun setting over the mountains. A view that should have lifted the soul but just reminded Alice how alone she was and how much danger she was in. She read the email again. The one that had been sent to the US government.

You wouldn't want anything to happen to your best analyst?… *Would you?*

The words made her gasp every time she read them. Every recent interaction with Jacob had felt like a little nudge toward her being dealt with. Killed. Wiped off the Earth with barely a whimper, but seeing it written down somehow made it worse. Made it real.

She picked up her phone. Still nothing from Ellie. Her heart was breaking. Had Ellie forgotten her? Betrayed her? Alice couldn't believe that Ellie could be so heartless, which led to only one other conclusion… something bad had happened to her.

*

Clark didn't like the waiting. The previous conspiracy he cracked had produced an immediate reaction. The Met Commissioner had responded quickly to his intel and everything happened within the same evening. This was different. The threats to life were more speculative. The intel he had was good, based on his somewhat biased opinion of the scumbag William Hardacre, but he needed others to believe it and this went beyond the Met Commissioner's influence. Clark hoped that he would have passed this to the intelligence services but he knew there was every chance it would get lost in the myriad of national security priorities. He had contacted Erica Mole to let her know what he had done. She seemed happy that someone was fighting her corner but Clark worried that he was giving her false hope. He ate another Jaffa Cake and stared at his dad's picture.

"I have to get him Dad. I have to get him this time."

60

President Caruso sat in the command bunker with Dirk Landsley, Janet Wallbrook, Jon Ruganzi, Mahindra Ahmed, Mike Charlington, his Chief of Staff, and Gareth Michaels, the Head of the US Military. Chad was dialled in from Switzerland. The room was full of nervous energy. The President spoke first.

"Dirk. You first. Tell me what we know about this Plutus Group and your missing analyst."

"Well, preliminary findings from our investigations suggest they are a front for whatever cock-a-mamie scheme they have cooked up that they think we are going to pay for. We are fairly sure that Alice Bidebecker, our missing analyst, is working for them, although we haven't been able to conclusively prove whether she is there under duress. The missing Professor, Carlton Jenkins, and his assistant George Mankley from the University of Minnesota are connected to this. We have a broad fix on the area we think they are holed up in, thanks to Chad's work in Switzerland, but have had limited support from the Swiss FIS, so this is all still a bit speculative. The critical gaps in our knowledge are who is really behind this and what exactly they are trying to sell to us."

The President didn't seem impressed with Dirk's progress and gave him a look that told him as much. He turned his attention to Janet.

"What has the CIA found out?"

"We have the CCTV images of a character called Shaun Lester or whatever name he is using this week, who was seen with Alice.

He is high on our watch list. I have spoken to our counterparts in British intelligence and they believe him to be a significant person of interest. Our analysts have a theory that Alice is providing the cyber security and Shaun is leading a team providing physical security for this Plutus Group. This is backed up by Chad's sighting of armed guards around the area that Dirk was referring to."

"Is that it?"

"Well no. There is one thing that has just come in from British intelligence that we are still evaluating but it does seem to have a connection."

"What?"

"The British received some intel from the Metropolitan Police Commissioner about suspect business practices by a William Hardacre."

"James Hardacre's father?"

"Yes, he was implicated but never charged in the conspiracy around his son stealing that woman's baby."

"I remember. A major fall from grace for the PM. I never liked him. He was weak and indecisive. I never met his father but I remember everyone telling me that he was the real power behind James. How is he involved in this?"

"As I said, we are still evaluating it, but there does seem to be some connection to this Plutus Group. William Hardacre has spent many weeks in Switzerland and the intel suggests he was in the broad area that Dirk's team have identified, based on his phone GPS. He has also got some connections to a Julian Watkins who runs a pharmaceutical company in the UK. Finally, there is some suggestion that he has been involved in trafficking some down and outs from the UK to Switzerland."

The President looked at the collective group. His mood was not improving.

"It's very nice Janet that the British seem to be doing all your work for you, but can you and Dirk explain why we haven't got the same level of intel on this?"

Dirk and Janet sat stony-faced, the spotlight very much on them, and the President in no mood to take any crap. Dirk broke the uncomfortable silence.

"Mr President, we do have a theory. Janet does need to evaluate this British intel but it could fit a scenario that we have been considering."

"Oh really, please explain. It would be nice for my extensive and very expensive intelligence network to actually deliver me some credible theories."

Dirk tried to ignore the sarcasm.

"They made reference to a drug development in their email. If the Professor is working for this Plutus Group, it follows that he is developing the drug because all his work has been about developing new treatments for infectious diseases. New wonder drug revenues are huge, multi-billion-dollar business, which would explain their obsession with cyber and physical security. The UK link suggests they are going to try to sell to the UK market as well, with this Mr Hardacre exactly the type of person that would salivate over the possible revenues. It also follows that they have holed up in some ultra-secure site in Switzerland to give them another layer of protection. The UK trafficking thing could fit a scenario where they have delivered some people for clinical trials."

"A nice theory Dirk but again, where is the US intel? Have there been people-trafficking issues in the US that match the UK's experience? Where is the US pharmaceutical link? Why did your analyst leave to work for them? You don't seem to have the answers to any of these basic questions. You seem content to ride on the back of some half-baked UK intel."

"I am sorry Mr President, we are working round the clock re-examining everything we have. The British intel—"

The President let out an exasperated sigh at the mention of the British again. Dirk tried to ignore it and soldiered on.

".... The British intel has given us a possible pharmaceutical link. Deepermeyer Pharmaceuticals. Preliminary investigations on this company have identified two brothers that run the company, John and Isaiah Deepermeyer. Flight records have them departing to Switzerland nearly six months ago. It seems a credible link to this whole conspiracy."

"What about people trafficking? What about your analyst?"

"Sorry Mr President. We haven't found any evidence of US people trafficking to Switzerland and we still don't know why Alice has betrayed the US."

Everyone sat uncomfortably round the table as the President's dissatisfaction with the whole situation was plain to see. He turned his attentions to Gareth Michaels.

"Gareth, what are our military options?"

"Well Mr President, we don't have a confirmed target yet and we don't have any satellite coverage over the area we suspect they are in, to justify making any military plans. We also can't just stroll into Switzerland with our guns blazing without co-operation from the Swiss and probably some sort of UN support."

"Jesus, this is ridiculous. Why are we so ham-strung on this? We are the fucking USA. We should be able to sort this at the flick of a switch. I do not like being so far on the back foot."

Everyone in the room was feeling the heat with increasing body language that said they all wanted to be anywhere but here. They all waited for the next person to be in the spotlight. It fell on Mike Charlington.

"Mike, please tell me that you have something positive."

"Not really Mr President. I have talked to all the Joint Chiefs and our advisory group and they do make one important point."

"Which is?"

"These people haven't actually done anything illegal, at least not that we can find. If the Professor and Alice have gone to Switzerland of their own accord, which our intel suggests, there is no kidnapping or abduction. They are perfectly entitled to develop new drugs wherever and however they want. Their obsession with security is understandable. Their association with William Hardacre, whilst concerning, doesn't actually constitute anything other than slightly dodgy business practices. The only thing they have done is ask us for money to reveal further information about what they are doing."

"Hold on Mike, they are holding us to ransom over this encryption and seem to think our missing analyst is some kind of leverage that we would be prepared to pay for. It's extortion, plain and simple. Their riddles over this drug are just plain stupid. Why on earth do they think we would give a licence for this drug when they are behaving this way? I don't care what the Joint Chiefs think. I want this group treated like any other terrorist threat."

"OK Mr President, I understand but whilst their methods of contacting the US government are, let's say, unconventional, we aren't compelled to pay up."

"OK, but what happens if we don't pay?"

"Well therein lies the dilemma. If we really want to know what they are up to, we might have to pay them to find out. Only then will we know if there is some criminality that we can hang our hats on."

The President looked around the room, taking in every face and giving them the kind of intimidating stare that came with being one of the most powerful men in the world. He eventually spoke.

"I am disappointed in all of you. The intel on this is shocking and I simply refuse to pay these bastards, based on what you have told me. You have another twenty-four hours to get me some credible answers. Now get out and do your jobs."

61

Chad got off the morning call with Jon and Mahindra. Everything was now at DEFCON 1 in terms of the President's mood and nobody had any more answers. The British intel seemed to check out and Mahindra had been tasked with looking into the Deepermeyers and re-examining everything they had around the missing Professor. Jon had asked Chad to do more reconnaissance around the suspected site but he knew there was little he could do without a full-frontal assault.

He knew it was time. He had to convince Alice to speak to him. He had to get her to admit she was Harlequin and he knew he might just have to break their golden rule and reveal his identity to her. It was their only chance. He logged onto Proton and messaged Harlequin.

BLOWFISH: Harley (Alice?). Things are serious. You are in real trouble and the US is under threat. Your bosses have written to the US government demanding money, but then you know that. Your encryption is amazing. I am sure you are pleased that we haven't managed to crack it. This is why I know it's you Alice. Despite what you think, we know no one is better than you. Your brilliance has ultimately revealed your secret to me. I'm in Switzerland and I know where you are, but I need your help. I don't believe you are a traitor but I don't know why you are working for these people... the Deepermeyers we think... and William Hardacre from the UK. If you cooperate you may get a deal, but I need something.

Chad was on the private message board so there was no chance of anyone else joining. She would get pinged to say there was a private chat message but there was nothing to compel her to answer, just like all his previous attempts. He waited. Ten minutes passed with no response. He was just about to give up when a notification pinged.

HARLEQUIN HAS JOINED THE CHAT

Chad held his breath, hoping that she would respond but after a minute she had not typed anything.

BLOWFISH: Come on Harley. Engage with me.

The cursor blinked. Nothing, until a few minutes later. His heart jumped with the excitement.

HARLEQUIN: Who is the boss of the NSA Senior Counter Intelligence Analyst Team?

BLOWFISH: Jon Ruganzi

HARLEQUIN: Who is the Director of the NSA?

BLOWFISH: Dirk Landsley

HARLEQUIN: Has Jon Ruganzi received a letter from the missing analyst?

BLOWFISH: No

HARLEQUIN HAS LEFT THE CHAT

"Shit!" Chad was so frustrated. She had begun to engage with him but what had spooked her? Why was she asking about a letter to Jon? He got up and paced around his hotel room, hoping that she would get back online.

*

Alice stared at the screen. She started to cry. The letter had not reached Jon. What had happened to Ellie? Had they hurt her, killed her... or worse, was she a fraud? Playing at being her friend, her lover but all the time just in it for... what?

She tried to control herself, focusing on how to escape the hell she was experiencing every minute of every day. It was clear that

Blowfish was in her old team. It just made sense. The fact they knew she had left so soon after it happened, knowing the names of their boss and the Director. Which one was it? Who would Jon trust to come to Switzerland? There was only one likely person. It had to be Chad.

Alice knew she had no choice. The constant simmering threats from Jacob and the vicious abuse that any one of Shaun's team were clearly capable of frightened her more than she cared to admit. Jake was still in her corner and George seemed more and more bullish about their situation. The email to the US government had started the end game. She needed to get out. Now.

She logged back onto the private chat area in Proton.

HARLEQUIN: OK Chad. I am listening

BLOWFISH: Chad?

HARLEQUIN: Come on. I know it is you and you know it is me

BLOWFISH: Well Alice, it is nice to finally get some honesty from you

HARLEQUIN: Cut the crap. Can you get me a helicopter?

BLOWFISH: A helicopter?

HARLEQUIN: Yes, it's the only way I can escape. There is a secret helipad at the back of the site and I think I can persuade one of the guards to get me there

BLOWFISH: Escape? Are they holding you against your will?

HARLEQUIN: At first no. They offered me lots of money to set up their cyber security but once I had delivered, I soon realised that I had made a huge mistake. They were never going to let me leave this place or honour their commitments. I am only still alive because they need me to watch the cyber security but soon... well I think it is obvious

BLOWFISH: You need to give me something Alice

HARLEQUIN: At midnight tonight, I will turn off the anti-surveillance. It will give you a chance to scan the site and you can see where the helipad is. You need to rescue me, the Professor and his assistant and to storm this place to stop these bastards succeeding in their corrupt money-making scheme

BLOWFISH: Ah?

HARLEQUIN: What do you mean... ah?

BLOWFISH: It's just a bit difficult

HARLEQUIN: Shit. Of course. They don't know you are in touch with me. Our involvement in Proton is against the rules

BLOWFISH: Yes

HARLEQUIN: Well, sorry but you are going to have to think of something. I will fall on my sword if you can get me out of this hellhole

BLOWFISH: OK, I will think of something. I will try to get everything ready for midnight

HARLEQUIN: Please Chad, make this happen. Tell them I'm sorry

Chad logged off. He stared out of his hotel window. What should he do? How could he admit to Jon that he had been in touch with Alice all this time, even though he only now had absolute confirmation it was her? He believed that she was really scared, that she had made a calamitous mistake and that she genuinely feared for her life. All the President's advisors seemed nervous about an act of aggression against these people but now he had clear evidence of criminality, even if it was just a threat. He knew he had no choice and picked up the phone to Jon.

"Jon, it's Chad."

"What have you got? The heat is really on here."

"I've found Alice. I am in contact with her."

"What? How?"

"Look Jon, I'd rather not say. I am not sure the NSA would really approve of the methods I have used."

"Chad, this is no time for games. Our heads are all going to roll."

"I know, which is why you just have to trust me. She is in real trouble. She did leave voluntarily at the promise of millions of dollars, but it was all a ruse. After she set up their cyber and satellite security, they betrayed her. She is convinced they are going to kill her, and soon."

There was a pause as Jon was clearly struggling with what to do next.

"What does she want?"

"A helicopter."

"What?"

"There is a secret helipad on the site. She wants to be rescued along with the missing Professor and his assistant."

"Oh, so she has confirmed that they are involved?"

"Yes."

"So, what is she expecting us to do?"

"She is going to turn off the anti-satellite security at midnight tonight. You need to get the team to do a full satellite scan of the site, including the helipad, so we can work out a plan to rescue her."

"She betrayed us Chad. Why should we help her?"

"She made a mistake Jon."

*

Jon Ruganzi pulled the blinds down in his office. He opened the locked bottom drawer of his desk. There it was. The bottle of Jack Daniels that always got him through these difficult moments. He slugged it straight from the bottle. There was no time for glasses. He winced at the harshness of it as it slid down his throat. He took a second slug. He re-orientated himself for a few minutes letting the alcohol give him the warm glow that would ultimately give him the courage to make the difficult call to Dirk. He just had to hope that this breakthrough would deflect from the suspect practices of his team.

223

Clay and Jacob sat in their office. The early evening sun was setting over the mountainous landscape.

"No contact and no payment?" said Clay with a sense of desperation.

"No, not yet."

"What about Hardacre?"

"No, nothing from him either."

"I don't like this Jacob. I don't like the waiting."

"I am sure our email has put the cat among the pigeons. I bet their intel teams are in overdrive trying to find out who we are and what we are doing. We'll get a reaction soon. I am sure of it."

"I hope you are right. You have put us in an impossible position. Something needs to happen and soon."

62

The President had reconvened the same group that had felt his wrath twenty-four hours earlier. Chad was still in Switzerland, dialled in on the video conference, but everyone else was sitting round the table, sullen faced, waiting for the uncomfortable scrutiny.

"Ladies, gentlemen, I hope we have made some progress over the last twenty-four hours."

There were a few furtive glances amongst the assembled crowd, but Dirk Landsley broke the tension.

"Yes, Mr President, Jon's team have made some good progress. I will let him explain what we have found."

The President fixed his attention on Jon.

"Thank you, Dirk. Mr President, we have two major updates. Mahindra has re-examined the Professor's disappearance and the links to the Deepermeyers. Our original review of the Professor's disappearance was inconclusive and shut down quite quickly when the university received an email from him stating he was OK and working in Europe. We had thought it strange at the time that there were no flight records for the Professor or his assistant on any commercial flights to Europe, around the time of their apparent disappearance. We examined the Deepermeyer link and found a private charter out of Minnesota on the day of the disappearance, linked to their firm. There are no details of passengers and no evidence that they went through any sort of passport control, which obviously makes this flight suspicious.

We also could find no CCTV of the Professor leaving the lab buildings on the day in question. Mahindra has though identified a laundry truck leaving the back of the lab building at about the right time. Now, we accept this is still a bit speculative, but we are developing a solid scenario that confirms the Professor and his assistant were taken against their will."

The President's face was not changing in a way that made Jon any less intimidated.

"Not exactly my smoking gun Mr Ruganzi. Doesn't give me enough to tell Gareth to blow them off their fucking mountain, does it?"

"No, Mr President, but we do have more."

"Go on."

"Chad has made contact with Miss Bidebecker."

"What! How?"

"She has been using a private chat room to communicate with like-minded cyber geeks. Chad tracked her down using the same chat room."

"OK, what has she given you?"

"Limited intel at the moment but she has admitted to leaving voluntarily to work for the Deepermeyers at the promise of several million dollars. She set up their cyber security and anti-surveillance. She is also responsible for the encryption that we have been unable to crack. It seems that once she had this up and running, they turned on her, threatening her life if she betrayed them. She seems genuinely scared and sorry for what she has done. She has offered to turn off the anti-satellite security at midnight tonight to give us a chance to scan the area. She says there is a secret helipad and has asked to be rescued along with the Professor and his assistant, by helicopter."

The President gave a snort of derision.

"Am I hearing this right? She has admitted to betraying the US on the promise of millions of dollars and now her little deal has gone 'tits up' she wants us to rescue her? Are you out of your tiny fucking minds? Let the bitch rot."

Dirk tried to deflect the heat on Jon.

"What about the Professor and his assistant, Mr President?"

"Your intel is still shabby Dirk. I accept your scenario is feasible but if the traitress bitch hasn't confirmed your intel, we have nothing to go on. At the moment, I have three US citizens who are betraying the US by working for this questionable pharmaceutical firm that is trying to extort money out of us. I can't see how rescuing them could ever be high on any President's priority list based on your appalling quality of intel."

He stared everyone down. "Am I wrong?"

There were a few faint "No, Mr President" comments from the audience. No one wanting to seem too bullish with everyone on the back foot.

"Janet. You have been very quiet. Has the CIA got anywhere?"

"We have validated the British intel. There is clear evidence that William Hardacre was working with the Deepermeyers a few months ago but he has not been in Switzerland for several weeks, adding credibility to the theory that he has fallen out with them. MI6 now has surveillance on him but he has not moved out of London for nearly a month. I have a direct contact in MI6 who will let me know as soon as that changes. As for the Deepermeyers, they seem to be squeaky clean, not even a parking violation. Either they are the genuine article or have connections in high places to cover up any illegal activity they may have been involved in. The security team is definitely a red flag to us. We have had Shaun Lester in our sights several times but have never been able to nail him for anything. The biggest frustration for both us and the British is that we can't find any credible intel on the so-called people trafficking issue."

The President stood up and shook his head. "This is totally unacceptable."

Everyone in the room tried to avert their gaze as the President walked out. As he passed Mike Charlington, he announced clearly to everyone, "Mike. We will not pay these people a dime. Let me know if we hear from them again."

63

It was around midnight and Alice had sneaked into the technology suite. She got the management software up for the anti-satellite security and hit the 'disable' button. Now all she could do was wait. Had Chad managed to convince Jon to help?

*

Dirk, Jon and Mahindra were in the technology centre attached to the White House. Chad was dialled into a secure conference call.

Jon spoke. "Right Chad, let's see if Alice was spinning you a line or not. The President may not be up for saving her, but a satellite scan of this area is vital if we are to form any sort of plan to resolve this crisis."

Mahindra was at the main console. She had moved their satellites into place, right over the suspected area. Jon leaned forward.

"Anything?"

Mahindra twitched at the close attention and the faint smell of alcohol on Jon's breath.

"Err no, not yet."

They all watched and waited. A few minutes passed and suddenly the screen jumped.

"Hold on. Here we go."

Mahindra tapped away at the keyboard, refreshing the screen. Suddenly a full satellite view of the area appeared.

"Well, Alice was true to her word."

Chad smiled to himself. Jon was manic with excitement.

"Right Mahindra, start scanning the whole of that area and get the footage stored and backed up."

As Mahindra started to work on the scan, Dirk came over to watch what she was doing.

"What are you seeing Miss Ahmed?"

"Well, there is the helipad that Alice was talking about. It is indeed the other side of the mountain from the main complex. There are several buildings in the main complex. I can pick up about thirty stationary heat signatures in this building…" she moved the mouse cursor to circle what she was referring to, "… which may be where the clinical trialists are sleeping. There is another block, which has about a dozen stationary heat signatures in it. I guess this could be where the staff are sleeping. There is a bigger building over to the right, which seems empty. A bit further round is the top of what looks like a cable car station. There is one heat signature there, moving around, which must be the guard on duty. If we follow the cable car line down… yes, there is the bottom and another mobile heat signature. They look like they have one guard at each end."

Dirk pondered what he was seeing and rubbed his chin.

"Miss Ahmed. Can you see any other way to access the site other than the cable car or helipad?"

"No."

*

It was 1 a.m. and Alice couldn't sleep. She had disabled the anti-satellite security for fifteen minutes, hoping that Jon and the team had used the time to scan the area. She logged onto the private chat area of Proton hoping that Chad was also still awake.

HARLEQUIN: Chad. Are you there?

There was no response. Alice rubbed her eyes. The tiredness was reaching her eyes but her brain wouldn't give in. She continued to stare at the screen but her head started to loll. As she came to, she suddenly realised he had responded.

BLOWFISH: What do you want Alice?

HARLEQUIN: Did it work? Did you scan the area?

BLOWFISH: Yes

HARLEQUIN: Thank you. Do you have a rescue plan?

BLOWFISH: No Alice. The President is not going to sanction a rescue. He thinks you are a traitor to the US. I'm sorry. He was very angry

HARLEQUIN: Jesus Chad. I am going to die. Does no one care about that?

BLOWFISH: At the moment... not really. They say you created this situation for yourself and it is not up to the US government to bail you out

HARLEQUIN: There must be something. Something I can do

BLOWFISH: Your only hope is to give me everything you know

HARLEQUIN: OK, what do you need?

BLOWFISH: What drug are they developing?

HARLEQUIN: I don't know. It's all a big secret

BLOWFISH: Oh, come on Alice, do you really expect me to believe that? You are in charge of the security, you must know

HARLEQUIN: I don't. I really don't but whatever it is they think they are going to make billions from it, so it must be big

BLOWFISH: OK, what about the Professor and his assistant? Are they there voluntarily?

HARLEQUIN: No, they were abducted from the university. Seems he had been working on something that started this whole thing off. The Deepermeyers were tracking his work and when the Professor made a breakthrough, they nabbed him and forced him to carry on the work here

BLOWFISH: Is it working?

HARLEQUIN: I don't think so. They have had some limited success but it seems like the Deepermeyers are expecting miracles from the Professor. He wants more time and more trialists but they seem to have refused

BLOWFISH: Interesting. Why have they approached the US government now?

HARLEQUIN: I don't know. I think they are impatient to do a deal. Jacob said something about starting negotiations

BLOWFISH: What about the gun-toting muscle?

HARLEQUIN: British. Ex-army. Team of six. All bastards, except for one who is helping me. They are well trained. Don't underestimate them Chad. Based on my experience they won't hesitate to do whatever they need to do to protect their interests

BLOWFISH: What about William Hardacre? Is he involved?

HARLEQUIN: Huh, that sleazy bastard. He was here but they had a big falling out over the UK trial volunteers. They were a bunch of drunks and drop-outs. The Professor refused to work with them and the Deepermeyers agreed. They had a big bust up with Hardacre over it and he was told to leave, along with the trialists

BLOWFISH: Where are they now? UK intelligence suspect that Hardacre trafficked them illegally but there has been no sign of them returning to the UK

HARLEQUIN: I don't know. They left here in a minibus and we didn't see them again

BLOWFISH: So, who is there? Are there clinical trial volunteers on site now?

HARLEQUIN: Yes, all from the US. This bunch are volunteers. We got them through social media and, after they registered on a secure portal, I did a security check on them before they were allowed on site

BLOWFISH: We couldn't find anything about them

HARLEQUIN: I am worried about something Chad. Seven of them were allowed to leave as they were successful in the trials.

BLOWFISH: So, what's that to you?

HARLEQUIN: I got close to one of them Chad. She was special to me. She was supposed to send Jon a letter but you haven't got it. I'm worried something has happened to her

BLOWFISH: Glad to hear you are still getting some

HARLEQUIN: Chad, this is serious. Her name is Ellie Baker. You need to find out what happened to her

BLOWFISH: OK, OK, I will. Now what about this encryption?

HARLEQUIN: If you get me out of here, it's yours

Chad logged off. The intel Alice had given him was brilliant. It might just make the next meeting with the President a bit less stressful. He would contact Jon in the morning and hope that they could convince the President to rescue her. As he lay down to get some much delayed sleep, he realised how much he cared about Alice, despite the revelation that she didn't seem to swing his way.

*

Alice lay down in bed. She had given it her all now. Chad had everything that could possibly convince the right people to rescue her. She had never met the President but hoped beyond hope that he could see through his anger. Was this the first day of the rest of her life or had she just signed her death warrant?

64

It was 7 a.m. and as usual Julian Watkins was in his London office, taking on board his first cup of Colombian slow-roasted coffee. Normally he would be hard into his paperwork and the never-ending stream of email correspondence at this point in the morning, to give him any chance of getting ahead of the usual meeting-heavy day. Today was different. His mind couldn't shake concern about Simon; the son that he had given up on was somehow occupying his every waking thought.

He had not heard from William Hardacre about this so-called wonder drug, despite having his team on standby to start production. William had promised him billions of pounds of revenue but Julian felt more and more that he was doing a deal with the devil.

He knew that he had many of the ruthless business traits of William, taking people, companies and competition out at a flick of a switch or a swish of the pen. It was what had made him the most successful CEO in Westbrook Pharmaceuticals' history but William just seemed to be on a different level. They had met three years ago at one of William's business functions in Mayfair, keeping in touch off and on until William approached him about this latest project, a secret drug development, so secret in fact that Julian still didn't know what it was supposed to be curing. Julian had been seduced by the money, as always, ignoring the questionable political manoeuvring that he was doing with Sir Henry White-Taylor as just part of the way that William did things.

The problem was their last conversation. He had been so dismissive about the UK volunteers, like they were just another annoying cockroach to be crushed under his shoes. William had got them from the Brighton area and he had strongly suggested that he had pulled a load of down and outs off the street. Erica's concern about Simon being missing was just too much of a coincidence and William would not even afford Julian the common decency of explaining where they were or what had happened to them. He had to do something to stop the worry about Simon invading every minute of his day. He picked up the phone to his good friend Mark Chesterfield, the Commissioner of the Metropolitan Police. He called him on his private mobile. Mark answered straight away.

"Julian. How are you?"

"Mark, we need to talk."

*

Clark was eating his breakfast; it was a day that needed the chocolatey milk heaven of Coco Pops. He was poring over the news feeds, desperately hoping to see anything about a scandal being uncovered in Switzerland or, even better, William Hardacre being arrested. He checked all the feeds. Nothing. Had Mark Chesterfield let him down this time? Was the information he had given him too flaky?

As his mind wandered to Erica Mole, he couldn't help but feel more guilty. The pain of not knowing was worse than the finality of knowing that one of your loved ones was actually lost to this world. Clark knew pain. His dad's suicide had never left him and he never wished that sort of waking agony on any other human being.

As he started to think about getting ready for work, he suddenly realised he had a message on Proton from Harlequin, after all this time. He was in danger of making himself late but he had to read what they had posted. He opened up a long communication addressed to him and SnapDevil.

HARLEQUIN: Krypto, Snap, I am sorry I have been off line recently and ignored your requests for help Krypto. The truth is that Blowfish was right. I am the missing NSA analyst. I am sorry Snap, because I know that goes against our code and how strongly you feel about this but I am in real trouble and something had to give. Blowfish and I work together, even though we didn't know it. It explains why he knew so much about my story so quickly. He got suspicious about the way I was reacting to our conversations about the story and, with his inside knowledge of what was going on, he worked it out. I have been a complete fool, seduced by the promise of millions of dollars to work on this secret drug thing in Switzerland. Once I had set up their cyber and anti-satellite security, they turned on me. I can't tell you how many times I have woken up recently thinking this is the day I am going to die. I am sorry about the hack Krypto. If I had not had this on my plate, I reckon I could have sorted the Zephyr thing, but if it is any consolation, I can give you something else. I worked it out you see. You have been tracking William Hardacre. I can't believe I didn't realise it before. You were the cyber geek they called the guardian angel on that cash for babies scandal, the one that William Hardacre got away with. You want to get him, I understand that, but he has fallen out with the Americans and gone back to the UK. I am sorry Krypto but I don't think you're going to get him on this one. I'm working with Blowfish to get me out of here. I have had to fall on my sword and hope my old team and the President will forgive me for my mistake. If it doesn't happen, I am dead. Whatever happens, Blow and I won't use Proton again. We know we have broken the code, so I have one last favour to ask as I know Snap is the genius when it comes to hacking bank accounts. There was a point where they gave me an account under a false name, which had just under $5 million in it. I squirrelled $80k away to pay off my mortgage but assumed the rest would remain there. I was promised $5 million more once the project was finished. Naïve, I know. Once they had done with me, the money disappeared. I know I can't really expect any favours from you both, but if I leave the bank details on the secure server with details of a new account, I have set up… can you get my money back? If you can, please take a fee, whatever you want. If I get out of this hell, I want some payback. I'm Alice by the way. Sorry again.

Clark quickly messaged Snap.

KRYPTO: Snap, have you seen this dude?

SNAPDEVIL: Yeh dude. So Blow was right all along

KRYPTO: Yeh, and the Hardacre thing. What a head fuck

SNAPDEVIL: Yeh crazy small world dude

KRYPTO: Are you going to help her?

SNAPDEVIL: I am pissed about them breaking our code but I can't let down a damsel in distress

KRYPTO: You are a legend

SNAPDEVIL: Yeh, all heart me

Clark logged off and rushed around to make sure he wasn't late for work. This conspiracy had just got a whole lot more interesting.

*

Alice got up and didn't know what to do. She had told Chad everything and revealed her nightmare to Krypto and Snap. All she could do was wait but the fear gripped her once again. Did she have time to wait for them to save her?

As she tried to control the involuntary shaking that started to consume her, she knew she needed to speak to Jake and George. She needed to implement her escape plan. She couldn't wait. As she tried to shake herself out of her growing terror, Alice wondered whether this was the feeling that death row inmates had as they awaited their fate.

65

After exchanging pleasantries, Julian knew he had to lay it on the line with Mark Chesterfield.

"Look Mark, I think I may be in to something that… well let's just say may not be quite legal."

"Jesus Julian, I am not doing you any favours here. If you are breaking the law, I don't want to hear another word."

"No, no, nothing has happened yet, well I don't think so anyway, but…"

"For God's sake Julian, spit it out man, you are rambling."

"Sorry, OK, I am on the cusp of a major business deal with William Hardacre."

"Fuck me Julian, why are you dealing with that scumbag?"

"Well, I have known him for a while and he approached me a few months ago about a new drug development he is involved in over in Switzerland. He wants my company to manufacture the drug."

"Switzerland?"

Mark's tone made Julian feel like this wasn't the first time he was hearing this story.

"Sorry, is that of some interest to you?"

"Maybe, go on."

"Well, the actual deal is not what I am worried about. I think he is just approaching it in his usual bullish way."

"I'd reserve judgement on that Julian. We have been after this bastard for years. Everything he does is dodgy but nothing ever touches him. You would do well to step away."

"Look Mark, as I said the deal is not what I am worrying about. The issue is my son, Simon."

"What about him?"

"He is a drop-out, left the family home in Scotland about eighteen months ago. His drinking was completely out of control. I threw him out. It broke up the family, ruined my marriage and alienated my daughter."

"I'm sorry to hear that Julian, I didn't know, but what has this got to do with Hardacre?"

"Simon was homeless but he dossed around Brighton. My daughter Erica visited him a couple of times a year to see if he was alright, but the last time she went he had disappeared. She spoke to the local homeless charity and the police. It seems that around twenty or so of the regulars have disappeared and not returned."

"What makes you think this has anything to do with Hardacre?"

"OK, Mark, this is where I am going to have to trust you to give me a bit of latitude, the 'off the record' bit, if you like. During my conversations with William about the drug trials, he mentioned he had pulled a load of down and outs from the streets and shipped them to Switzerland to be the UK clinical trialists. He got them from Brighton. When I asked what happened to them, he said they had been dealt with."

"And you think your son was one of them?"

"It's too much of a coincidence. I know I had given up on my son, which I am ashamed about, but he does not deserve to be treated like an insignificant piece of dirt. I am sure William has something to do with his disappearance and I need to find out what has happened. I need your help Mark."

"I can't divulge national intelligence Julian, I am sure you understand, but I can say that your story does add weight to something that was sent to me a few days ago. I can't answer your question but I will add your intel to the case notes. We will try to find out what happened to your son."

"Thank you."

"Oh, and Julian, in the meantime, cut ties with Hardacre. I don't want to have to come and arrest you."

Julian Watkins pushed back in his plush leather chair and puffed out his cheeks. It was done. He had probably just pissed several billion pounds down the drain but maybe today was the day when he remembered what a decent human being should be. What a father should always be.

He opened up his email and composed a message to Erica.

Erica, I am sorry. I know you are ashamed of the way I treated Simon. I am ashamed of myself. I realise that now. I have looked into what you have found and I believe that something has happened to Simon. I spoke to Mark Chesterfield, the Met Commissioner, he is a friend of mine. He is going to look into it. Sorry again. Dad.

*

Erica saw the email. A tear escaped and rolled down her cheek. She wasn't sure whether it was the realisation that someone else believed her about Simon or the fact that her father might actually have a caring bone in his body. Either way, she now had two people fighting her corner.

*

Mark Chesterfield picked up the phone to Sarah Bressingham, the MI6 liaison that he had spoken to when the original intel had come through from the self-styled 'guardian angel'.

"Sarah, it's Mark Chesterfield. I have some more intel about that drug development thing in Switzerland. I have just taken a call from a friend who is worried about his son. Seems he may have been one of the people that were allegedly trafficked. My intel suggests a clear link between the Swiss thing and William Hardacre."

"Oh, right. Do you have a name of the alleged victim?"

"Yes, Simon Watkins or maybe Simon Mole."

"Thanks, I will liaise further with the Swiss FIS and the CIA. Now we have a name, it may open up some stronger avenues of investigation."

"What about Hardacre?"

"We have him under constant surveillance and I am linked in with the Head of the CIA. If he moves out of the country, we will be tracking him."

"Excellent, thanks Sarah, it would be good to nail that bastard, once and for all."

66

The Professor sat in Clay and Jacob's office, nursing a strong coffee, trying to stop his head from thumping. George sat next to him, impassive, while Jacob probed their unwilling guest.

"What are you doing Professor? George here tells me you have been hitting the bottle hard these last few days."

"Yes, is that a crime now?"

"No, but don't you think all your time should be spent on finalising this cure?"

"Finalising! Finalising! Have you listened to anything I have been telling you? This is NOT working. The conditions you are forcing me to run these trials under are pathetic and have no sound scientific basis. We are going backwards."

"But Professor, you have a cure. You have thirteen patients that were completely cured within twenty-four hours. Don't you realise what you have done? You have cured the common cold."

The Professor stood up unsteadily and glowered at Clay and Jacob.

"No, I have not. You are completely insane. How can you even begin to make statements like that? I admit that I was seduced by the breakthrough I made in Minnesota. The scientific outcomes of that small alpha group were amazing but all we have done is isolate one strain of the rhinovirus and managed to find a way to cure a very small percentage of the trial group. That is not a cure."

"Sit down Professor. You don't seem to understand that we are not patient men—"

241

"Oh, I do, trust me."

"... Which means we take a business view of your progress rather than a scientific one. You do have a cure and we are going to start manufacturing it. Good business sense and clever marketing will make this the must-have drug. By the time anyone realises it is less than effective, we will have made billions of dollars."

The Professor's head was pounding and he really wanted to sit back down, but he was determined to remain standing. Remain as defiant as he could.

"I am sorry, I will not have any part of this. I am done. I will not put my name to a scam."

The room fell silent as the Professor gave in and sat back down. Clay and Jacob looked at the Professor with mild amusement. George remained quiet and unruffled.

After a few moments, the Professor made a noise. A faint, rising laugh, which grew into a booming guffaw which Brian Blessed would have been proud of. Jacob was curious about the Professor's sudden change of mood.

"Something amusing you Professor?"

He tried to calm his laughter. "Oh, I have just realised, it doesn't matter what I do or say. You don't have the first hope of getting this drug licensed. You need full scientific evidence before the US drugs licensing committee will let you start manufacturing. Ha, you're fucked and I am not going to work on this shambles a minute longer."

Jacob turned his attention to George.

"George. Do you have the full scientific breakdown of the successful cure, including all the ingredients and measures required to meet the drug production specifications?"

"Err, yes, it is all fully documented."

"I thought so."

67

Alice sat in the bar, nervously twiddling her hair. Her paranoia was growing by the minute. Any interaction, any snide look from Jacob or anyone in Shaun's team made her gut tighten. It was like they were all in the know, goading her... 'today you are going to die... today you are going to die...'

She took a big slug of her vodka and tonic, just as the Professor, George and Jake arrived, making a beeline for her quiet table in the far corner of the bar.

They all sat down but Jake was bouncing around like an excitable puppy. Alice was immediately irritated. She was not in the mood for his stupid boyish attitude.

"What's the matter with you soldier boy?"

"Well my beautiful Alice, I can get the key to the helipad door. Shaun does not keep it locked up and I know where it is."

"The helicopter's not coming Jake."

"What! Why?"

"Well, apparently the President thinks I'm a traitor and isn't inclined to save me. To be honest, I don't fucking blame him."

George interjected.

"We need to get out Alice. The Deepermeyers are going to stop the trials. They think we have a cure. Our days are numbered."

Alice looked at the Professor. "Is this true Prof?"

"Yes, it is Alice. They are completely insane. It is clear to me now that they never intended to complete proper clinical trials.

They are going to deceive the US public by marketing a scam drug, based on the formula we had a small breakthrough with."

"Can they do that?"

"Well, I have no idea how they will get it licensed but they don't seem the sort of men to let obstacles like that get in the way."

Alice sat and mused on it. Now she understood why the email was sent to the President. She refocused on the collective audience.

"So, what's going to happen now Prof?"

"I don't know for sure but, as I have refused to do any more work on it, I think they will send the rest of the trial patients home and close it all down. They have forced George to provide all the specifications."

"Shit, so we really are in the end game. We have now all become dispensable."

The mood had darkened as they all focused on the bottoms of their glasses, hoping the alcohol would somehow transport them away from this hell. After a few minutes, Jake spoke.

"If your helicopter's not coming Alice, we only have one option."

"And that is?"

"We are going to have to fight our way out."

Alice looked at the collective group and put on an amused expression, which belied her ever-present terror.

"Good luck with that soldier boy. I know you have a gun and I can kick some butt when I need to, but I don't think the Prof and George are quite equipped for your plan."

Jake tried to ignore the mocking tone.

"Look, in three days' time, I am doing the night shift with Gav. I will be stationed at the top cable car and he is at the bottom."

"Have you got Gav on side then?"

"No, he didn't seem interested in anything I had to say about what was going on here. He is either stupid or too loyal to Shaun to rock the boat."

"So, how is that going to help our plan?"

"As I said, we will have to fight our way out. He is only one man and I will have my gun. If we play this right, I can disarm him with the minimum of fuss."

Alice looked at Jake, trying to work out whether this was the dumbest plan in the world or maybe their only hope.

"Seems risky to me. Surely, he will be on guard if the cable car suddenly starts moving down the mountain in the middle of the night. We'd be sitting ducks."

"Not necessarily. If we can hide you and just have me visible as the car approaches, he will just think it is me doing a routine check."

Alice looked at George and the Professor who both shrugged, seemingly up for this mad plan. It wasn't Alice's helicopter plan but she realised it was maybe all they could hope for.

"Three days. Well, I don't think we have a choice. I just hope we are all still alive to even give this a go."

They all picked up their drinks and tried to lose themselves in the numbing effects of the alcohol.

*

Clark sat in his usual spot, empty Chinese takeout containers and Jaffa Cake crumbs festooned across his desk. He read Harlequin's communication over and over. She had confirmed most of what he suspected but he couldn't bring himself to contact Erica Mole to tell her that he now had almost conclusive evidence that something bad had happened to Simon.

The apparent lack of action from Mark Chesterfield also bothered him. Was he doing anything about this? It sounded like Alice was engaging with the US intel service but were the British liaising with them? Had any connections been made?

He drummed his fingers on the desk. Impatient. Frustrated. The thing that was really bothering him, as he once again caught himself looking at his dad's picture, was William Hardacre. Alice had suggested that he was out of the game. Clark had to admit it was strange that he hadn't moved out of London for weeks. He still had the Zephyr hack running but it was not giving him anything. He rubbed his eyes and shook his head. This wasn't over. There was no way that William Hardacre was done.

68

The collected group sat nervously in the White House conference room, waiting for the President to arrive. The same group of people that had been there for the past two evenings and who all knew they were on borrowed time. The President had been less than impressed with their intel and many of them knew this meeting might be their last chance to save their jobs.

Dirk Landsley, Janet Wallbrook and Jon Ruganzi were making small talk, hoping that the significant progress they had made in twenty-four hours would indeed appease the President. Chad was still in Switzerland and dialled in on the video conference.

They all jumped as the door opened and the President walked in. They all went to stand and he quickly commanded them to sit, clearly eager to get on with the meeting.

"Dirk, I understand you have made some good progress?"

"Yes, Chad has been in direct contact with Alice Bidebecker and she has given us everything she knows. She is desperate to be rescued."

The President's face was serious but did not flinch at Dirk's attempt to persuade him to change his mind about Alice. The stare told Dirk he should just carry on.

"Alice has confirmed that the Deepermeyers are developing a wonder drug, which they expect will make them billions of dollars. She is unsure what it is for. She has confirmed that the Professor and his assistant were taken against their will and are being forced to develop this drug, based on some recent breakthrough he had when he was at the university. All records of his work were taken, so we have not been able to verify anything with the university. There are a number of US citizens currently on site voluntarily, who are involved in the clinical trials. Seven of them were allowed to leave and Alice is worried about them. She got close to a lady called Ellie Baker, who is missing. There are no records of her catching a flight back to the US. She confirmed the UK intel but it seems as though they have broken ties with this William Hardacre over a disagreement with their trial volunteers. The UK seem to have a people trafficking issue but we clearly don't. Physical protection is being delivered by six ex-British army who are fully armed. She was unsure why they had approached the US government in the way they did except for saying that they had told her they wanted to start negotiations."

The President sat and stared at Dirk. Picked up his coffee and took a deep swig. The lack of any response ramped up the tension in the room, as no one dared to fill the uncomfortable silence. After what seemed like an eternity, the President finally spoke.

"So, you believe what this traitor is saying?"

Dirk looked at Jon for help, neither man knowing what to say. The President's response was not what they had hoped for. Just as it looked like the President was about to leap from his seat and shake an answer out of someone, another voice cut through the air.

"I believe her."

The President spun away from Dirk and Jon to look at the video conference screen. Chad sat there and repeated his point.

"I believe her Mr President."

The President's expression changed from simmering rage to something more relaxed.

"Mr Brown. I am glad that someone has finally got the balls to give an opinion. Why do you believe her?"

"She is a good person Mr President. She made a terrible mistake, seduced by the promise of several million dollars to work for these people. She is one of the cleverest people I have ever met but in this case she has been stupid. Once they got her to do what they wanted, they betrayed her, threatening to leak a story to the US press that she is a traitor selling national security secrets. More recently they have been making threats on her life. She is convinced they are all going to be killed when they close down the Swiss operation. I am also fairly sure that the UK and US trial volunteers that left the site have all been killed."

The President rubbed his chin.

"The problem is Mr Brown you don't actually have any evidence. You just have the 'say so' of one woman, who may be a nice person, may have made a mistake, may have been uncharacteristically stupid but still chose to betray the US. She was one of our Senior Analysts for fuck's sake, committed to honour and serve. It's not like she was some two-bit admin clerk."

Chad was on the verge of trying to respond when the President spun his chair away from the screen, seemingly dismissing Chad's attempts to justify Alice's actions as a mere irritation.

"Mike. What is the latest view of the Joint Chiefs?"

"To be honest Mr President, their view hasn't changed. They agree with you that we do not have anything to corroborate Miss Bidebecker's intel and given her actions she is considered unreliable. Whilst US citizens are involved, there does not seem to be any direct threat, with most of them apparently in Switzerland voluntarily. There is no corroborated evidence of any criminality and even if there were, this is surely an issue for the Swiss police or at worst the Swiss FIS. This situation just does not tick the boxes as a national security threat. Yes, we have lost one of our best analysts but she does not seem to have taken any national intelligence secrets with her. Unless we get some tangible evidence of a clear threat or act of aggression against US citizens, the Joint Chiefs recommend this case is closed down."

"What about this encryption?"

"The Joint Chiefs are confident that Jon's team will crack it. They don't think we need to pay to get it back."

The President looked at Dirk, moved his gaze to Jon and raised his eyebrows. A look that said he clearly didn't share the faith of the Joint Chiefs.

"And what about their attempts to extort money from us? Does anyone have any idea what we are paying for or what will happen if we ignore them?"

"No Mr President. Their approach seems fanciful and lacking in any credibility."

"So, what on earth do they hope to achieve?"

"Well, if it is a new drug, they will need it licensed to manufacture and distribute in the US. We are guessing that this is just some play to get this fast tracked."

The President grunted, clearly unimpressed with everything he was hearing. He turned his attentions to Gareth Michaels, the Head of the US Military.

"Gareth, I presume your view is unchanged?"

"Correct, Mr President. Our discussions with the Joint Chiefs were unequivocal. There is no military imperative here. No tangible threats to US soil or US citizens that would require our intervention. We would always consider a request for support from the Swiss, but that is as far as it goes, unless the intel picture changes."

The President sat back in his chair and looked around the room, not speaking, just sizing everyone up. After another uncomfortable few minutes he spoke.

"OK, thank you to everyone for their work on this over the last twenty-four hours. I am inclined to agree with the Joint Chiefs' recommendation. This situation is closed. This Plutus Group are complete fantasists if they think they can extort money from the US, based on some half-baked riddle. Mr Brown, if you do talk to Miss Bidebecker again, please make it clear that I considered your plea for clemency but her actions cannot be rewarded with the full force of the US government wasting time on an unnecessary rescue mission."

With that he stood up and marched out of the room.

*

Chad logged off the video conference and stared out of his hotel window, up towards where he knew Alice was sitting, high up in her mountain prison, hoping that someone would save her. Chad wanted to help her but he was no super hero. He didn't know how to hold a gun, let alone use one and he didn't think those were the credentials for taking on six highly trained soldiers.

"Fuck, fuck, fuck! Alice, I'm sorry."

*

Dirk, Jon and Janet walked out of the conference room along the marbled hallway toward a row of other meeting rooms, either side of the corridor. Gareth was just up ahead. Dirk beckoned him into one of the meeting rooms.

"Gareth. We need to talk. We need your help."

Gareth looked at the concerned faces of the three people that were now staring at him.

"And just exactly what does that mean?"

"We need to rescue her Gareth and we need to save the Professor and his assistant."

"Hold on. Were you not just in the same meeting as I was?"

"Don't be flippant Gareth. The Joint Chiefs are passive and ineffectual. The President always does what they say, but they are wrong. We have one of our own about to be killed by some money-making lunatics who don't seem to care what gets in their way."

"The President thinks she is a traitor and I tend to agree with him. And, anyway, it doesn't matter what I think. He gave us a direct order to close this down and the one thing I have to do in my role is follow orders."

"For God's sake Gareth. We have worked together long enough to know that there are orders and then there are the creative solutions that the President doesn't need to know about."

Gareth screwed his face up like he had just bitten into a very sharp lemon. "I really hope you are not suggesting we sanction a black op."

*

Clark was about to shut down for the evening. His lumpy bed was calling, relief from the fatigue that consumed him. As he closed down his consoles, he noticed the Zephyr app alerting him to a text exchange on Hardacre's phone.

Sarah. It's William. I trust you are making sure that everyone that matters has the right intelligence picture on me?

Yes William. They all think I have you under constant surveillance. I am sure I can keep them on the hook while you do what you need to do

Good, look forward to dinner with your folks this weekend. I hope your dad's golf handicap is still going in the right direction

Clark couldn't believe it. Who the hell was Sarah?

69

Alice sat in her mountainside 'prison' not knowing what to do with herself. She had a message from Chad the previous evening. The President had closed down all hope of her being rescued and was refusing to engage with the self-styled Plutus Group that the Deepermeyers had created for their little stunt. She was absolutely on her own. She checked her phone in the vain hope that Ellie may have been in touch but that yielded nothing. Was she even alive? Would Chad still look for her now the President had closed the op down? She had forty-eight hours until Jake's mad escape plan could be put into action.

As she sat, stressed and wired, she almost jumped out of her skin as there was a knock on her apartment door. Should she answer it? What if this was it? Time for her to be dealt with? As she hesitated, a voice came booming from the other side.

"Miss Bidebecker. Please open the door. The Deepermeyers require your presence."

It was Shaun.

She tried to stifle a scream. She paced around the room. What could she do?

"Miss Bidebecker."

She had no choice. She opened the door. Shaun stood there stony faced, accompanied by Maverick who immediately leered at her breasts. Alice tried to show defiance.

"What do you want?"

"The Deepermeyers require your presence. Immediately."

"And what if I am not inclined to grant them my presence?"

Shaun smiled, lunged forward and grabbed Alice roughly before she could even react. Maverick took one side, making sure his hand was placed firmly on her arse. She flashed a glare at him that said 'I will break your hand off', but he just laughed and continued to force her forward.

Alice had no chance against the strength of the two men. As she was manhandled down the corridor, she thought she caught a glimpse of someone, seemingly watching, unconcerned. Weird.

They eventually arrived in Clay and Jacob's office. Alice was bundled into a chair with the two of them looking at her with a sense of pity on their faces. Jacob spoke.

"Miss Bidebecker. I think you know you have almost served your purpose here."

"So pay what you owe me and let me go."

"Hmm, I am afraid it doesn't work like that."

"Well, kill me then. Get it over with. Just like you did with Ellie."

"Ellie? Who is Ellie?"

"One of the trial volunteers. You killed them all. Didn't you?"

There was a subtle look between Jacob and Shaun that told Alice what she needed to know. The pain almost overwhelmed her. She wanted to leap up and strangle them. Holding on until their lives were snuffed out, just like they had done to Ellie, just like they were going to do to her.

"I have no idea what you're talking about Miss Bidebecker. The volunteers were escorted to the airport in Austria and as far as we know got on their flights to the US, as will the rest of the volunteers when we release them tomorrow."

Alice couldn't believe it. She knew he was lying and now they were going to kill the rest of the volunteers. She made a mental note to contact Chad, if she survived that long.

"Anyhow Miss Bidebecker, I did say 'almost'. We have one more thing you need to do, before…"

Jacob's sentence drifted off, almost like it was distasteful for him to actually say the word.

Alice was stunned. What could she possibly still do for these bastards?

"We are disappointed in the US government's refusal to engage with us and we know you have been in touch with a member of your old team."

Alice's stomach hit the floor. How did they know she had been in touch with Chad? She tried to front it out.

"'Been in touch'. What a quaint way of putting it, but I assure you, my only contact with the US government is the email you asked me to send. I can't be held to account if they have refused to respond."

"Oh dear Miss Bidebecker. Are you really going to add lying to your list of misdemeanours?"

Alice was in pieces but she did her best to keep her expression firm and unruffled, despite the body blows coming with every sentence.

"I don't know what you mean."

"Cut the crap Miss Bidebecker. We know everything you have been doing and I mean... everything. We want you to set up a secure video conference this evening at nine p.m., which I expect the President of the United States and all his cronies to be on. Make it clear to them that this is their last chance to engage with the Plutus Group and do a deal. Please explain that there will be consequences if this does not happen. Do I make myself crystal clear?"

Alice stood up. "Consider it done."

She walked out, not giving them a second more to threaten and intimidate her. At least she knew she might survive the day but she agonised over whether they would they keep her alive long enough to execute her escape plan the following night. As she walked back to the security suite, Jacob's comments troubled her... *we know everything you have been doing.* Alice was sure that there had not been any technical surveillance on her. After all, she was the cyber expert. Which left only one explanation. Someone was betraying her, feeding back everything she was doing. After catching a glimpse of who she thought was watching her, as the goons led her away, she now had a pretty good idea who it was.

70

Alice logged straight onto the private chat room of Proton and messaged Chad.

HARLEQUIN: Chad, things are moving fast here. I need your help

A few agonising minutes passed as the cursor just sat blinking at her like some impetuous child refusing to do what their parents had asked of them. Alice began to think that maybe Chad had abandoned her too. Five minutes passed. Nothing. Ten minutes. Fifteen minutes. Alice's heart was in her mouth. *Come on Chad, don't give up on me.*

BLOWFISH: I told you we have orders not to help you

Alice punched the air with relief. Despite what he had just messaged, she knew there was hope.

HARLEQUIN: Look Chad, there are two things you need to do. Please. Firstly, they are closing this down. They are sending the final volunteers away tomorrow. You need to get someone to track the coach as they are going to kill all these people. I know it. They will lead you to where they killed Ellie and the others. I am sure of it

BLOWFISH: Alice, I have no resources. I am the only one on the ground here and the President will not authorise any US resources on this thing. The Swiss are being passive and will only work with us if we have clear evidence of criminality

HARLEQUIN: Do they need my dead body before they will believe this thing? Following that coach will give them what they need

BLOWFISH: I'm sorry Alice, my hands are tied. What is the second thing?

Alice screamed at her terminal. Did no one care that she was on borrowed time? She calmed herself and launched into her final plea. The one that might just give her enough time to escape.

HARLEQUIN: I can't believe this Chad. I really can't. If you can't do that you have to do this second thing or I am dead by the end of the day

The conversation was killing Chad. All his suppressed feelings for Alice were threatening to overwhelm him. Never had he felt so insignificant.

BLOWFISH: I will try. What is it?

HARLEQUIN: I have set up a secure video conference for 9 p.m. tonight Swiss time, 3 p.m. DC time. They want to speak to the President and his key advisers. They said this is his last chance to engage or there will be consequences

BLOWFISH: What does that mean?

HARLEQUIN: I don't know but you have to persuade the President to take that call

BLOWFISH: I can't see this happening Alice. The President has made his position quite clear and we only have four hours to make this happen

HARLEQUIN: You have to try Chad. For me. Please

BLOWFISH: I will

Once again, Alice had put it all out there. She now had to rely on others to give her the time she needed, to get to tomorrow evening, to have the chance to escape. She walked back to her apartment and waited, wondering whether this beautiful mountain view was the last thing she was going to see on Earth.

*

Chad got straight on the phone to Jon and explained Alice's latest request. Jon was not surprisingly sceptical but left Chad curious with the last thing he said.

"I will speak to Dirk about the requests. Don't lose faith. You never know where help might come from."

*

Mike Charlington resumed his usual position, waiting outside the Oval Office for the President to be ready. A few minutes later, the door opened and he was ushered in.

"Mike, what can I do for you?"

"Sorry to trouble you Mr President, but there has been a development with this Plutus thing."

"I thought I gave clear instructions to close that down yesterday."

"I know Mr President but Mr Brown has had further contact with Miss Bidebecker. She claims they have insisted on having a conference call with you at three p.m. today or, as they stated, there will be consequences."

"You know I don't respond to 'sabre rattling'."

"I know Mr President but it seems that Miss Bidebecker believes she will be killed if you don't comply. She is also convinced they are going to kill the final volunteers after they release them from these so-called trials tomorrow."

"We have been over this Mike. You as my Chief of Staff and the Joint Chiefs have dismissed her as a traitor, assessed her intel as unreliable and this Plutus Group's claims as fanciful and opportunistic. I am not hearing anything new."

"I am sorry. The request came up the line from Dirk and he asked me to speak to you. It seems he does have some loyalty to his team and does not want anything happening to Miss Bidebecker."

"To what end Mike? Does he really think if we comply with

her requests or execute this ill-conceived rescue plan, that I would ever let her work for the US government again?"

"Err, no, I guess he just doesn't want her to die."

The President turned his seat away from Mike and looked out of the Oval Office windows. Mike wasn't sure if this was a good sign. Was the President actually considering his pitch?

Several minutes passed, Mike sitting uncomfortably in his chair staring at the President's back. The President had not moved or spoken a word the whole time. The tension was palpable. Just as Mike considered getting up and leaving, the President turned around and floored Mike with what he said.

"OK Mike. I will participate in this video conference but only because I am curious to see what these lunatics have to say for themselves. I have not changed my position on Miss Bidebecker or the request for resources to rescue her. I simply want to see what this Plutus Group looks like in the flesh."

71

It was 2.55 p.m. DC time and Mike had gathered Dirk, Janet and Gareth in the conference room ready to join the President on the video conference. The President walked in and sat front and central, ready to see the 'whites of their eyes'.

At 3 p.m. precisely the screen refreshed and they were confronted with the faces of the two men they had heard so much about.

*

It was 9 p.m. in Switzerland and Chad sat in his hotel room, wondering how this thing was going down. He couldn't believe that Jon, Dirk and Mike had convinced the President to take the call. Would he really negotiate with these men? Had he bought Alice the time she needed?

As he tried to occupy his mind, he jumped as there was a knock on his hotel door. He got up, peered through the spy hole. Outside were a man and a woman, dark glasses, suited and booted. Government types. What the hell was this?

He hesitated but the knock came again, more insistent.

Chad opened the door. They both removed their glasses. The woman spoke.

"Mr Brown. I am Special Agent Sandra Lockwood and this is Sergeant Dylan Westfield, US Special Ops. Can we come in please?"

"Oh, yes, of course. Why are you here?"

"We are here to help you Mr Brown. With this situation."

"Situation? I was told the President had refused to allow any resources on this thing."

Sandra stiffened her facial expression.

"The orders to help you did not come from the President. He doesn't know we're here."

"Oh… Oh, I see, so this is what Jon meant."

"Jon?"

"Sorry, Jon is my boss. Just something he said."

"Well, Mr Brown, I suggest you fill us in on what is happening here and we can see what we can do to help. Order up some coffee please, this may take a while."

*

There was a moment of stand-off as both sides stared at each other on their respective screens. The President broke the impasse.

"I presume I am talking to John and Isaiah Deepermeyer?"

"You are relatively well-informed Mr President but only our dear ole mom calls us by those names. I prefer Jacob Deepermeyer and this is my brother Clay."

"Gentlemen, can we cut to the chase. I had informed my team to shut down any engagement with you as I do not respond well to threats and I do not negotiate with terrorists."

"Gee Mr President, harsh words and yet you are on this call."

"Yes gentlemen, I was intrigued to see the type of men who thought they could extort money from the US government."

"You really have some colourful language Mr President. Terrorists? Extortion? These are not words we would use to describe our attempts at engaging you in our once-in-a-lifetime opportunity."

"OK, humour me. How would you describe your attempts at engagement?"

"We are businessmen Mr President. We are patriots. We have a scientific breakthrough that could inject significant productivity into the US economy and yet you and your cronies cannot sniff out a good business deal when it's right in front of them. We are willing to trade your analyst and her excellent new encryption for a drug licence and an upfront payment to smooth the deal."

The President tried to ignore the increase in volume and subtle menace that was now evident in Jacob's voice.

"You are talking in riddles, insisting on us paying for the privilege of hearing your pitch before we even knew what we were supposed to be paying for. I fail to see how that could be construed as a good business deal."

"You lack faith Mr President. Do you not believe that our almighty God can guide you through these moments of doubt, to see the greater good, to help all US citizens to have a better life?"

"Geez, you really are insane. What the fuck has God got to do with the fact that you are terrorists trying to extort money from the US? That sort of crap might work with your workforce but it means squat to me."

There was a short pause as the two stags stepped away from butting heads and the collective audiences held their breath, fascinated to see where this was going next. Jacob sat back in his chair and looked at Clay, whispering something behind his hand. The President sat staring at him, stony faced and determined not to be intimidated by these goons. Jacob broke the impasse.

"Your attitude is tiresome Mr President. We are offering the US an opportunity to licence a new drug we have developed, which will significantly reduce absences from work. This will inject billions of dollars in productivity into the US economy as workers' return to work is dramatically speeded up. You had a chance to do this deal at fifty million dollars. You have one final chance to do this deal, which guarantees exclusivity to the US market. The cost is now a hundred million dollars."

"So, you have stopped working with Mr Hardacre from the UK?"

The President could see Jacob flinch at the mention of William Hardacre's name.

"The cost is a hundred million dollars for an exclusive deal in the US. You have forty-eight hours to make the payment or we will have no choice but to negotiate a deal for this drug with the UK, China and Russia. These negotiations will also include the potential sale of the encryption. If you delay, I can't guarantee the safety of your analyst. It's your decision Mr President."

With that, the video conference call was abruptly ended and the President was left staring at a number of perplexed faces.

*

They were now into their second cup of coffee as Chad relayed everything that had happened with Alice, to Sandra and Dylan. They listened intently and seemed genuinely engaged in what Chad was saying. Chad was relieved to have someone else to talk to, but couldn't get out of his mind that someone had ordered a black op to rescue Alice. How on earth did they think they would keep this from the President? Sandra broke his train of thought.

"OK Chad, it seems like we might need to be guided by Alice on when to intervene but it seems like her suggestion to follow this coach tomorrow may be the first step. The Swiss FIS are not engaging and have not supplied us with any intel to suggest that they have found a load of dead bodies by the roadside. We don't have the evidence of criminality that everyone seems to need to move this thing forward."

"Alice is pretty convinced. They must have covered their tracks well."

"Don't worry Chad, we are with you on this. Our orders are to treat all Alice's intel as credible and bring her home safe and sound."

Chad visibly relaxed. Sandra and Dylan excused themselves for the night and they all agreed to be operationally ready for whatever was in play tomorrow.

*

The President looked around the room, expecting some sort of comment, but no one spoke.

"Are none of you going to say anything?"

Mike Charlington put his head above the parapet.

"Err, Mr President, I am not sure we have learned much more from that conversation, except that the price has gone up."

"How credible is their threat about negotiating with other countries?"

"Difficult to say. They seem fairly uncompromising in their attitudes."

"Can we really afford to play 'chicken' with this encryption? My so-called best intel team have not been able to crack the work that Miss Bidebecker seems to have done, so what gives you and the Joint Chiefs any assurance that we will sort this mess out? And, as for this wonder drug injecting significant productivity into the US economy, can we really ignore that and risk the Chinese or Russians getting it ahead of us?"

The body language once again spoke volumes. Nobody was comfortable. Nobody had the real answers to the President's questions.

"Does anybody have an opinion?"

The President was seething but calmed his voice to give a clear direction.

"Mike. Convene the Joint Chiefs. We need to make a decision and if this goes wrong you can all consider this your last meeting with me."

*

Alice had been watching the consoles, making sure that the video conference call was working. The last thing she needed was for Clay and Jacob's call to drop out at a crucial moment. All of a sudden, she noticed that the Deepermeyers had ended the call. The familiar sense of dread hit her stomach. Had they got what they wanted? Would it be enough for her to survive the night? She scuttled back to her apartment and went to bed, hoping that sleep might give her respite from the constant fear and anxiety. As she tried to induce sleep, thoughts of Ellie and Chad filled her sub-conscious. Would her world ever get back to normal? Would Chad find a way?

72

There had been darkness for so long but something was changing. She felt heavier, like she was suddenly connected back to the real world. She could feel her limbs, people were touching her, speaking in a language she didn't know. Was it German?

The sounds in her head were changing, like wind whooshing through her brain. A light. What was that? Her world was becoming lighter, shapes were forming, people's faces. A voice, not speaking the foreign language but English, of sorts.

"Hello, mystery lady. Welcome back to the land of the living."

She tried to orientate herself. Where was she? Her head was full of cotton wool but her eyes were adjusting. The faces were forming into better, clearer images. She was lying down, machines all around her. Doctors? Yes, doctors and nurses all around her. She was in a hospital. The voice came again.

"Can you speak?"

She tried but nothing came out. They gave her some water, which rasped against her throat. She coughed and spluttered. They told her to take it slowly. After a few more sips, she managed to form a coherent sentence.

"Where am I?"

The voice spoke again. The doctor.

"You are in a specialist trauma unit in Geneva, Switzerland. You have been unconscious since you were admitted. You were found on a ledge of a steep mountain, right next to a sheer drop. You were very lucky to survive."

The memories started flooding back. The minibus, panic, the Hummer pushing them off the road toward the drop. She was at the back. The emergency exit. She had pulled on the handle with all her might. It gave and she tumbled out, smashing into a large expanse of rocks. She smashed her head but she remembered the minibus going over the cliff, before the trauma sent her world into darkness.

She was crying and shaking at the memories. The doctors and nurses looking concerned, fussing over her, asking if she was OK. She mustered up as much volume as she could.

"I need to speak to the police. Now!"

The doctor seemed surprised by her sudden burst of energy.

"Err, yes OK, I will get someone to contact them, but you need to rest. You have been unconscious for some time. You need to give your body time to adjust."

"Look, I'm fine, just get me the police. Something terrible has happened."

"OK, OK, we will get them. One thing though. We don't have your name. None of your personal belongings were on your person when they brought you in."

"My name is Ellie Baker."

73

Alice jolted awake. It was morning and she did that thing where you touched different parts of your body to make sure everything was still in place. She was alive. No one had come for her in the night.

Half an hour later, a bang on the door filled her with the familiar feeling of outright panic. She didn't even try to resist this time. She just opened the door and accepted her fate. Thankfully, it was only Shaun, no Maverick to leer at her and touch her up.

"The Deepermeyers want to see you."

Alice walked out of the room with no comment. Did the fact that they wanted to see her mean she was still useful to them? All she needed was twenty-four hours.

Jacob spoke as she walked into their office.

"Ahh, Miss Bidebecker, it seems you haven't exhausted your usefulness to us after all."

Alice's heart gave a little jump. She tried not to show too much excitement but hoped against hope that they were going to give her the time she needed to escape.

"Oh, really."

"Yes, we had the video conference with the President and his cronies last night. A bunch of losers but we gave them forty-eight hours to make a payment or we will be taking the deal off the table."

"And why does that affect me? Why don't you just get it over with and kill me? Stop playing your stupid psychological games. It doesn't impress me and just makes you look and sound stupid."

Clay and Jacob looked at each other with an amused expression.

"We don't really care what you think Miss Bidebecker but we need you available to set up another video conference with the US at short notice, once they hopefully see sense and pay up."

"So, you can guarantee me that I won't be harmed for at least the next two days?"

"Yes, why do you ask?"

"No reason."

Alice walked out, trying to suppress a smile. She had done it. She was going to be alive long enough to implement her escape plan. All she had to do now was deal with the traitor in her midst.

As Alice walked back to her apartment, a sudden wall of noise emanated from the accommodation building. The remaining volunteers were leaving, all chirpy and excited about going home. Alice stood and watched them weave their way to the top cable car station, immobilised by her complete inability to do anything about their situation. They were all going to die and they were all bouncing along like they were going on holiday. What could she do?

She ran back to her apartment. She had to warn Chad and hope that he could follow them and stop this thing. More than that, she wanted him to find out what had happened to Ellie. She got back to her apartment and left him a message on Proton. She looked at her watch. Fourteen hours to go.

*

Chad sat in his hotel room with Sandra and Dylan, waiting for something to happen. A notification pinged on his laptop. A Proton message.

"What is it?" said Sandra.

"It's a message from Alice. The coach is about to leave with the other US trial volunteers. She wants us to follow them."

"OK, let's go then. We'll use our vehicle. I think an SUV is better than that thing you hired."

Chad smiled and followed them to their vehicle. He had never been operational in the field. His churning guts told him he probably wasn't cut out for it but Sandra and Dylan looked like they could more than handle anything that would get thrown at them. He settled in the back seat and tried to relax as they sped up the mountain to try to catch the trail of the coach.

*

Erica Mole sat idly scrolling through her social media feeds. She didn't really expect to see anything different. Days and weeks had gone by and there had been no news about Simon. She had spoken to the local police in Brighton and the homeless charity. There had been no return of any of the homeless people. She had emailed Clark but he seemed as frustrated as she was. He had passed all the information he had to his police contact but everything was annoyingly quiet. And lastly, the route she never expected would bring any support, her father, had been speaking to his people in high places but even his influence didn't seem to be bringing any joy.

Where are you Simon? What has happened to you?

*

The SUV sped up the mountain, certainly eating up the terrain better than Chad's little hire car. They had hardly gone any distance up the incline before they saw it. The small coach was coming down the mountain followed by a Hummer. They drove past, trying not to be too obvious but a few metres further up, they found a small widening in the road, just enough to do a

271

U-turn. Dylan was driving and completed the manoeuvre with some aplomb. Chad was impressed and tried to settle in to the very comfortable back seats.

Within a few minutes they had caught the mini convoy, keeping a discreet distance as it drove along the main road toward Austria. After about half an hour, the convoy suddenly took a sharp right up a steep incline. Chad bolted up. The SUV took the turn.

"Where are they going? This has to be it. This has to be where they kill them."

Sandra looked round. "Let's hope your ri—"

Sandra didn't finish her sentence. To Chad, the next few seconds seemed to play out in slow motion. An earth-shattering noise. Sandra's head slumped forward, blood dripping from a bullet wound. Someone had shot her. The noise was the sound of the bullet shattering the windscreen as it made its way into Sandra's skull. Chad and Dylan both looked at Sandra. A second later, another sound, just the same and Dylan slumped forward as the SUV careered off the road and all the airbags engaged as the vehicle crashed into a large rock.

74

Mike Charlington convened the Joint Chiefs for an early morning meeting, at the President's request. The President wasted no time in getting to the point.

"Ladies, gentlemen, I presume Mike has updated you on our recent video conference with the Deepermeyers?"

There was a general murmuring in agreement.

"We have gleaned limited information from this interaction other than to put a face to our enemy. These so-called patriots have increased the bill to a hundred million dollars for some wonder drug that they refuse to divulge the details about unless we pay up. They are threatening to sell it to the UK, the Russians and Chinese. They are also threatening to sell the enhanced encryption that our missing analyst has developed for them. You seem confident that this risk can be mitigated but I have been singularly unimpressed with the results from the NSA on this matter. My personal view is that we should not be held to ransom by these lunatics. I am ashamed to see US citizens acting in this way, claiming to be businessmen, claiming to be patriotic. But, as always, I am interested in your views."

The conversation flowed around the room but after a frank exchange, the Joint Chiefs' view had not changed. They felt there was no tangible evidence that what they were offering was really going to help the US and without some threat to US citizens or US soil, or indeed some corroborated evidence that US citizens had been harmed, they felt there was no military imperative.

They held their line that the encryption issue would be resolved by the NSA team, despite the President's concerns.

The President listened intently. The noise died down as the room waited for the President's response.

"Thank you for your constructive comments. I tend to agree with your views. There still does not seem to be a military imperative here. Their claims of economic benefits coupled with their threats to sell these benefits to other countries still seem fanciful. I am concerned about the encryption issue but I will bow to your counsel on this matter. I'm not—"

The President was stopped mid-sentence by Mike Charlington.

"Mr President, I am so sorry to interrupt you but I have just received an email from Janet Wallbrook. Her contact in the Swiss FIS has been in touch. They have a US citizen called Ellie Baker in one of their hospitals. She is claiming that the US trial volunteers were murdered. Their minibus was deliberately driven off the road over a massive cliff. She managed to jump out just before it went over the edge. She knocked herself out and has been unconscious since the accident. She has just woken up and directed the Swiss police and FIS to where she thinks the accident happened. They are reporting evidence of multiple vehicles sitting at the bottom of a ravine near where Miss Baker claims the incident took place. The site is very difficult to access but they are getting specialist teams in to try to find out what is down there. The crucial point is this does seem to corroborate part of the intel from Miss Bidebecker."

The President visibly flinched at the mention of Alice's name. His response was terse, clearly irritated by the interruption to his thought process.

"Thank you, Mike. This doesn't change anything. I have not changed my mind about Miss Bidebecker. There will be no military intervention and we will not pay these bastards a dime. If you get any further intel from Janet or Dirk about this development, I am prepared to listen to it but there is to be no action on this until further notice."

He stood up and walked out of the room.

*

Janet Wallbook and Dirk Landsley were having a coffee together when the message from Mike Charlington came back to Janet.

"Huh, the President and the Joint Chiefs haven't changed their mind. He is still ordering no action on this situation. It seems this Ellie Baker news has not been enough to change his mind but he has said he will review any new intel we get from the Swiss FIS, once they have been able to examine the crash site."

"Why is that man such a jerk? This Ellie Baker development is clear evidence that Alice's intel checks out. Why can't he see that?"

"I know. I am hoping that Sandra and Dylan are on it. The last sit rep I had from them was that they were following the coach that had just left the site. The timing is weird though. If the Swiss FIS were up at the alleged crash site a few hours ago, surely there is a good chance that the coach and our team would have run into them."

"Have you heard anything from them?"

"No, that is the strange thing. As soon as I got the call from the FIS, I tried to contact them both. I can't get through to them. All messages just go to voicemail."

"That is weird because I can't get through to Chad either."

Janet and Dirk looked at each other, their expressions confirming that their minds were going to the same place. Were their team at the bottom of the ravine with all the other alleged victims? Janet quickly called the Swiss FIS contact. She needed them to find out what had happened to the team, two of whom were not even supposed to be there.

75

Nine hours to go. Alice sat in her apartment, full of nervous energy. Why was time going so slow? She had arranged to meet the Professor, George and Jake for dinner around 6 p.m. Two friends and a traitor. She mulled over how to handle the situation. She couldn't afford to let them know she knew but it was a huge risk to keep them in the inner circle. They all knew the escape was planned for tonight. What could she do to shake them off?

Seven hours to go. Alice sat around the table with her three escape 'buddies'. She decided to play it cool. There was no change to the plan. At 1 a.m., they would convene at the top cable car station. Jake would take them down to the bottom and disarm Gavin. Jake would have the keys to the Hummer and they would make their escape. The traitor would be dealt with by force.

Five hours to go. Alice sent a message to Chad. She wanted him to be there with whatever resources he could muster. A contingency plan? A welcoming committee? Whatever. She just wanted a friendly face at the bottom cable car station when they drove away from the hellhole. Maybe some firepower if things went wrong. She waited for his response.

Three hours to go. The tension was building. No one had disturbed Alice. No knocks at the door. Maybe the Deepermeyers were going to be true to their word, but the doubt remained. If she was right about the traitor, why hadn't they come for her, to mess up her plan? Something felt wrong about the situation but it was the only plan she had. What made her doubts worse was the lack of contact from Chad. Why hadn't he responded? Why hadn't he updated her about what they found after following the coach yesterday?

One hour to go. Alice was pacing around. Her doubts were multiplying by the second. The traitor would spoil the plan. Chad had abandoned her. Gavin would put up a fight. Nag, nag, nag. She was rapidly talking herself out of going ahead, but then her phone pinged. Chad? As she saw the text message she almost fainted on the spot. She sat down before she fell down, and read the text over and over.

Babe, are you OK? You were right. They tried to kill us all. They pushed our freeking minibus over a cliff. I leapt out at the last minute. Someone found me and took me to hospital. I have been unconscious since the accident. As soon as I woke up, I told the police everything. They have killed them all babe. The officer dude told me they think there are three vehicles down there. OMG, I can't believe this has happened. Please tell me you are still alive. Love Ellie xx

Tears were streaming down Alice's face as she tried to direct her fingers to craft a reply. She sent a text right back. Her faith in the plan was restored. It didn't matter who knew what and who did what. She was now going to fight her way out of this hellhole if it was the last thing she did. Now she had something to fight for.

*

His eyes blinked open. It was dark. Where was he? Chad tried to orientate himself. He was in the back of the SUV. *Shit!* He suddenly bolted up. A mistake. His head was pounding. He felt along his hairline. Massive bruising. The memories came flooding back in waves. He gingerly turned on the torch on his phone, hoping that his memories had tricked him. The horrific image as the torch lit up the vehicle quickly dispelled that happy notion. Sandra and Dylan were slumped in the front of the car. The smell of death seemingly permeating every pore. Chad tried to ignore the smell and replayed what had happened, so quickly and so brutally. As the SUV careered off the road, Chad had seen guns being drawn back into the Hummer. They had murdered his colleagues. He looked at the time; 12.08 a.m. He was dizzy and disorientated but he had to contact Jon. As he opened up his phone, he realised he had a message from Alice. She was going to escape. Tonight. In less than one hour and she wanted his help. He got on the phone to Jon.

*

It was just past 6 p.m. Janet Wallbrook and Dirk Landsley were still together in Janet's office. Their day had no prospect of ending any time soon as they waited for updates from Switzerland about the crash site. They had also been unable to contact their team on the ground and the Swiss FIS had no information about their whereabouts. As they considered what to do next, two things happened simultaneously. Janet had an email from the Swiss FIS and Dirk had a message from Jon.

"Shit, Dirk, we have our smoking gun. The Swiss FIS have confirmed that there are three vehicles at the bottom of the ravine. The whole site is burnt out but there are multiple charred remains in the wreckage. This confirms Alice's intel. They have killed the UK trialists and the two busloads of US volunteers."

Dirk was tapping away at his phone. "It gets worse. Jon has just received a call from Chad. Sandra and Dylan are dead. They shot at their vehicle when they were following the coach. Chad survived but knocked himself out in the accident. He has only just woken up. It also seems as though Alice has hatched an escape plan, which she is executing tonight... in less than an hour's time. She asked Chad for help but he is in no fit state."

"Holy crap. This is it. Get Gareth in here. We need to mobilise some more resources."

"Are you going to brief the President?"

"Hell no. Him and his chiefs of staff will just find another reason to stall. We are on our own and anyway this just got real personal. Sandra was a dear friend of mine."

"You know we'll lose our jobs over this."

"So be it."

76

The clock ticked past 1 a.m. and Alice was mobile. As she quietly crept out of her apartment, she could see the outline of two figures further up the corridor. The Professor and George. One friend and one traitor. She acted as cool as she could but her heart was racing, palms were sweaty and her head was pounding with the stress of whether such a stupid, risky plan was going to work.

They all gave quiet acknowledgements to each other as they walked toward the exit, out into the cool summer air and over to the cable car station. Jake was waiting.

"Are we ready soldier boy?" Alice said with the merest hint of desperation.

"Yes ma'am."

They all got in the cable car. Apart from Jake, they all crouched down in the hope that Gavin wouldn't see them as they arrived at the bottom. The cable car mechanism started up and Alice winced at the noise. It sounded like a herd of elephants. Surely this would wake someone?

The cable car made its slow descent. Alice looked at the Professor and George, trying to read their expressions but both of them had their steely, determined faces on. Someone was keeping their mask well and truly on.

As they reached the bottom, Alice tensed. This was it. They stayed put as Jake exited the car. Gavin was immediately on the move to find out what was going on.

"Watcha doin' Jake?"

"Oh just...", Jake used the light tone to catch Gavin off guard. He smashed the butt of his rifle into Gavin's head and he went down immediately.

"Come on," Jake shouted at the other three. They all stood up and quickly jumped out of the cable car. As they started down the hill toward the Hummer, Alice grabbed Jake and hung back, letting the Professor and George walk ahead. She wanted Jake to take out the traitor.

Alice started whispering furiously at Jake, trying to relay her wishes without giving her game away but, as she did, her world fell apart.

The Hummer doors opened. Within seconds Shaun, Maverick and John were twenty yards away with automatic rifles aimed at each of the escapees, except for the traitor. George.

They were closely followed by Jacob and Clay.

"Well Miss Bidebecker, you clearly did think we were stupid," said Jacob. "Did you really think we didn't know everything you were up to? For one of America's finest brains, you have been incredibly naïve."

Alice looked at George.

"You fucking bastard George. What the hell did they promise you to betray us? Does the Professor mean nothing to you?"

George just stared at her, an amused arrogant expression on his face. The Professor was staring at George, hardly believing what was happening. Jacob cut across the tension.

"Please don't talk to my son like that, Miss Bidebecker."

Alice and the Professor looked at each other in horror.

"Your son!" they chorused.

"Yes, let's all go back up to our offices. We have a little story to tell you... before we kill you, of course."

77

Alice was trying not to completely break down. She knew the plan was risky but she just hoped that she had been wrong about George and that somehow the escape would work. How wrong had she been and where was Chad with the cavalry?

Alice, Jake and the Professor were unceremoniously dumped in chairs, the three guards in close proximity, their rifles locked and loaded to deal with anyone who had heroic intentions.

Jacob, the classic narcissist, launched into his story, clearly revelling in the moment.

"You really are a hapless bunch. The three amigos, plotting and planning. Jakey boy, clearly Miss Bidebecker's obvious charms were a better bet for you than loyalty to your team. I am sure they will have fun reminding you of what it means to break ranks. Miss Bidebecker. I kinda liked you. You stood up for yourself and there is no doubting you are America's best cyber expert. Your work was exemplary but ultimately, you had to be dispensable. And finally, the Professor, where my story really comes to life."

They all tried to resist the urge to launch themselves off their chairs and smash his smug face in, hoping that the time he was taking to glory in his cleverness might present an opportunity to escape.

"You see the thing is Professor, we have been watching you for many years. We knew you had the potential to discover something amazing and we had to be a part of it. We needed an inside man, someone that could feed back everything you were doing. You see it's funny how life works. George was the result of an affair I had with my secretary at the time, George's real mum, Mary Mankley. She agreed to raise George, stayed married to a nice boring man and I made sure he was always taken care of… financially, at least. She eventually told him the truth about me and we developed a relationship. A good relationship. I could tell quite quickly he was a 'chip off the old block'. When I mentioned my plan, he practically bit my hand off."

"But we…"

"Yes, his sexuality was a real bonus. We knew you had a penchant for young men and George seemed happy to oblige. My son is a true professional."

The Professor looked at George with a mix of pain and hatred.

"Why George? Why did you do it? All that time we were together. How long was it? Two years and all the time you were just buttering me up, planning to betray me and sharing my bed."

George smirked. "Yeh, you know you weren't bad for an old man."

The rest of the Professor's questions went unanswered as Jacob continued his ramble.

"You see Professor, George was perfect, gaining your trust and playing his part oh so well. There was never any surveillance in your labs. George just kept us up to date with all you were doing and made you paranoid by moving things around in your office. Messing up that weird Feng Shui thing you have going on was a nice touch."

"You bastards – what was with all the apparent terror when we first got here George? Was that all an act too?"

Jacob laughed. "Yes George, I did think you played that particularly well, especially the part where you had a gun to your head. Oscar-winning performance."

The Professor was broken. Alice tried to reach over and comfort him, but her efforts were quickly stopped by the guards. Jacob carried on, revelling in every second of his 'moment in the sun'.

"You see Professor, despite what you think, we are very patient men. We knew, and George came to understand this too, that you make money by playing the long game. You don't become billionaires by flapping about, knee jerking at every situation, hoping a deal might land in your lap. You plan, you prepare, you negotiate, you deal, you know your enemy and you take them out."

"Is that right Jacob?"

Everyone turned to where the new voice had come from. Jacob and Clay stood staring at the uninvited guest. Absolutely gobsmacked.

78

Clark was raging. Within the last twenty-four hours, William Hardacre was on the move, leaving the UK and arriving in Switzerland several hours later. This was what Clark had been expecting. He knew William wasn't done and he was now making his move. Alice had implied that the US and UK were working together to keep an eye on him, so why was he moving freely across Europe? He had sent another anonymous email to Mark Chesterfield, telling him about William's movements but this didn't seem to have any affect. William was still moving toward his target. As Clark looked at his dad's picture, his mind took him to a place he didn't want to go. William's influence was everywhere. Did he really have MI6 in his pocket as well? Had Mark Chesterfield been turned after helping him with the 'cash for babies' scandal?

*

Julian Watkins sat in his office. It was late but he couldn't stop reading the email he had received from William Hardacre. The game had started. William would have the formula within twenty-four hours and he expected Julian to start manufacturing it straight away. He put his head in his hands. What the hell should he do? Mark Chesterfield had promised him this was all under control, so why was William acting like nothing had happened?

*

Mark Chesterfield sat in his corner office, looking out over Victoria Street, sweating profusely as the dodgy air conditioning hardly touched the stifling heat that this June evening hung onto in Central London. William Hardacre had once again invaded his workload. His mystery guardian angel had emailed him to say he was on the move to Switzerland. Julian Watkins had contacted him to say the deal with William was about to land and he didn't know what to do. His efforts to contact Sarah Bressingham at MI6 had failed. If William had moved out of the country, Sarah was supposed to have deployed resources to stop him. Mark suddenly had a very bad feeling about this.

*

After the initial shock of seeing William standing there, Jacob composed himself and got back into command mode.

"Well William, as nice as it is to see you, we are a bit busy here, as you can see. Shaun, can you escort Mr Hardacre back off the premises. You can shoot him if you want."

William's expression didn't change. He just stared at Clay and Jacob with a look of a predator eyeing up his prey. Nobody moved.

"Shaun. I think I just gave you an order. Can you escort Mr Hardacre off the premises?"

Shaun looked at William, then turned to look at Jacob.

"I'm sorry Jacob. I'm afraid I can't do that."

With that Shaun and his team aimed their guns at Clay, Jacob and George. There were multiple audible gasps from the people in the room. Jacob was the first to react.

"Just what the hell is going on here? Point your guns away. Where is your loyalty?"

William Hardacre gave a snort of derision. "That's the thing Jacob. In my experience loyalty can be bought and your little gang of soldiers are loyal to me, because I am paying them to be. Simple really."

Jacob could see he was on the back foot but still tried to talk his way out of the situation.

"OK, William, if it's all about the money. Tell me what you want."

"What I want is for you stupid Yanks to shut up."

Jacob looked at Clay, desperately looking for a way out. An angle that would get them back in the game.

"Come on William, we are all businessmen here. I'm sorry if you felt we acted hastily but we had to concentrate on what we thought was right and now we have the US government ticking over nicely. Billions of dollars are at our fingertips."

William shook his head. "Did you really think I would just walk away from this? You treat me like garbage, like some second-class citizen and expect me to just roll over because you say you are sorry? You two are more stupid than I thought."

Jacob tried to up the bravado but in reality he was shitting himself. He knew they were in deep trouble.

"William, we will make billions more if we work together on this. You know that. If you have the UK ready, we can launch this thing across both sides of the pond. The US are just about ready. I have been leveraging their economic paranoia. They will sign up real soon."

"Is that right? From what I've heard, they have consistently refused to play your games. Your optimism seems wildly misplaced, a bit like many of your decisions on this little project."

"Decisions? What do you mean?"

"Well, making an enemy of me, employing that bitch and thinking the US would just roll over. You two are a liability."

"Oh, I suppose you could have done it better, could you?"

William laughed.

"You arrogant prick. While you have been playing stupid cryptic word games with the US government, I have been doing what is needed. I have a pharmaceutical firm ready to start production tomorrow and I have a licence from the UK government to manufacture this drug because I paid off the right people. What is it you Yanks say? I have hit a home run while you have struck out."

Jacob's mind was racing, trying to find a way out. Clay was frozen to the spot. Jacob's contempt for his brother came flooding back. He had always been the weak one.

"You are making a mistake William."

"Am I?"

Just as everyone was tensed up, the powerplay in the room ratcheting up to the max, there was a sudden burst of movement. George lunged forward, trying to grab the gun off John. His efforts took John by surprise and he stumbled back. Jacob saw the opportunity and lunged at Maverick. William stepped back away from the commotion but gave Shaun a look that made it clear what he expected him to do.

There was a sudden burst of automatic gunfire, the sound deafening in the small space. Everything stopped. George and Jacob were on the floor, blood seeping from their bullet wounds. Alice and the Professor, seemingly forgotten in all the carnage, instinctively got up and grabbed at George's prone figure.

The guns were re-directed at them but William stood them down. Alice felt for a pulse. She looked up and shook her head. "He's dead."

Clay just sat there. Frozen in fear. Not daring to look at his brother. William kicked at his body. Nothing. He grabbed Clay by the throat. "Now maybe you will take me seriously."

Clay tried to talk through the firm grip. "What do you want?"

"You are going to join me in a conference call with your government. It's time for the big boys to play. Time to tell *el Presidente* that the deal has changed."

79

Contact was established with the US government surprisingly quickly and William was pleased that his request for a one-to-one call with the President was met with affirmative action. The call was arranged within the hour.

As Alice and the Professor tried to take in everything that had just happened, William proceeded to carry on like this was an everyday event.

"OK, John, can you take this poor excuse for a soldier away and do with him what you like. I am sure the guy I met at the bottom cable car station would like to get re-acquainted. Professor, can you come with me to your lab? We are going to put together all your information on this wonder drug and get it off to my team in England. Production will start tomorrow. Oh, and Maverick, can you take Miss Bidebecker back to her apartment and guard her until I am ready for her."

As William walked out of the room with the Professor, he leant over and whispered in Alice's ear. "You are about to find out what it means to disrespect me. Warm the bed up for me."

He looked at Maverick. "Don't touch her. I don't want your sloppy seconds."

*

The Professor's mind was racing. So much had happened in such a short time. Having to cope with George's betrayal, followed by his and Jacob's brutal murder. And now, William Hardacre was back on the scene, exacting his revenge for the souring of the business relationship. He hoped that in a moment he would wake up and marvel at this vivid dream.

As he walked in a daze being pushed along by William, he suddenly started to laugh.

"Something amusing you Professor?"

"They haven't told you have they?"

"Told me what?"

"It doesn't work. The cure doesn't work."

The Professor was caught off guard by William's response.

"I know. In fact, I know everything Professor. As much as I hate those Yanks, they were right about one thing. This drug doesn't need to work. We can focus on the small number of success stories and make it sound like a wonder drug. People are stupid. They will buy this drug because it will promise the impossible and by the time people realise it is less than effective, we will have made billions. We can spin it that the drug has cured the current strains of the common cold but, like all viruses, it has mutated, meaning more development is needed. And, guess what? I can then sell them the new and improved version. It's just good business Professor and clever marketing. Oh, and don't forget that I already have a licence to manufacture this in the UK. I don't need to play silly political games with my government."

As they made their way into the lab, the Professor started pulling all the paperwork and electronic files together. William watched on like a cat who got the cream. The Professor's mind was racing. Would he get out of this situation now the game had changed? He decided to try the straight-talking approach with William. He seemed the type of guy that might just respect a bit of honest bravado.

"What are you going to do to me now? Are you going to kill me?"

"Well that really rather depends on you Professor. I want you to work for me in the UK, with my pharmaceutical team. As I said, you have more work to do. But, if that upsets your morals, well... I think we know the answer, don't we?"

The Professor just put his head down and didn't say another word. Were these going to be the last moments of his life, giving away his most precious work to a bully? He continued to put the information together, desperately hoping that something would change as he pondered the fate of Alice and Jake.

*

Alice was bundled back into her apartment, Maverick clearly enjoying another opportunity to manhandle her.

"I suggest you go into your bedroom and get ready, bitch. Mr Hardacre won't be long."

Alice sized up her options. There was nothing in the immediate vicinity that could help her. She decided to wait in the bedroom, anything to get away from the leer of Maverick's gaze.

She paced around the bedroom, trying to stay calm. Her head was spinning with the events of the last hour. How could it have gone so wrong? Why did she not see that Hardacre would be back? She thought about George, his betrayal. She didn't like to think she had been naïve but the signs were there, she just didn't want to see them or believe them. And what of the Professor? Was he already dead? She needed a new plan. It seemed that Chad had let her down. She was on her own and whether she lived or died came down to her own ability to get out of this latest fucked-up situation. She lay down on the bed, hoping that inspiration would find her.

As she stretched out, her hand touched something under her pillow. She bolted up. This was it. If she could get William off guard, she had a chance. She freshened herself up and stripped down to her bra and panties. She lay on the bed and waited.

After dealing with the Professor, William went back to the video conference suite and waited. He was looking forward to re-acquainting himself with that bitch but this little bit of business had to take priority. Clay sat next to him, passive and broken.

*

In the US, President Caruso sat in the VC room with Mike Charlington.

"What is this all about Mike and why haven't I heard from Gareth, Dirk or Janet?"

"Well, we had a communiqué from this Plutus Group but this time from William Hardacre, requesting a private one-to-one call with you."

"This is most irregular Mike. I thought I had made it clear that I would do no more on this until Dirk and Janet had established any new intel."

"I'm sorry Mr President, but I can't get in touch with Gareth, Janet or Dirk."

"What! Where are they?"

"I don't know Mr President."

The President was simmering but refocused on the here and now.

"Why are you advising me to take this call, Mike?"

"I just think the Mr Hardacre link is an interesting development. I am intrigued as to what he has to say."

"OK Mike, I will do this thing but I am not happy that my three other key advisors seem to be AWOL."

*

A few minutes later the call was established and the President sat staring at a new face, sat next to one of the Deepermeyers, who looked decidedly unkempt and no longer in command.

"Mr Hardacre, I presume. I hope the Deepermeyers have told you that I don't negotiate with extortion terrorists and I don't respond to threats."

"Yes Mr President, my name is William Hardacre and I will make this brief. I am in charge now and I apologise for the Deepermeyers' silly games. I don't need any money off you to reveal what I am selling. The deal is simple. We have a cure for the common cold and I will start manufacturing the drugs in the UK from tomorrow. The US has an opportunity to sign a contract with my company to start buying and distributing this drug as soon as you are ready. I will get contracts emailed to you overnight. It is your decision whether you sign them but be aware that the UK will be benefiting from this immediately. You can have your encryption back. I have no interest in it. I will also take care of your little analyst problem."

With that William Hardacre disconnected the call.

The President looked at Mike with absolute astonishment. "A cure for the common cold. My God can that be true? And what does he mean about 'taking care of our analyst problem'? Find Gareth, Dirk and Janet now and get them in here. We have a lot to talk about."

80

After what seemed like an eternity, Alice heard her apartment door open. She heard a muffled conversation between William and Maverick, which amounted to him being told his presence was no longer required.

Alice tensed up. If she was ever going to see Ellie again, she had to get this right. Her bedroom door opened and William stood there. His expression changed, trying not to show the surprise he was clearly feeling at seeing Alice spread out on the bed in just her underwear.

"So, what is this Miss Bidebecker? Have you finally decided that I am worth your attention?"

"Well, you know, it's only a shag. How bad can it be? I don't suppose you'll last long looking at these." She cupped her breasts trying to pretend she was vaguely enjoying this when all she wanted to do was vomit at the prospect of this old, fat, disgusting man being anywhere near her.

William didn't move. He was sizing up the situation.

"Oh, sorry William, did you want me to resist? Do you like it if we fight back? Do you get off on raping women?"

Without warning William suddenly lunged forward and grabbed Alice by the throat, his weight immobilising her.

"Do you think I am stupid, you little slut? Whatever game you're playing here is not going to work and yes, I do prefer it when they fight back."

William kept his right hand on Alice's throat as he fumbled around with his trousers and boxer shorts. As he yanked them down, exposing his hardening penis, Alice strained to look down at what he was doing. As he started tearing at her panties, clearly getting ready to force himself on Alice, her mind started to shut down almost as though her consciousness was trying to block out the horror of what was happening. As the assault continued, she felt disconnected from the moment, but she knew she had to stop it. Her plan had to kick in. Now. Her brain suddenly clicked back into gear. She could hardly move with his weight on her, but crucially he had left her right arm free. As the horror of the assault came close to his rough penetration, she reached under her pillow and grabbed the knife that she had kept under there ever since the last assault by Maverick.

In one sweeping move she swung her arm out from under the pillow and plunged the knife into William's neck.

Everything stopped. Blood starting pouring from the wound. William let go of Alice's throat, fell off the bed and clutched his hand to the wound. His hand was not stopping the blood but he was still alive.

Alice got up, knife still in hand and looked at William. In that moment, the stress and rage of the last few months came flooding out. She stabbed him again, and again and again. The frenzy continued until she had no more energy to spare. She dropped the knife and let out a howl, like some wild animal in pain. She slumped on the floor next to William. Was he dead? She kicked at him. Yeh, he was dead.

She was covered in blood, but now she had to move. Find the Professor and get out of here. She had a sudden pang of guilt for Jake. She had wound him round her little finger to get him to help her to escape and now he was suffering God-knows what, at the hands of his so-called mates.

As she contemplated her options, she suddenly heard a loud repetitive throbbing noise. As she tried to focus on the noise, it got louder. It was getting closer. What was it? She tried to wipe the blood off her hands as she grabbed her clothes. She gingerly moved out of her apartment, along the corridor to the outside door. She could hear the noise more clearly now. She suddenly realised what it was. Helicopter rotor blades.

In a few seconds the main compound was in complete chaos. Three military helicopters were dropping soldiers onto the ground with speed and precision. Guns were firing from all directions. Shaun and his team were out and engaging the intruders, but their firepower was nothing against the might of whatever was coming in. Within a minute, all of Shaun's remaining team were dead.

Alice stood in the doorway watching the horror unfold. As the soldiers from the helicopters gained control, she risked walking out into the courtyard. Suddenly, a voice shouted across the din of the rotor blades.

"Alice!"

She turned to see a familiar face bounding towards her.

"I'm sorry I'm a bit late."

She jumped on Chad and gave him the biggest hug. "You did it! You persuaded the President to save me."

"Err, not exactly, but there is plenty of time to explain. Let's get you out of here and cleaned up."

As Chad helped her to the helicopter, she stopped a few feet from the door. "The Professor, Jake. Are they still alive?"

Chad pointed over to the other side of the compound. Soldiers were helping the Professor and a battered and bruised Jake into another helicopter.

Alice belted herself into the back seat of the helicopter and closed her eyes. The nightmare was finally over.

EPILOGUE

Clark was transfixed to the news. Something had happened in Switzerland but the US were trying to cover it up and there was no news on Hardacre. The latest news bulletin started.

US President David Caruso is coming under increasing pressure to explain an apparent US/Swiss joint military operation in the mountains above the village of Boden in Switzerland. Reports suggest that US military helicopters were seen landing in what has been described as an old spa retreat, followed by the noise of automatic gunfire. The President is insisting that this was not a US government-endorsed mission but the triple resignations of his Head of the US Military, Gareth Michaels, his Director of Intelligence, Dirk Landsley and the Head of the CIA, Janet Wallbrook, have got conspiracy theorists frothing at the mouth at what might have happened. Many are suggesting that these three individuals have gone against the President's orders to work with the Swiss on whatever this mission was and have been ordered to resign. The US administration is refusing to comment on these developments.

Based on information leaked from a reliable source, there is also a suggestion that these developments are linked to the burnt-out remains of several vehicles in a ravine about forty miles away from this site, which has resulted in mass casualties, currently being investigated by Swiss police. A social media campaign by a mother from Pennsylvania, whose daughter went missing after allegedly travelling to Switzerland to take part in a clinical trial, has garnered several more concerned families who also have loved ones missing. Commentators are making a clear connection between this situation and these tragic circumstances. These suspicions have been heightened by the arrest by Swiss police of billionaire pharmaceutical magnet Clay Deepermeyer, who is alleged to have been working out of the site that was stormed by US forces. The whereabouts of his brother Jacob Deepermeyer are unknown, adding to the intrigue around this whole situation.

It is unclear whether any other nations were involved in this operation but some people are linking the apparent disappearance of UK billionaire William Hardacre to these events. Mr Hardacre has not been seen for several days and we understand that he travelled to Europe, possibly to Switzerland, around the same time as the US military operation. The UK government and Mr Hardacre's office have refused to comment.

Clark sat back in his chair. *Missing! Missing!*

He thumped the table with his fist and immediately regretted it. *Shit. Where are you Hardacre? What have you done now? What have you got away with… again?*

Just as Clark felt like smashing the place up, anything to quell his rage, he suddenly realised he had a message on Proton. It was from Harlequin.

He realised tears were rolling down his face, but he wiped them away as he fumbled his fingers across the keyboard, desperate to see if Harley, *Alice,* had any news. He opened the message and his heart leapt.

HARLEQUIN: He's dead Krypto. I know because I killed him myself. Thought you might wanna know.

The tears came again but this time with unbridled joy. He picked his dad's picture up and kissed it.

"We did it Dad. We did it."

*

In the UK, the Prime Minister discreetly moved Sir Henry White-Taylor off the front benches and into a dead-end international development job. Away from the prying eyes of the public, Sarah Bressingham, the MI6 agent, was arrested on allegations that she was on William Hardacre's payroll and had turned a blind eye to his trek back to Switzerland. His death sparked a crisis within his business empire, as there was no heir to his fortune that wasn't already incarcerated at Her Majesty's pleasure. The crisis was deepened by the absolute delight that Mark Chesterfield and DCS Jenny Ragnor had at starting a full investigation into the Hardacre empire, successfully getting a court order to freeze his assets.

*

Several weeks after the events in Switzerland, Erica Mole stood with her father Julian Watkins next to Simon's grave. They never did identify the body, it was too burnt to provide the possibility of a positive ID, but old dental records were enough to convince the authorities that the remains were of Simon and should be returned to the family for burial. They put fresh flowers down and hugged each other.

As she walked away, Erica gave her dad a new business card. The name on it was Erica Watkins. Julian smiled and watched his daughter go. As he stood by the grave, tears welled up.

"I'm sorry son."

As he turned to leave the graveside, Julian Watkins saw a familiar face standing at the edge of the cemetery. The Met Commissioner, Mark Chesterfield. He walked up to him, resigned to his fate.

"Hello Mark, I assume this is not a social visit to pay your respects?"

"I'm afraid not Julian."

"Am I under arrest?"

"If you come willingly Julian, we can say that you are helping us with our enquiries. If you tell me everything you know about Hardacre, and I mean everything, I might just be able to keep you out of jail."

"Thank you Mark. Let's go."

*

Professor Carlton Jenkins was welcomed back to the University of Minnesota with open arms. The work he had done on finding a cure for the common cold was properly documented and registered with the scientific community in the US and their partners in other countries. The Carlton Jenkins Foundation was set up to co-ordinate work on proper clinical developments and trials. The Professor was heard to say several times that he would no longer be seduced by short-term results. His mantra was clear. If science willed it, they would find a way, even if it took another twenty years.

*

At about the same time, in a luxury house overlooking Montego Bay in Jamaica, Alice sat on a sunbed applying copious amounts of sun cream.

"Can I help you with that babe?"

Alice smiled at Ellie, drew her close and kissed her. "I love you."

"I know. I love you too."

Alice lay back down and took in the rays.

Ultimately her betrayal of the US government meant there was no chance she would ever work for the intelligence services again. Despite the shit storm between the President and his senior team, most of whom had resigned in protest at his handling of the events, Alice had negotiated herself out of any jail time. Full cooperation with the relevant authorities in Switzerland and the US, together with full technical specifications of her brilliant new encryption standards, had just about been enough. The seventeen stab wounds that were on William Hardacre's body were harder to explain but some diplomatic manoeuvring between the US and the Swiss police had somehow managed to get Alice off with a plea of self-defence.

As she discreetly walked away from the drama, she met up with Ellie back in the US and immediately took off for Jamaica. What nobody knew was that Snapdevil had delivered. He had found the near $5 million by hacking through the Swiss bank account that the Deepermeyers had been using and moved it back to Alice's account before the authorities had seized the money. Less his ten per cent fee of course.

A $2 million sprawling mountainside house was quickly purchased. Ellie and Alice settled down to a long life together with no need to ever work again, if they didn't want to.

As they continued to soak up the sun, a voice broke their semi-slumber.

"Can I get either of you anything?"

Alice looked at Jake.

"No thanks soldier boy, you can go now."

Alice felt guilty about her treatment of Jake and employed him as a general butler/handyman across the massive property. He seemed grateful for the change of pace as he recovered from the vicious beating at the hands of Shaun, John and Gavin.

Alice smiled at Ellie and put her sunglasses back on.

Life was good. Finally.

ACKNOWLEDGEMENTS

Firstly, a belated thank you to Thomas Wade and Ben Jackson for the creation of my website – www.colinwade.co.uk – it wasn't quite ready when the first book was launched but is now fully operational.

Thanks again to my alpha readers – Ray Wade, Jacky Wade, Hannah Wade, Anthony Cooper and Karen Warner - for their time and dedication in reading multiple versions of the manuscript.

Thank you to my family for their unflinching support.

Thank you to Jericho Writers and in particular, Russel McLean, for the manuscript review which once again ironed out the rough edges.

Thank you to Troubador Publishing for all their support, particularly Fern Bushnell, Jonathan White and Imogen Palmer. Imogen's work on the copy edit was once again exceptional in finding all those spelling and grammatical errors that inevitably creep in when writing.

Thanks should also go to the local independent shops in Oxfordshire that have helped me by stocking my first book in their stores. Particular thanks to Frog Orange in Headington, Mostly Books in Abingdon and the Wallingford Bookshop. I look forward to working with you on getting this book sold.

Finally, a massive thank you to my small but perfectly formed readership. Your enthusiasm and support for my writing has been amazing. I hope you enjoyed this book!